TASTES LIKE MURDER

BOOKS BY CATHERINE BRUNS

Cookies & Chance Mysteries:

Tastes Like Murder

Baked to Death

A Spot of Murder
(short story in the Killer Beach Reads collection)

Burned to a Crisp

Frosted with Revenge

Realtor for Hire Mysteries:

Killer Transaction

Priced to Kill

TASTES LIKE MURDER

a Cookies & Chance mystery

Catherine Bruns

Acknowledgements:

There are several people to whom I owe a debt of gratitude for their help with this book, beginning with retired Troy, NY Police Captain Terrance Buchanan for sharing his knowledge and wisdom with me. Patti and Frank Ricupero and Susan Bellai were beyond generous to donate the use of their delicious family recipes. Special props to critique partners Diane Bator and Dani-Lyn Alexander who always gave it to me straight. Beta readers Constance Atwater and Krista Gardner had great ideas and never tired of listening to me ramble on about "my story." To my family for their support, especially my husband Frank for his infinite patience. Last but certainly not least, a huge thank you to publisher Gemma Halliday for believing in my writing and helping me to realize my dream.

CHAPTER ONE

———

Mrs. Gavelli wagged her stubby finger. "You no forget my free fortune
this time. I tell your grandmama if you cheat me."

My mouth fell open in surprise, but I knew better than to argue with the elderly, Italian lady who stood before my display case, dressed in a drab, gray housecoat. It was shocking how well her outfit matched her coarse hair, pulled back from her stern face in a severe bun. As she reached down to scratch her leg, she succeeded in pushing her knee-highs farther down her calves. One more movement and they'd be level with her black Birkenstocks.

"No, Mrs. Gavelli. You have my word."

My best friend and partner, Josie Sullivan, appeared in the doorway. She'd been icing cookies in the back room for a delivery tomorrow. "Mrs. G, you're fogging up the glass on our case with your breath. Are you buying something or not?"

Nicoletta Gavelli snorted as she pointed at the tray of chocolate-dipped fortune cookies that lined the bottom shelf of our display case. They had been my idea to lure more business into the shop, giving us a unique flair. The sign written in blue Magic Marker on the glass read: *Buy a cookie—get a free fortune.* They were easy enough for Josie to make, but she thought I was wasting my money on them. I didn't care. Although frugal about other matters concerning my business, this small expense didn't worry me. I enjoyed seeing the delighted expressions on children's faces when they opened them.

Mrs. Gavelli continued her tirade in broken English. "You no fool me, Sally Muccio. You be up to no good since you work your wiles on my grandson."

She'd never let the incident with Johnny go. As tempting as it was to throw her out of my shop, I had a soft spot for the old lady and her sharp tongue, though it was pretty obvious she'd never cared for me. Nicoletta had lived next door to my parents ever since I could remember and was good friends with my Grandma Rosa. To this day, she still insists I tried to take advantage of her grandson, Johnny, when in fact it was Johnny who had lured me into their darkened garage at the tender age of six. Johnny, much more mature and reckless at the ripe old age of eight, informed me there was a great game called Doctor which we should play. He even went so far as to say he'd give me an ice cream cone afterward. I was foolish enough to believe him. Even then it was all about food for me.

"No fortune cookie till you buy something." Josie folded her arms triumphantly across her chest.

Mrs. Gavelli let out a loud harrumph. "Josie, you never change. No respect for elders. That mouth, she never stop. Why you not home with babies?"

"My husband's there, Mrs. G. He works nights, remember?"

"Yah, sure he home. I bet he drink the beer till he pass out."

Josie narrowed her blue eyes. "We're running a business here. Are you buying something or not?"

Mrs. Gavelli snickered at her. "Some business. You bake cookies all day. Is no real job." She turned to me. "You need new husband. I see why old one leave you now."

I wasn't sure which of her remarks stung the most, the one about my ex-husband or the one that insulted our new profession, which I happened to be very proud of.

Josie's face turned as red as her hair. "Colin was a cheating bum. Sally left him, not the other way around."

"It's okay, Josie." I was afraid she might start flinging cookies at Mrs. Gavelli's head. "Let it go."

Mrs. Gavelli waved her hand. "Whatever. Give me Italian butter cookie. And why so many American cookies? You Sicilian, for God's sake. Why you got chocolate chip cookies touching Italian ones?"

"Because they're a huge seller, and we do have other

customers besides Italians." I reached for a piece of waxed paper.

"Italians rule this town, missy."

I laughed. Her statement was true enough. I placed the cookie in a small, white bag. "That'll be one dollar and twenty-five cents."

"Is too much. Why you cheat me?"

"Oh, dear God," Josie muttered under her breath.

I didn't want to fight with Nicoletta. Deep down inside there was always a tiny flicker of hope that maybe someday she'd approve of me. "Okay, Mrs. G. There's a special today. Two cookies for one seventy-five."

Mrs. Gavelli sniffed and reached inside her leather handbag. "Good, I take. And you give me free fortune." She rapped on the glass with her fingernail. "I take those two on end."

I tried to explain. "Mrs. G, it's one free fortune cookie per person, with purchase."

"Yah, but I buy two cookie."

She was confusing me. I already knew I was going to lose this argument.

Josie wrinkled her nose. "Mrs. G, you get one free fortune cookie. It doesn't matter if you buy a dozen cookies. You only get one."

She stomped her foot. "You crazy? What the matter, you cheap or something?"

I gave in and placed the two fortune cookies in the bag with the others.

Josie made a face. "Sal—"

I shook my head at her. "Never mind." These two were going to be the death of me.

Josie whispered a curse word as Mrs. Gavelli grabbed her loot, reached for a fortune cookie, and immediately broke it apart. The lines in her face deepened as she read the paper and then stared at me with disgust.

"What this?" She waved the piece of paper.

I blinked. "Um, the fortune, Mrs. G."

"This no fortune. This crap." She sneered and read aloud from the strip of paper. "May you always have good appetite?" Mrs. Gavelli grunted and threw the paper on the blue-and-white, checkered vinyl floor. "Garbage."

"Pick that up." Josie's face was scarlet.

Mrs. Gavelli placed her hands on her well-rounded hips and glared stubbornly back at Josie.

I grabbed my friend's arm before she could move forward. "You can't hit the customers. It's bad for business."

Josie's mouth twitched in a smile, and she laughed. Mrs. Gavelli watched us suspiciously, bringing her index finger to her head in a circular motion. "Crazy loons."

"Have a pleasant day, Mrs. G," Josie managed to say with a straight face.

Mrs. Gavelli huffed. "You girls better be good. I keep an eye on you."

The bells over my door tinkled in the waft of humid air, which rushed inside after her much-needed departure.

Josie leaned down to pick up the paper and waved it at me. "Why do you let her talk to you like that?"

"Oh, her bark is worse than her bite." Maybe. "You have to ease up. What if there had been another customer in here?"

She frowned and walked into the back room. "I'm sorry. You know I wouldn't have hit her. But it *was* tempting."

I followed Josie out of the storefront, into the area designated as our kitchen or prep area. As my principal and only baker, Josie spent most of her day back here. In addition to the ovens, there was also a large wooden block table in the center of the room used for making doughs and decorating cookies. Surrounding the table was a stainless steel refrigerator, upright freezer, two-bowl sink, and dishwasher.

I grabbed a spoon and lowered it into the steel bowl standing underneath the commercial mixer filled with buttercream frosting Josie had recently prepared.

She held her arms open wide. "That's why you wait on the customers, and I stay back here. I have no patience for her sort."

With a grin, I flicked the spoon and watched as the frosting splattered against Josie's cheek. Surprised, she laughed and picked up another spoon, dipped it into the buttercream, and smeared it down the side of my face before I could react.

"Don't get me started, girlfriend. Even on my worst day,

I can still manage to kick your scrawny butt."

That was an understatement. Josie had always been tough as nails.

I reached for a dishtowel to wipe my face. "Correction. The only reason you are back here is because of your amazing talent. But we can't afford to offend any customers, especially when the place is brand new. I want this to work more than anything."

"Me, too. And it *will* work. We've got a cookie delivery scheduled for tomorrow night. Maybe more on the way, too."

My pulse quickened. "Awesome. Did you call Vido? Is he available?"

"He's going to pick them up tomorrow night before we close." She laughed. "Vido worships the ground I walk on. He's always available."

"You'd better not let Rob hear you say that."

"Oh, please. He's fine." Rob and Josie had married nine years earlier, almost right out of high school, when Josie found out she was pregnant with the first of their four adorable boys. "When you've been married as long as we have, you know what the other one's thinking. Trust me."

I avoided her eyes and stared down at the table, but she was quick to catch my expression.

"Oh gosh, Sal, I'm sorry. That was a stupid thing to say."

I managed a smile. "It's okay. I mean, hey, we were only married five years."

"That's still a long time."

I refilled the spoon and brought it to my lips, savoring the sweet, creamy taste. "Your buttercream is the best. And apparently five years wasn't long enough. I didn't know him like I thought I did."

"Now that the divorce is final, you can start making yourself available for the opposite sex again."

"No, it's way too soon. I don't want to rush into anything. Plus, I need to concentrate on the business. That's all I have time for right now."

Josie's eyes gleamed. "I think we ought to concentrate on celebrating your newfound freedom. Let's go out for drinks tonight."

I started to wash the dishes in the sink. "How're you going to do that? What about the kids?"

"Rob's off the next couple of nights."

"Gee, maybe he'd like to spend some time with his wife for a change."

Josie made a face. "Oh, please. He gets poker night with his buddies. I deserve a night out with my friends, too."

I adored Josie but also envied her. Rob was a loving husband who only had eyes for her. Not that Josie was shabby to look at. After four kids, she still had a great figure, was a good mother, and a fantastic baker.

I did okay with the doughs but was terrible when it came to decorating. Even though I'd put up the capital, this business wouldn't have been possible without her. I glanced at my watch. Nearly seven—closing time. "All right. One drink. And don't invite everybody in town, either. Only a couple of friends. I can't stand to hear one more 'I'm sorry.'"

Josie shook her head at me. "You can't keep hiding from people. Besides, pretty much everyone already knows anyway."

You had to love small towns. Everyone knew everything about your life. I turned off the water. "Did you finish the dough for the baby shower on Saturday?"

"Yes, ma'am. I'll bake and frost them early that morning. And please don't ignore me. You know I hate that."

"I said I'll go. And I'm not hiding from anyone. I want to forget about the past and move on." For the first time in over a year, I was starting to get excited about what the future might hold in store for me. My dream of a happily-ever-after life with Colin may have been shattered, but it was time to start over. A new beginning.

Josie had her cell phone in hand. "That's my girl. Okay, I'll call Ellen. She's back on days at the hospital, so I think she's around. What about Gianna?"

"I'm not sure. She's been studying like crazy for the bar. I'll send her a text and ask."

My baby sister was a recent graduate of Harvard Law School. Besides being drop-dead gorgeous, she was also brilliant. Those were two valid reasons to hate her, but I couldn't do it. We'd always been very close. The state bar examination was being held in a few months, and Gianna was sick with worry she wouldn't pass. I knew otherwise. She'd ace it, the thought making me want to burst with pride.

My fingers flew as I typed out the words. *Going to Ralph's with Josie and Ellen George. Quick drink—wanna come along?*

Gianna must have had her iPhone by her side as I received a *See you in a half hour* within seconds.

I texted back a quick *K*, which I knew she loathed.

Josie's lilting voice filled the room. Her cell phone was carefully balanced on her shoulder while she expertly removed a tray of raspberry cheesecake cookies from the oven and placed them on a cooling rack. She was taking them home to her kids tonight.

I drooled at the smell. Growing up in an Italian family, food had always been plentiful and a passion for me. No one ever left the table hungry. My mother loved telling people the story of how I'd sneak downstairs in the middle of the night to empty my grandmother's cookie jar. Ever since the shop had opened, I seemed to hear it more often. "We should have known then you'd wind up owning a bakery," she'd laughed.

Josie snapped her phone shut. "All set. Ellen will meet us there in about an hour." She turned the oven off and threw her apron in the laundry basket next to the sink. She undid the knotted bun on top of her head, and her auburn hair spilled over her shoulders in a thick, rich curtain.

The bells over the door rang, announcing we had a last-minute customer. I glanced at my watch. It was 6:59, but hey, a sale was a sale. Josie started to put her apron on again, but I held up my hand.

"Allow me." I walked through the doorway into the storefront and immediately froze, my mouth dropping open in surprise.

Amanda Gregorio stood there, a sly smile on her Botox-filled lips. She wore a white, lace blouse and black miniskirt, displaying perfectly-shaped, tanned legs. Her high cheekbones were pink with excitement, resembling Goldilocks in an eerie sort of way. And that was where any similarities ended.

Josie and I had gone to high school with Amanda. We'd

never been friends, and from day one she'd developed a strong dislike toward me. I didn't know why. She'd done everything from spreading lies to tripping me during cheerleading practice. Josie offered to beat her up countless times, but I didn't want any more trouble. I figured once high school was over I'd be rid of her forever.

Until the day I came home early from work and found her in bed with my now ex-husband.

Bile rose in the back of my throat. My initial experience of shock was quickly replaced with anger. Was she here to rub more salt into my still-open wounds?

"What are you doing here?"

Amanda gave me a quick once-over. "I heard you were back in town. How are you, Sal?"

A loud gasp sounded behind me. Josie stood there, hands on hips. "The nerve of some people."

Amanda pressed her palms onto the display case as she stared into it. "Lovely to see you too."

"Hi, guys. Uh, Amanda, maybe this wasn't such a good idea."

Charlotte Gregorio stood behind her cousin, peering out at us over horn-rimmed glasses. I didn't know her well, but at least she didn't seem to be of Amanda's lethal caliber. She'd been ahead of us in school by a year and was always what we'd considered a nerdy type, her mousy, dark eyes poring over textbooks.

"Hi, Charlotte." I managed to force a smile.

Josie muttered a curse word under her breath. "Amanda, shouldn't you be prancing around that overpriced spa of yours, giving someone a bikini waxing?"

Amanda tossed her long, blonde hair in defiance. "That's what I have employees for." She glanced at Josie's hair. "You should come by for a color sometime. Those grays are really starting to show."

Josie gritted her teeth. "Get out of here before I throw you out."

She giggled. "I don't know what you mean. I'm a paying customer. Besides, Charlotte wants to try some of those yummy cheesecake cookies everyone in town is talking about. Don't you,

Char?"

"Um, sure." Charlotte hung her head, voice barely audible.

"I'm sure you wouldn't want people to think you were throwing customers out of your shop. Might be bad for business." She tapped her slender index finger against the side of her head. "Oh, did I mention a friend of mine is an editor over at *The Daily Bugle*?"

I could take a hint, applied with a fingernail that appeared to have been dipped in blood. All I needed right now was bad publicity, especially when we were trying to establish our clientele. Amanda's family was rich and powerful. As much as I hated her, I didn't have the luxury of throwing her out on her ear. How unfortunate.

Josie started forward, but I pulled her back. "It's okay. I can handle this."

Amanda waved a ten-dollar bill in front of me. "When you two are done chatting, I'd like my cookies, please. Six would be divine."

I turned my back on Amanda and grabbed a piece of waxed paper, pausing for a breath. There was no way I'd give her the satisfaction of knowing how devastated I'd been the night I'd found her and Colin together.

Josie folded her arms across her chest as she stared Amanda down. "I think you should let me wait on her. I'll give her a cookie she never forgets."

"Why all the hostility?" Amanda stuck her lips out, and I had a sudden urge to pop them like a balloon. "You guys weren't even getting along. Colin told me so."

My breath caught in my throat, but I wasn't about to indulge her with a reply. "Six dollars, please." It was difficult to look at her without my stomach churning.

Amanda laughed as she handed me the money. "You're so jealous of me it's pathetic. Perhaps if you run to Florida and beg, you can get him back. Then again," she said as she looked me up and down, her gaze coming to rest on my stomach, "maybe not. Gravity hasn't been kind to you. Speaking of weight, Josie, you're looking thin these days. Oh, wait a second. You're not knocked up like usual."

Josie's face flushed a deep crimson as she started forward again. I grabbed her with one hand and gave Amanda her change with the other. "I think it would be best if you left now."

Josie shook me off. "Charlotte, there's a swimming pool down the street. Maybe you could do all of us a favor and hold your cousin's face underneath the water until it turns blue?"

Charlotte's eyes went wide with horror. She looked from us to Amanda with a confused expression.

Amanda gave a halfhearted wave. "There's really no need to threaten my life. We're leaving."

"Good." Josie clenched her jaw.

"Well, girls, it's been fun. But I'll be back. I just love sinfully sweet things." She tossed the bag at Charlotte and waited for her to open the door. I immediately turned and walked into the back room as the bells began jingling away.

The room started to close in, and for a second, I was afraid I might throw up. I grabbed a glass and turned on the faucet. My hand trembled, and the glass slipped out, crashing to the floor. Sighing, I bent down to pick the pieces up.

Josie appeared at my side with a broom and dustpan. "I've got this." Her eyes were somber as she stared into mine. "Are you okay?"

"I will be. Seeing her just brought it all back for me." My mind was still fuzzy when it came to the details after I'd found them together. All I remembered was calmly shutting the bedroom door, walking outside, and getting back into my car. I drove most of the night, until I somehow managed to find myself in Georgia. Then I'd called a lawyer.

Josie put her arm around me. "We'll put up a sign saying *No skanks allowed.*"

I laughed. "What would I do without you?"

"Let's go have some fun. You need to forget about that dirtbag ex-husband of yours and find someone else who'll treat you like you deserve."

"I don't need a man right now. It's way too soon."

"Honey, every girl needs a man sooner or later. They do tend to come in handy at night once in a while." She winked. "Come on upstairs and freshen up so that we can get going. I definitely need a drink that's stronger than water."

Josie's eyes gleamed. "Now you're talking. And I bet there's a biker at Ralph's with your name on him."

I chuckled. "Gee, maybe it's my lucky night."

We walked out to the front room, and I shut off the lights, turned the sign around to say *Closed*, and locked the front door. I started up the wooden stairs located behind the display case that led to my apartment on the second floor. In my head, I was busy calculating today's and yesterday's sales for about the tenth time. Thanks to a life insurance policy I inherited through my great-aunt Luisa, I had a few weeks' time in which the business needed to be turning a steady profit. If not, I'd be forced to move back in with my parents. My stomach revolted at the mere thought.

"Don't let Amanda upset you," Josie said as she followed me up the stairs. "One of these days, that witch is going to get her just desserts. No pun intended, of course."

We laughed together.

Then a chill ran down my spine.

CHAPTER TWO

———

Ralph's was a bar we had frequented on a regular basis since high school. Although we hadn't been of legal drinking age then, Ralph let us stop in for the occasional burger and soda or to shoot a game of pool on the oak-finished table located in the back room. This was the first time I'd been here since I had moved back to town.

I'd received my first kiss in front of Ralph's. I remembered that glorious fall evening with equal amounts of fondness and sadness. As we'd watched the multicolored leaves and full moon with love in our eyes, I was convinced I'd found my one true love.

Ugh. I pushed the memory away. That was the first time my heart had ever been broken, before Colin, and sometimes I still wasn't sure I'd gotten over it. *Don't think about him anymore. That was another lifetime ago.*

Colwestern was a small, quiet town in New York, directly outside of Buffalo. The name was appropriate since it was in the western region, and we usually had bitter cold for more than half the year. Houses were close together, but for the most part, people maintained their properties and got along well with their neighbors. Several streets were zoned both commercial and residential, like Elk Street, where my cookie shop was located.

Wednesday was a slow night at Ralph's. Most of the clientele appeared on the weekends. A few men sat at the bar watching a Yankees' game on the solo flat-screen. A young couple shot pool between embraces. Two women enjoyed a dinner of hamburgers and beers while they chatted. Josie and I settled at a table near the front door.

There was a rustic feel to the place. During the summer, Ralph would line up all thirty Major League Baseball team hats and suspend them from the oak beams in his ceiling. During the fall, he replaced them with NFL helmets. He declared with pride that he ran a sports bar now. Someone needed to tell him to invest in a few more televisions first.

We'd barely settled in and ordered a couple of beers when Ellen George arrived. This was the first time I'd seen her in years. She came over and enveloped me in a warm embrace, which surprised me a bit since I hadn't known her well in high school. I hugged her back.

"Honey, you look great!" She smiled at me.

"So do you."

Ellen was petite and slender, her short, blonde hair cut in a style reminiscent of Dorothy Hamill's. She was a year older than Josie and me. Her father was strict and hadn't allowed her to go out much in high school. She and Josie had become close a couple of years ago when Ellen had helped deliver one of her boys by C-section. It had been touch and go for the baby for a while, and Josie herself had been in the hospital several days. Ellen was now a nurse in the emergency room at Colwestern Hospital.

When her mother had died, she'd taken over as caregiver for her father, who was in fragile health from a stroke. She'd never married, and Josie suspected she didn't even date. I admired how devoted she was to her father's care. It was obvious she adored him.

"How's your dad?" I asked.

Ellen sat next to me and made a face. "As controlling as ever."

Whoops, seems I'm wrong about that one.

Josie frowned. "Why don't you get a full-time aide to come in so you can have your own place? God knows he can afford it."

Ellen's eyes widened in surprise at the suggestion. "Oh, no. We have an aide that comes in three times a week already. As the only child, it's my duty to take care of him in his old age."

Josie and I exchanged glances. It sounded like Ellen's father had been feeding her a guilt trip for years.

Ellen grabbed my hand in a tight squeeze. "I'm so sorry about Colin. I thought you guys made a great couple."

Yeah, me too, once upon a time. "Thanks." Her fingers continued to close around mine, and I grimaced from discomfort. "Uh, Ellen?"

Josie shot Ellen a dirty look. "Jeez, it's not like he died. Stop being so dramatic."

I tried to pull my hand away, but she tightened her grip. "Hel-lo, Ellen?"

"But I thought—" She gazed at me with pity in her eyes.

I jerked my hand free and shook my fingers, thankful there was still feeling in them. "Ouch." Good grief. I hoped she treated her patients more gently.

Ellen's face was puzzled. "Did I hurt you? I'm sorry. I forget my own strength sometimes. I lifted a man who weighed over two hundred pounds today." She snapped her fingers. "Nothing to it."

Josie laughed. "You sound barbaric. And the talk is scaring Sal. Look at how pale she is."

Wrong, that was from sheer pain. "No worries. I'm fine."

As the waitress delivered our beers, Ellen flushed and then ordered a glass of white wine.

"Oh." I stopped the waitress. "Can you bring a glass of red as well? We have someone else joining us." I turned to Ellen. "Gianna will be here in a little while."

"I haven't seen your baby sis in ages. This is so great." Ellen narrowed her eyes at Josie. "You're glowing. Are you expecting again?"

Josie almost spat her beer out. "No fear of that. Rob finally got a vasectomy."

"No way." Ellen was shocked. "You said he'd never get one."

Josie folded her hands on the table. "Yeah, well, he had a sudden change of heart."

I covered my mouth to hide my smile. I knew all about Josie's recent scare. Rob had been so upset that he was more than willing to make the dreaded trip to the doctor. Even though it turned out to be a false alarm, both seemed at peace with their decision. Josie pretty much got pregnant if Rob happened to look at her the wrong way.

"Check this little guy out." Josie tapped her phone and proudly displayed a picture of her youngest baby, now three months old.

Ellen squealed as she clutched the phone between her hands. "What a cutie. I can't believe how he's grown since I last saw him."

At that moment, the door opened, and Gianna breezed in. As if on cue, every man at the bar turned around. By her appearance, no one would have ever guessed she'd been buried in law books since the wee hours of the morning. She greeted Josie and Ellen, then gave my ponytail an affectionate tug, settling in the chair to my immediate left.

Gianna fanned herself with a napkin. She looked spectacular in a yellow sundress that went well with her olive skin—cool and crisp, despite the sweltering September humidity. "Holy cow. They said this heat might finally break tomorrow. Hottest summer I can remember in a long time."

I laughed. "Give it a couple of weeks, and we'll have three feet of snow outside."

When the waitress brought Gianna's wine, Josie gestured toward her friend. "You remember Ellen, don't you?"

"Of course." Gianna smiled, displaying perfect, white teeth. "So nice to see you."

Ellen had been texting on her phone, but looked up to return the pleasantry. "You too, sweetie. How's the studying going?"

Gianna made a face. People frequently mentioned how much we looked like twins. We both had large eyes the color of milk chocolate, but hers were almond-shaped and draped with curly lashes I'd always envied. She in turn said she preferred my longer ones.

She sipped at her wine. "I don't think I can cram one more fact into this big dumb brain of mine. How's the store? I was going to stop by today for one of those dark chocolate cookies. Or maybe half a dozen. God, I must have PMS."

Josie shook her head. "We sold out of those before noon today. They're one of our most popular. I'll make more tomorrow and set some aside for you."

"You're the best. It sounds like things are going well." Gianna tossed her rich, chestnut hair, letting it envelop her shoulders in soft waves.

"We've been busy." I put my hand up to smooth my own ebony hair. It was as long as Gianna's, but with slightly more curl. On humid days like this, it became a frizz fest. "Every day seems to bring in a few new customers. Little by little, we're getting there."

"Well, that's because the place rocks." Gianna beamed.

"We need to find your sister a man." Josie signaled to the waitress for another round. "Who's available in this town?"

Gianna shrugged. "How would I know? Law books and prep classes are my life these days." She gave my arm a nudge. "Mom and Dad are upset you haven't been over for dinner all week. By the way, Jake O'Brien stopped by the house yesterday to fix the dishwasher. Mom tried to call you about a dozen times. Smells like a possible setup to me."

I groaned. "Give me a break. Jake's a nice guy, but we're just friends."

"Grandma's making your favorite tomorrow." My sister took a sip of her wine.

I licked my lips with anticipation. "Braciole?"

"Darn straight." She grinned.

If there was one thing I couldn't resist, it was Grandma Rosa's braciole. My mouth watered, and I could almost taste the thin slices of beef, pan fried with a filling of herbs and cheese, then dipped into her rich tomato sauce. A definite comfort food since I had been a child. "Okay, I'll think about it."

"Mom's worried about you. She said to forget the apartment and move back home for a while."

I pressed my fingers against my temples. "Yeah, she's told me that about a thousand times." I was renting the building with an option to buy and had no intention of moving back home. Ever.

"Have the divorce papers come through yet?" Ellen asked suddenly.

My favorite topic. "It was final a few weeks ago."

"Wow, that was fast, wasn't it?" Ellen observed.

I nodded mutely. What else could I say? It was a huge

relief to be done with the legal tangles. The divorce process had been an emotional roller coaster. I'd suspected Colin's indiscretions for quite a while before actually catching him with Amanda. He'd sworn it had only been the one time, but since Amanda owned a condo in Florida, I had no idea how long they might have been enjoying each other's company. When I refused to give him another chance, he became cruel and belittled me at every opportunity possible. I'd shed more than my fair share of tears and only wanted to move past it all.

Gianna squeezed my hand while she addressed Ellen's question. "No-faults usually don't take very long because there's no children or property involved."

"Would you believe that skank Amanda had the nerve to stop by the shop this afternoon?" Josie asked.

"Get the heck out," Ellen said. "What did she want?"

Josie reached for another beer. "Only to get in Sal's face and remind us how she wields all the power in this town."

"Sickening," Gianna breathed.

Ellen shook her head. "Some people are just born evil."

Josie took a long sip. "She'll get hers eventually, if I have anything to say about it."

I stared at my best friend. "Look, I'm fine now. It was a bit of a shock seeing her at first, but I think I did okay."

"You were amazing." Josie grinned. "Calm, cool, and collected. But that skank won't go away. I know her. She'll keep tormenting you."

"This town is big enough for the both of us."

Josie snickered. "I don't think any town that contains Amanda has spare breathing room. Hell, she could suck the air out of China."

We laughed.

Disgust was written all over Ellen's face. "She wouldn't even make a donation to Hopeful House when I asked her to." Ellen and a group of other nurses served on a committee that provided help to families of children with leukemia.

Gianna's mouth fell open. "With all the money she's got? And it would be a tax write-off for her anyway."

Ellen nodded. "Exactly. I don't know how anyone could be so selfish. What a useless turd."

We all stared. Ellen had been quiet in high school, and I'd never known her to speak ill of anyone. She didn't have any children, but Josie had told me Ellen adored the boys and was great with them on the few occasions she'd been to my friend's house.

I shook my head in amazement. "How can she refuse to help children, especially sick ones? I don't get it. Come by the shop tomorrow, and I'll give you a check."

Ellen's eyes widened. "Look, Sal, I didn't mean to imply anything."

"You didn't. I want to help. Please."

Gianna stood and wrapped her arms around me in a warm bear hug. "You put that rich snob to shame with your generosity."

I hugged her back, embarrassed, and tried to change the subject. "We should have invited Amanda to join us tonight. Oh, wait, I left my poison back at the shop."

Everyone giggled.

Gianna slung her purse over her shoulder. "I've got to get back to my studies. Will we see you tomorrow night for dinner?"

I took a long sip from my bottle. My sister seemed slightly out of focus. Maybe I needed glasses? "I'll be there. Drive safe, and stop worrying about the silly test. You've got it in the bag, girl. I'm so proud of you."

"Love you, Sal." Gianna grinned and waved to Josie and Ellen. "Later, chickies." She headed for the exit.

"Bye, kiddo." Josie winked.

A biker sitting on a bar stool spotted Gianna leaving and ran to hold the door open for her. He was rewarded with a sparkling smile.

Josie shook her head. "Your sister sure knows how to attract the opposite sex. If I didn't love her so much, I'd hate her."

I raised my bottle in the air with a flourish. "To my beautiful baby sister. She's going to make one heck of a lawyer." The room started to spin, and I shut my eyes for a second.

My best friend frowned. "You can't be drunk yet. There's no way."

I suppressed a laugh. "I'm feeling pretty good."

Josie leaned toward Ellen. "She's such a lightweight."

"Puh-leeze." I raised my bottle in the air again. "Another toast. To my new life." I clinked my bottle with their beverages and then downed the rest of my beer in a flash.

"I will definitely drink to that." Josie grinned. "And how good it is to have you back."

"And to the most fabulous cookie designer in the world. My dearest friend Joshie. Er-Josie." I was having difficulty locating my tongue.

She sighed and pushed her beer aside. "Looks like I just became designated driver."

I reached for another beer and snorted, unladylike, into the bottle. "Hey, I should go play some pool and see if I can pick up a biker or two. Maybe I'll take both home with me."

I expected Josie to crack up, but she remained silent, fixated on something behind me. I whirled around too quickly and slid off my lacquered chair onto the floor. Everyone seemed to stop what they were doing to gawk. Embarrassed, I tried to stand. A pair of strong, muscular arms lifted me in a single swoop. Confused, I found myself looking directly into a pair of midnight-blue eyes I would have known anywhere. They belonged to my ex-boyfriend Mike Donovan.

He gazed at me, a playful smile on his lips. "Nice move."

Annoyed, I pushed his hands away and stumbled back into my chair. "Yes, nice to see you too." I touched the back of my head gingerly.

"Are you all right?" Josie asked, concern in her eyes.

"I'll be fine." I hoped I sounded more convincing than I felt. Seeing Mike had sobered me up in a hurry.

He stood there, hands in his jeans pockets, eyes wandering over me. My breath caught in my throat. *What does he want?*

He nodded to Josie and Ellen. "Ladies."

"How's it going, Mike?" Josie asked.

He grinned at her. "Hey, Mrs. Sullivan. How's the new baby? What's that make, a dozen now?"

She smirked. "Wiseass. No, number four."

They all seemed to be waiting for me to add something to the conversation, but I continued to sit there in silence. I didn't know what to say or how to react. My stomach twisted into a giant pretzel as I looked at him.

Josie cleared her throat. "Would you like to join us?"

"No, thanks." Mike's eyes searched mine.

Ellen spoke up. "Um, I've got to be going. Early day at the hospital tomorrow. I'll see you guys later." She moved with the speed and agility of lightning.

Josie rose. "I'll go get some ice for your head. Be right back." She glanced at me with a question in her eyes. I got her unspoken message and gave her a halfhearted wave, indicating I'd be fine with Mike. I wasn't sure if the sudden queasiness in my stomach was from the beer or seeing him. Probably both.

Mike and I had dated for the last two years of high school. He'd been my first serious boyfriend, my first love. He had been my first everything until the night of the senior prom when I'd found him in the backseat of Brenda Snyder's Buick.

When I decided to leave Florida after the divorce and return to my hometown, I had known this day would come eventually. In such a small town, I was bound to run into Mike sooner or later. I wished it had been much later though.

"Well, that wasn't awkward." Mike watched me. "Mind if I sit down?"

I gestured toward Gianna's discarded chair. As he sat, my eyes did some wandering of their own. I hated to admit it, but he'd grown better looking in the eight or nine years since I'd last seen him, and that had been at a respectable distance. Not that he'd ever been a slouch in that department. His black hair curled slightly over the nape of his neck, and he still sported his usual five o'clock shadow. He'd always hated shaving and done it as little as possible. The look worked well with his rugged, tanned face.

Mike was no longer the skinny boy I'd dated in high school, but a muscled and powerful-looking man. Josie casually mentioned once that she'd seen him running a marathon. I hoped it helped him blow off steam. In our two years of dating, we'd had several fights caused by his jealous and insecure ways.

A tingle ran through my body, and I hated myself for it.

"I heard you were back in town." He lowered his voice. "You look terrific. How've you been?"

"I'm fine. And you?"

"Never better." His gaze didn't waver from my face.

The room was growing warmer, and perspiration started to collect on my forehead. Perhaps the air-conditioning had stopped working, but more than likely it was from my extreme discomfort. I glanced away, embarrassed.

Mike edged the chair a little closer to me, scraping it on the floor.

Panicked, I tried to move mine backward and, in the process, hit my head on the wall. "Ouch."

His face broke out into a huge grin. "Still a bit klutzy, I see. You haven't run over anybody's foot lately, have you?"

I bristled at the comment. "Why'd you have to bring that up? You know how upset I was after it happened."

Mike had always been a conscientious driver, unlike me. One time we'd had an argument, and I'd taken off in my usual, impatient huff. I'd accidentally hit him with my car as he ran beside it, trying to stop me. He'd broken his foot, and I'd been hysterical. Fortunately, he forgave me, and we'd experienced a great make-up session afterward. Heat rose through my face as I remembered the intimate details.

"I was sorry to hear about your divorce. It must have been rough on you."

I shrugged. "It's over with, and I'm fine. Thanks for your concern though."

His face fell, and I knew my tone conveyed sarcasm, which hadn't been my intention. So many emotions ran through my head as I stared at this man. In the past ten years, I'd thought of him often. Too often.

"Sal, you never gave me a chance to explain."

I took another sip of beer. "Please, Mike. It was a long time ago. I don't want to get into this now."

"I was drunk that night. I didn't know what I was doing."

I blew out a sigh. "Leave it in the past, okay? Ancient history."

"I never did anything, I swear. She kissed me. I always—"

I dropped my empty beer bottle on the table and stood, albeit shakily. "Nice seeing you. Excuse me. I have to get up early." I started toward the door. Why was he doing this to me? Here I was trying to make a new life for myself, but the old one kept haunting me.

Mike caught my arm as I tried to move past him. His expression changed from forlorn to annoyance in a split second. "What the hell is the matter with you?"

Furious at his tone, I spun around to face him. I moved a little too fast and almost lost my balance. His strong arm steadied me, and I stared into his eyes. Their beauty had always managed to hypnotize me. They were still breathtaking but had hardened, perhaps from a life too full of pain and devoid of happiness. Similar to mine the last couple of years.

I hadn't known it would hurt this much to see him again. "Please let me go."

Mike said something inaudible under his breath. Even in my inebriated state, I knew he was becoming irritated as his tanned face turned the color of flame. He released his grip on my arm and stood there motionless, hands on hips, continuing to watch me. "You haven't changed a bit. Stubborn and pigheaded, as always."

I desperately tried to clear my foggy head. "Did you just call me a pig? That's extremely rude."

His mouth twisted upward in a smile. "You're sloshed. Does it still only take two beers?"

I tossed my head and held up three fingers. "I beg your pardon. For your information, I had this many."

Mike gave a low whistle. "Wow. A new record for you."

Is he making fun of me? I couldn't tell. *And why is the floor on the ceiling?* Again, I started for the exit.

"You're not driving, girl," Josie yelled. "Let me pay the bill, and I'll be right there."

Ignoring her, I pushed through the door and stood on the front steps, inhaling the warm, sticky air with several gulps. My head throbbed, and my stomach was starting to do flip-flops. Suddenly my arm was grabbed from behind, and I whirled around. Mike.

"Sal, talk to me. I'm not the monster you think I am."

I didn't want to dredge up our history again. Maybe my biggest fear was that I might have always been wrong about that night. It was no secret how much Brenda had wanted him. She'd possessed stalker tendencies where Mike was concerned and a reputation that preceded her. Heck, she wasn't called Backseat Brenda for nothing.

I yanked my arm free and pushed at his chest, but couldn't budge him an inch. He was over two hundred pounds of solid muscle. He smirked at my futile attempt, and this infuriated me. Was I some kind of warped entertainment for him? Furious, I reached up to smack him across the face.

In a single motion, he captured my fingers and held them against his chest. His heart drummed rapidly beneath my hand. He placed his other arm around my back, pulling me toward him. Again, I stared into those deep-set eyes and was lost. Mike didn't hesitate as he pressed his soft lips against mine. I closed my eyes and, for a few split seconds, let myself enjoy the tender kiss. It was so natural to be in his powerful arms again, safe and protected. Two words I'd learned to live without.

I quickly came to my senses and struggled to free myself from his grip. Mike released me without protest, but didn't move away.

"What the heck do you think you're doing?" I grabbed my stomach in sudden pain.

Mike didn't reply as he reached a hand up to stroke my hair. I immediately swatted it away.

Then I threw up all over his shoes.

CHAPTER THREE

———

"Drink this." Josie stood beside my bed with a glass of tomato juice.

I removed the pillow from my head. "Ugh. I hate the taste of that stuff."

"Too bad. It helps restore antioxidants and vitamins you lost last night. It'll help you feel much better, trust me."

I took a small sip and grimaced. "Save the health talk, please. I may throw up again."

"If you've got anything left, which I pretty much doubt, you'd better make it quick. The store opens in ten minutes."

Groaning, I handed the juice back to her and put the pillow over my head again. "Tell me the truth. Did I make a fool out of myself last night?"

"Yes."

I peeked out from the pillow, looking for any trace of a smirk on her face. "Stop joking."

"Who's joking? Don't I always give it to you straight? And who the hell gets a hangover and pukes after only three beers?"

"Well, I'm sorry. You know I've never been able to hold my liquor."

"Winnie the Pooh could drink you under the table."

I rolled my eyes at her. "He might have been there last night, for all I remember."

"By the way, you owe Mike a new pair of sneakers." Josie's mouth curved upwards into a sly smile.

Panicked, I pushed the pillow aside and sat up with a start at the mention of his name. "Say what?"

"You do remember barfing on his feet, don't you?"

I shut my eyes. "I had hoped it was a bad dream."

Josie chuckled as she picked my comforter up off the floor. "Sorry. No such luck. You should have seen his face. Absolutely priceless. Then again, you were too busy falling over into the bushes to notice."

My stomach rumbled and not from hunger. "Was he really angry?"

Josie grinned. "He didn't seem too happy. After he helped pack you into the car, he walked off toward his house. Good thing he lives close by. He was barefoot."

My mouth opened in astonishment as she stared back at me, arms folded over her chest. Her mouth started to twitch, and soon we both burst into laughter.

I rolled out of bed, wincing. "Everything hurts."

"We can say you're officially back in town after last night's performance."

"Well, please don't alert the presses. I can't remember the last time I was so embarrassed."

"I can." Josie's voice was wicked. "Does Sal the Mooch ring a bell?"

I threw my pillow at her head, and she ducked. "You promised never to call me that again."

In junior high, I'd lost my snack money one day and borrowed a dollar from another student. Somehow I'd forgotten to pay her back, and thus my new nickname was born. Even after I finally did return the dollar, the name stuck with me throughout high school.

"Yeah, so I lied." Josie paused for a moment. "Um, you might not want to hear this, but—"

"Please tell me I didn't do anything else repulsive." I rubbed sleep out of my eyes.

"I think Mike still has feelings for you."

This was the last thing I expected to hear. "Why on earth would you say that?"

"It was the way he was looking at you. I've always suspected, anyhow. Oh, and for the record, I witnessed the kiss too. It was like you guys were back in high school again."

My cheeks were hot underneath my fingertips. "I was drunk. I didn't know what I was doing." Great. Hadn't Mike said the very same thing to me last night?

Josie gave a low chuckle. "Yeah, it definitely looked like that."

"It doesn't matter. We've been over and done with for years." My stomach was growing queasy again.

Her eyes grew soft. "He hasn't been serious with anyone since you, Sal."

"Oh, please. Don't tell me he hasn't been with a woman in ten years."

She snorted. "I didn't say he was a monk, moron. I'm saying he hasn't been in love with anyone since you."

Although deep down I was pleased to hear this, I wasn't about to let anyone—not even my best friend—know. "It's too late. We could never be together again."

"Uh-huh." Josie's tone was dismissive as she walked over to my linen closet, reached inside, and threw a towel at my head. "Come on, go take a quick shower. I can manage everything until you get downstairs."

* * *

The day passed uneventfully. Sales were a bit slow, so in between customers I balanced the books from my seat at the front, next to the large window. We'd set up three small tables there so that customers could linger and enjoy treats with a cup of coffee. I already had visions of expanding and maybe one day offering a small lunch menu too. Perhaps some egg rolls to go with the fortune cookies? I smiled to myself. My dream of owning a business had finally become a reality. I was still pinching myself at times.

I cleaned the display case, polishing the glass until it shone, and helped Josie make up two baskets for local deliveries while she worked on the upcoming baby shower order. I glanced in awe at the sugar cookies in the shapes of ducks, rattles, and baby carriages, piped in her homemade strawberry icing, honoring our client's soon-to-arrive baby girl. Josie had started culinary school, but left when she got pregnant with her first baby. Her talent was rare, and I never ceased to marvel how, without her, I wouldn't have been able to carry out my dream.

There was a rap on the back door, and I opened it. Vido Falzo waited in the alley. Tall, dark, and greasy, he was on permanent disability for a back injury sustained a few years ago, which made him a terrific part-time employee. He worked cheap and was always available. At Vido's request, we kept his name off the books. I never asked why.

The trunk of Vido's Ford Focus was open and ready for action. Rumor had it, he and his brothers were the type of people you didn't want to annoy since they had mob connections. As I watched, he removed the cigarette from his mouth and threw it on the ground, grinning at me with tobacco-stained teeth. Voice hoarse, he spoke in a stage whisper. "You got the baskets?"

Suddenly, I felt like I was in an episode of *The Sopranos*.

"They're on the counter, Vido," Josie called out as she washed trays at the sink.

Vido looked her up and down several times as a sly grin formed under his dark, wiry beard. He turned to me, and his attention immediately focused on my chest.

I crossed my arms over the front of my low-cut, white V-neck shirt. Sure, I'd known Vido for years, but he still had the ability to make my skin crawl.

I picked up one of the baskets, and he grabbed the other two. While we placed them in his trunk, I tried desperately not to think about what else might have been in there recently. I handed him two twenty-dollar bills that he stuffed into the pocket of his faded jeans, riddled with holes.

Vido took one last parting look at my chest and whispered, "Have a blessed day." He grinned and sped off in his car.

I shut the back door and turned to Josie, busy untying her apron. "Why does Vido still scare the crap out of me?"

"Oh, he's harmless."

"I'm pretty sure he's a pervert." I picked up the container of double fudge cookie dough I'd prepared earlier and placed it into the refrigerator for Josie to use tomorrow.

"No, he's not. I went out with him once, remember?"

"You went out with everyone."

Josie laughed as she wiped down the prep table. "I've

been hearing rumors about him lately."

"Do tell." I grabbed a broom and dustpan from the corner.

"I heard he's been spending time at skanky Amanda's house. Definitely a match made in heaven."

"Maybe he's doing some work for her," I added teasingly, "taking out the trash or something."

She smiled wickedly. "I'm guessing it's something else, all right."

I shook my head in amazement. "I can't picture those two together."

"Who'd want to?"

"Gross. That's all I have to say." I emptied the dustpan into the garbage.

Josie glanced at the clock. It was after 6:30. "Hey, is it okay with you if I take off a few minutes early? Rob and I are having a date night."

I smiled. "Aww, that's sweet."

"Yeah, well, I do like to see him once in a while without four kids hanging off me. My mom agreed to babysit too, which you know is rare. We'll probably go see a movie."

I gestured toward the front door. "Go. I'll finish cleaning up. Have fun."

"Aren't your parents expecting you for dinner?"

"Honestly, I don't know if I can hold anything in my stomach."

"You'd better eat something. You know how they get if you—" The bells on the front door jingled, and we both peered through the doorway to see who our latest customer was.

Josie gritted her teeth. "Am I having a nightmare?"

Amanda was back. *Mental head slap.* Minus Charlotte this time, she seemed so involved in checking the place out that we weren't positive she had noticed us. Or perhaps she liked the idea of having a ready-made audience. She glanced at the newly painted, cream-colored walls and the silver-framed artwork I'd bought discounted from a local shop. Next, Amanda ran her blood-red manicure all over the cute wooden wall shelf Rob had made for us, as if testing for dust. The shelf held two porcelain figurines seated at a table with a plate of cookies and a teapot between them. She picked up each figurine, turning them around in her hands, then returned them to the shelf in opposite spaces.

"Oh, great." I groaned under my breath. "Is this going to be an everyday thing?"

Josie balled her right hand into a fist. "I'll take care of her."

"No. You go. Rob's waiting for you."

"Are you sure?"

"Positive. She's here to get a rise out of me, anyway. Don't worry. I'll be nice."

Josie grinned. "But I don't want you to be nice."

"Ha-ha. Look, if she doesn't get a reaction from us, she'll stop coming in eventually." *I hope.* We walked out of the back room together.

Amanda had her nose pressed to the glass of the display case like a child. I cringed, having polished it less than an hour ago.

"Oh, look who's here. Again. Too bad I'm leaving. We could have spent quality time together." Josie winked. "Call me later, babe." Josie's code for *let me know what happens, or else.*

"Bye. Have fun." I turned to Amanda. "What would you like?"

"Mm." Amanda licked her lips. "Josie is a bitch, but she sure can bake. What are those cookies?"

I clenched my fists. "Sugar with sprinkles."

While Amanda continued her browsing, I tapped my foot. The bells over the door rang again, and Mrs. Gavelli strolled in. I had a sudden urge to smack my head against something hard.

"Hello, Mrs. G." Amanda waved.

Mrs. Gavelli's face lit up. "Amanda, sweetie, how you are? And so pretty. How your spa do?"

Amanda beamed. "Wonderful. I'm thinking about adding a Jacuzzi."

"Mama Mia! I need to go there."

I clasped my hands together and smiled at the old woman. "What can I do for you, Mrs. G?"

She glared at me. "You give me two more butter cookies."

"Of course, but no more specials. If you want them, you have to pay full price." I grabbed a piece of waxed paper from the counter behind me.

Mrs. Gavelli clucked her tongue and reached inside her purse for money. "You a cheat. Okay, I take. But I'm gonna tell your grandmama. And you give me fortune this time. Real fortune."

I prayed she'd get a good one, or she'd really make my life miserable.

"Ooh." Amanda pointed her finger at the case and squealed. "I want one of those too. You forgot to give me one yesterday."

Mrs. Gavelli nodded gravely. "She always forget."

I reached down to grab a fortune cookie for each of them, trying to push the negative thoughts away. *I can do this.*

They both eagerly broke their cookies apart at the same moment. Mrs. Gavelli's lips moved silently then she looked at me in disbelief. "Why you give me lousy fortune again?"

Good grief. "Mrs. Gavelli, I don't put those in there on purpose. We buy the fortunes from a novelty store, and Josie stuffs them into the cookies. I have no idea what they're going to say."

"Yah, sure," she spat out, and then read aloud. "*Be nice or leave.*"

Poetic justice. I turned around to ring up her sale, hoping she wouldn't see my smile.

Mrs. Gavelli glanced over Amanda's shoulder. "What you get?"

Drawing her eyebrows together, Amanda stared intently at the strip. "I don't understand this."

"They don't mean anything." Why did people keep putting so much emphasis on these little pieces of paper?

Amanda frowned as she read aloud. "*No fortune for you. Wrong cookie. Your luck is just not there.*"

"Aha!" Mrs. Gavelli pointed a finger at me. "You see? She get bad fortune too. Is setup."

I closed my eyes and leaned back against the wall, defeated.

"Well," Amanda sniffed. "I know you're jealous of me,

but it does seem like kind of a childish thing to do."

Count to ten, Sal. Nope, didn't work. "Buy something now or leave."

Mrs. Gavelli shook her fist at me. "You rude. Is no way to treat customer." She flounced out the door, bag in hand.

Amanda didn't even look up. "Ooh, I think I want one of those vanilla yummy things with the chocolate drops on top. What the heck. Give me six of them."

"Fudge," I corrected her. "They're called Fudgy Delights. And that will be six dollars." I scooped the cookies into a bag.

Amanda's chin dropped. "Don't I get a discount?"

She had to be kidding. "Why on earth would I give you a discount?"

"I was in here yesterday as well," Amanda said. "Shouldn't volume count for something?"

"Six dollars, please." I clenched my jaw, praying she would leave soon. I didn't want another confrontation.

Amanda shook her head in disgust while she pawed through her mammoth-sized Gucci purse. She handed me six singles and snatched her bag, reaching inside to remove a cookie. "You really should lose the attitude. It makes you ugly. Oops, I mean uglier."

I gritted my teeth as I turned away from her to ring up the sale, praying for more self-control. If I could wait on Amanda and manage not to lose my temper, I knew I'd be successful with any other customer who walked through the door. "Good night. It's closing time."

She took a bite and moaned, closing her eyes. "But I'm not done enjoying my cookie yet."

"Enjoy it outside on the porch. Now, please."

My cell phone started ringing from the back room where I'd left it. "Good night, Amanda."

She shot me a dirty look and turned on her heel, pushing the front door open with force, bells jingling away merrily at her departure. I quickly locked the door before she decided to return.

Good riddance. I ran into the back to grab my phone and glanced at the number on the screen before answering. "Hi, Mom."

"Hi, sweetheart," she purred into the phone. "You're still

coming for dinner, right?"

"Yes, I'll be there."

"It's already getting dark."

I surveyed the kitchen area one last time and shut the lights off. "Mom, I think I can drive in the dark."

"Did you want to bring a guest?" Her voice was thick with hope.

"You mean a date? Who on earth would I bring?"

"Jake was here yesterday. He's such a nice—"

I pinched the bridge of my nose between my thumb and forefinger. "I'm not ready for this. Please ease up, Mom."

She sighed loudly. "You're nearing thirty. You should get married again and have a couple of babies. Your biological clock is ticking."

"Okay, I'm hanging up now. Do you need anything?"

"The newspaper didn't get delivered today. Can you bring yours? Oh, and why don't you bring your father some of those *genettis* Josie makes? They might cheer him up." My mother was fooling herself.

"Sure. I'll see you soon." I hung up and walked out to the bakery case. As I placed a dozen of the Italian, glazed cookies sprinkled with nonpareils into one of my pink bakery boxes, I knew they wouldn't do the trick. My father had recently turned sixty-five and was convinced he'd die soon. It didn't matter that he was in excellent health. Domenic Muccio said his time was coming soon.

His latest hobby consisted of scanning the obituaries and attending random wakes so that he'd know exactly what he wanted when the fateful day arrived. My mother was happy to leave him to his own devices. His total opposite, she acted like a teenager most days. I loved them dearly, but they were both certifiably nuts.

I walked to the front door and changed the sign over to *Closed*. Amanda sat in one of the wicker chairs, nibbling away. She must have sensed my presence because she suddenly turned and waved at me gaily. I ignored her as I shut the light off and lowered the blind on the door.

Once upstairs, I stepped into the shower for a quick rinse and changed into a pink T-shirt and white shorts. I grabbed a pair of sandals from my closet and blew dry my hair. After adding some blush and mascara, I was good to go.

Darkness had fallen in the twenty minutes since I'd closed the shop. Thunderstorms were expected later, the reason for the pitch-black sky. Perhaps then the heat wave would be over for the year. Fall was right around the corner, and soon enough winter would beckon with snow and cold, northeastern temperatures.

I sighed. Come January, I'd really be missing the Sunshine State.

My car was parked out in the alley. I started toward the back door of the shop then remembered the newspaper. It would be a shame if my father couldn't read the obituaries during dinner. Shaking my head, I unlocked the front door and pushed to open it. Something held the door firmly in place from the other side. Convinced the heat was making it stick, I pushed harder. The door moved forward but only slightly.

What the heck? I reached along the inside wall to turn on the porch light. I sucked in a sharp breath, and my blood ran cold.

Draped across my woven welcome mat lay Amanda's lifeless body.

CHAPTER FOUR

My legs went numb. For a minute, all I could do was stare. I forced myself to move forward and managed to squeeze out the doorway while trying not to disturb her body. I knelt beside Amanda and felt for a pulse in her wrist. Nothing. *Oh my God.*

I fumbled in my purse for my cell phone and immediately dialed 9-1-1. I sat there, hyperventilating, trying not to look at her, but it was impossible.

"Nine-one-one, what is your emergency?"

I started to babble. "Please. She collapsed. On my front porch."

"Who collapsed, ma'am?"

"A customer. Her—Amanda Gregorio. I-I came downstairs and opened the door, and she was lying on my porch."

"Name and address, ma'am?"

I was aware of my breath coming in shallow gasps. "Sally Muccio. It's my bakery. Samples. I mean, Sally's Samples."

"What's the address, ma'am?"

I couldn't think. "Um. Thirty-nine Elk Street. Please hurry."

"The medics are on their way. Is she breathing?"

"I don't think so."

"Can you tell if her airway is clear? Do you know CPR?"

My pulse was racing. I leaned close to Amanda's face, looking for any sign of life. There was visible swelling around her eyes and lips, definitely not Botox related. A wave of fear traveled through my body. Was there something wrong with the cookies she'd eaten?

"Ma'am?"

There was a huge lump in my throat. "I'm sorry. I don't know CPR." I rocked back and forth on my knees, praying she'd sit up and insult me. Had I wished her dead once upon a time? Probably, but I hadn't really meant it. *Please let her be okay.*

I glanced toward the chair where she'd been sitting a short time ago and noticed her purse, upside down, with all the contents spilled out, almost as if she'd been searching for something. What had happened to her?

Flashing lights and a bevy of sirens captured my attention. An emergency vehicle screeched to a halt in front of my shop. A police car pulled up right behind them. A man and a woman rushed toward me with a gurney.

"Have they arrived?" the 9-1-1 operator asked.

"Yes. Thank you." I clicked off and got to my feet.

"Stand back, ma'am," the man ordered.

I stepped off the porch and crossed over to the sidewalk while they attended to Amanda. A small crowd had started to gather in the street. The wind whipped through the trees, shaking them back and forth, and warning of the impending storm. I shivered.

"What happened here?" The woman medic addressed me while her partner administered CPR.

I looked at her, dumbfounded. "I don't know. She was eating cookies and then collapsed on my porch."

"Do you know her?"

I nodded. "Her name is Amanda Gregorio."

"Do you know if she has a pre-existing medical condition, ma'am?"

From the corner of my eye, I could see a policeman standing behind me. "I-I don't know. Her mouth looks swollen—"

"Allergic reaction?" The woman medic addressed her partner.

"Possibly." He shook his head. "I'm not getting anything."

"Let's go!" the woman shouted. They lifted Amanda's body onto the gurney and hurried past me toward the ambulance.

Within seconds they were gone, amidst a brilliant cascade of lights and wailing sirens. I stood there, trembling with fear, unsure what to do next.

There was a gentle tap on my shoulder. "Miss Muccio?" A policeman about my age gestured toward the shop. "Can I ask you a few questions?"

I watched him in a foggy haze. "Questions?"

His warm green eyes stared at me, full of concern. "Are you okay, miss?"

I shuddered. "I don't know. I guess."

The policeman placed his hand on my elbow and guided me up the steps into the shop. He shut the door behind us. My inquisitive neighbors wouldn't be able to hear our conversation now.

"I'm Officer Jenkins. You are Sally Muccio, the owner of Sally's Samples?"

I stared out the window into the darkness. "Huh? Oh, right."

He held out a chair. "You don't look very well. You'd better sit."

I sank heavily into the chair. He sat across from me, notebook and pen in hand. Even in my shocked state, I couldn't help but notice how good looking he was. Thick, dirty-blond hair and an aristocratic-looking nose. Broad shoulders and a slim waist. One of those guys who made women swoon over men in uniform. He must have been new to the local force. All of the cops I remembered around here were old, balding, and cranky. I'd always admired the dark blue uniform New York officers wore, but he would have looked hot in a paper bag.

"Would you like me to get you some water?"

I shook my head. "No, thank you." I watched while he made some notes. "What happened to Officer Cowell?"

He grinned, displaying teeth well suited for a Crest commercial. "He retired earlier this year. Actually, his leaving created an opening so that I was able to transfer here from Boston."

"He tried to arrest me once for jaywalking."

Officer Jenkins' mouth twitched. "Yeah, sounds like him." Then he frowned. "Your lips are turning blue. Do you want to grab a sweater, Miss Muccio?"

My teeth started to chatter. "No, I'm fine. Please call me Sally."

"Only if you call me Brian."

I hesitated. "But you're a cop."

"We won't tell anyone." He chuckled and reached for his pen again. "So you know Miss Gregorio?"

"We went to high school together. Today was the first time I'd seen her in a while." The memory of finding her and Colin together in a compromising position flashed through my mind, and I trembled. "Well, actually, yesterday was."

"Oh, right. I heard you moved back recently."

I raised my eyebrows. "How did you know?"

Brian's cheeks reddened. "I was in here last week. Your coworker was telling someone you'd recently relocated from Florida."

"I don't remember seeing you." *And I definitely would have remembered.*

"You were on the phone with someone in the back room." He toyed with his pen. "Your sister's name is Gianna, right?"

I had to hand it to my sister. She always knew where to find the good-looking ones. "How do you know Gianna?"

"I've talked to her a couple of times at the sub shop. I gather she and the owner, Frank Taylor, go together?"

I nodded. "For about a year."

"She's very nice—and almost as beautiful as her sister." He watched me expectantly and smiled slowly.

My heart skipped a beat. The hot cop was flirting with me. "Uh, thank you. And you can call me Sal if you like. Everyone does."

The cleft in his chin deepened as he grinned, perhaps a bit longer than necessary to convey politeness. I was amazed how at ease I felt with him, despite the impressive badge on his chest, which flashed in the bright lighting of my shop, and the intimidating Glock attached to his belt.

Brian glanced at his pad again. "Was Amanda okay while she was in the shop?"

"Yes, she seemed fine."

He shifted in his seat. "I overheard you tell the medic her lips were swollen?"

"Yes. There was swelling around her eyes, too."

"Did she buy any cookies from you?"

My voice started to shake. "Nothing in the cookies would have caused her to become sick. I'd never do something like that."

Brian put his hand on my shoulder. "Hey, relax. I'm not implying anything." He peered closely at me, as if he understood my agitation. "You guys didn't get along, did you?"

"It's a long story." I stared at the floor, refusing to meet his gaze.

Brian leaned forward across the table on his elbows. "Care to enlighten me?"

Heat crept into my face. I couldn't believe I had to say this to a member of the opposite sex, much less a cop. I raised my head and met his eyes, a brilliant green with golden flecks. They were kind and encouraged me to proceed. *Why does he have to be so darn good-looking?* "Sh-she had an affair with my husband."

Brian's eyebrows shot up. "Husband?"

"Ex-husband. The divorce was final a few weeks ago."

"I'm sorry, Sally." His face was full of sympathy. "That's quite a lot to deal with." He jotted something down on his notepad.

A knot tightened in my stomach. I didn't want anyone to pity me. "Don't write that down!"

He put his hand on my shoulder again. "Relax. I have to record all the details."

"But everyone will think I tried to hurt her because of Colin." My throat tightened, and I was afraid I was going to lose it soon.

"No one is accusing you of anything." Brian's voice was soft.

His gentle tone did the trick, and I immediately burst into tears. "I'm sorry. I don't know what to do. I've put every dime I have into this business. Once this story gets out, people might not want to come here anymore."

Brian reached into his pocket. When he handed me a

handkerchief, I was amazed. I'd always associated that act of chivalry with people of my father's age group.

"Thanks." My mascara had to be running everywhere, and I probably looked like a rabid raccoon.

"Anytime. So do you know how long she might have been out on the front porch?"

At that moment, Josie flung the door open and stumbled in. She glanced at me, wild-eyed, then at Brian. Rushing to my side, she threw her arms around me. "What the hell happened? Your parents called. They were worried when you didn't show up or answer your phone. We were getting ready to go into the theater, so I told Rob I wanted to stop by. The neighbors said someone fainted outside?"

I nodded and gestured toward her. "This is my partner, Josie Sullivan."

Josie reached out to shake Brian's hand. "Hello, officer. Yes, I've seen you in the shop. Chocolate chip, right?"

"Good memory," he grinned.

She grabbed my arm. "What happened?"

I blew my nose. "Amanda collapsed on the porch."

"Oh my God." Josie's mouth dropped open. "This is all we need for business now."

"Not fond of her either, are you?" Brian asked.

Josie's cheeks turned scarlet. "I'm sorry. We didn't wish her any ill will, officer. Amanda's—well, she's not a very nice person. She pretty much ruined Sal's life."

Brian made more notes on the pad until his cell phone rang. "Excuse me, ladies. I'll be right back." He went outside to take the call.

Josie knelt beside me. "What happened? Did you and Amanda have a fight?"

I shook my head. "Of course not. She bought some cookies and took them out on to the porch. I closed up the shop, and she stood there, waving and trying to annoy me. I went upstairs to change, and when I came back down, I found her—like that."

"Well, what do they think happened?" Josie plopped herself in Brian's chair.

I shrugged. "They're wondering if it could have been a

reaction or an allergy."

"To what? There's nothing here that would have triggered that."

"I know. But can we prove it?"

The color drained from Josie's face. "Okay, maybe we're worrying for no reason. She might come out of this fine. Then she can tell everyone what happened, and we're not responsible. Right?"

I stared at her, unconvinced.

Brian came back in the shop, his expression grim.

"What is it?" I held my breath.

He glanced from me to Josie with hesitation. "Amanda's dead. She was already gone when they put her in the ambulance. They tried to resuscitate her on the way to the hospital, but it was no use. I'm really sorry."

Josie put her hands to her mouth in an expression of horror while I continued to sit there, immobile, asking myself how this could have happened. And one other question came to mind. *Will everyone think I killed her?*

CHAPTER FIVE

———

"Okay, now tell us everything from the beginning again," Mom said.

Bleary-eyed, I finished chewing my mouthful of spaghetti and stared around the cherry wood dining room table at my family. It was near midnight, and my parents had insisted I spend the night. My mother was seated at my right and Gianna to my left. My father sat at the head of the table, the newspaper spread out in front of him. Grandma Rosa bustled back and forth between the kitchen and dining room.

No way was I going back to the shop alone tonight, they had declared. It was useless to argue, and I was too exhausted from the day's activities to try. The fact that I hadn't had much sleep the night before due to my alcoholic binge wasn't helping my situation, either. After having found Amanda's body, rest would now be impossible.

Of course, I wasn't allowed to go to bed until I had eaten and shared the story of my horrific night with everyone. I took a sip of water and glanced up at the dark paneling that held my father's favorite painting, an imitation of da Vinci's *Mona Lisa*. Her eyes seemed to tell me she understood what I was going through.

"Oh, honey, wait until I get you some more to eat." My mother already had the top off the china tureen and had scooped out another slice of braciole for me before I could protest. She flashed by me in record time on her four-inch stiletto heels. Even at this time of night, she was decked out in a sparkly, silver mini dress. I had to admit she looked terrific at the age of fifty-two. The face-lift she underwent last year certainly hadn't hurt her, either. My mother has always had a fantastic figure, despite giving birth to two children. The other day we'd been shopping at the local farmer's market together, when our cashier asked if we were sisters and who was older. Mom wasted no time. She said I was.

"Mom." I covered my plate. "I really don't have much of an appetite."

She pushed my hands away and placed parmesan cheese and the plate with the braciole in front of me, then scooped more spaghetti from a bowl. It was a losing battle. "Sweetie, you need to keep up your strength. You've had a traumatic evening."

Gianna's delicate features were masked with worry. "Why don't you sleep with me tonight? You know, in case you have a nightmare?"

My father tossed the paper aside, frowning. "You see? That girl, she had it coming."

"Domenic!" my mother cried. "How can you say such a thing?"

Dad rubbed his balding head in exasperation. "After what she did to our daughter, Maria? It's karma. Simple as that."

"Sounds like it may have been an allergic reaction." My sister took a sip of her wine.

My father grunted and pointed at Gianna. "Someone wanted her dead. They fixed it so she'd have a reaction. God, she was a rotten little thing." He pounded his fist on the table. "You should never cross people. Or else someday you, too, might wind up lying on someone's porch."

"Oh my God." My sister rolled her eyes at the ceiling.

"I wonder if she'll get a huge crowd at her funeral," my father mused aloud as he stared at his painting. He was probably wondering if his service would be larger.

"Dad," Gianna said. "Her mother is the town socialite. They have more money than God. Amanda owned the only spa around here. Even if people didn't like her, they'll still go to the wake, at least for her mother's sake."

He waved her off and studied the paper again. "When I go, I want my obituary to take up an entire page. You'll write it, Gianna. You've always been good with words."

"Dear Lord," my grandmother muttered under her breath. "All you think about is death! It is like living with the

Grim Reaper."

Dad shot his mother-in-law a look of exasperation. "You should be thinking about it too, old lady. You've got at least ten years on me. You're liable to go anytime."

"Sei pazzo." Grandma Rosa shook her head.

"You're the one who's crazy." My father frowned at her. "I bet you don't even have a burial plot yet."

I groaned. "Enough, please? Can we stop talking about funerals for one night?"

"Poor sweetie." My mother wrapped her arms around me as I stared, eyes pleading for help, at my grandmother.

"Stop smothering her, Maria." Grandma Rosa walked into the kitchen. "Sally is not a baby anymore, for crying out loud. She is a grown woman."

My father snorted as he reached for his wineglass. "A divorced woman. I knew you never should have married that bum. Now his tramp is dead. They're ruining your life."

I put my weary head in my hands.

"You didn't finish telling us what happened." Gianna refilled her glass.

I blew out a breath. "There isn't much more to tell. Brian made a call to the station and another policeman showed up. They searched the shop and waited while Josie and I locked the door, and then they left."

"Will they close the place for a while and call in a forensics team?" Gianna, lawyer-in-training, asked.

I ate a small bite of braciole. "I don't think so. They can't be sure of the cause of death until the autopsy results come in, so they don't know if it was an accident or—" I stopped myself, unable to say the word.

Gianna looked at me in surprise. "They actually think she might have been murdered?"

"Of course she was murdered," my father bellowed. "The girl was evil!"

Grandma Rosa reappeared, setting a cup of espresso in front of me.

"If I have coffee now, I'll be up all night."

She handed me the cream and sugar from the nearby buffet table and shook her snow-white head. "Sally, my love, who are you kidding? There is no way you will sleep tonight, coffee or no coffee."

I hated to admit it, but she was right. Sighing, I took a sip of the strong drink and almost choked, then cocked one eye at my grandmother. "What did you put in here?"

She shrugged. "Maybe a little sambuca. It is good for you."

My mother reached inside her cosmetic bag and pulled out a compact. She started removing her false eyelashes at the table. "Sal, the police don't think you have anything to do with it, right? I mean, do they know what she did to you?"

I finished chewing another bite before answering. "I told Brian about our, shall we say, differences. He said they can't speculate on anything until the autopsy comes back."

"Who is this Brian?" Grandma Rosa raised one eyebrow and sat down across from me.

Gianna winked. "He's the new cop on the force. I see him at Frank's place all the time. He's very nice. Cute too."

"What are you talking about?" Heat rose through my face.

"Maybe we should invite him over for dinner." My mother held the mirror out in front of her while she primped her long hair. It was dark like mine, but not as curly.

I looked at her in disbelief. "Mom, you don't invite cops to dinner."

"Why not? They have to eat too, you know."

A small gurgle escaped from my mouth before I could stop it.

My mother stood, yawned, and stretched. "I need to get some sleep. I'm showing houses tomorrow morning." She enjoyed dressing up and wearing her gold-plated name badge as she viewed homes with prospective clients. My parents didn't need the extra money. Their house was paid off, and my father received a generous pension from the railroad, which was a good thing because in the six months since my mother started her real estate career, she'd made exactly zero in sales.

Mom ran around the table, kissing each one of us on the cheek and ending with my father. "Don't be too long." She wrapped her arms around his neck. "You know how I hate to sleep alone."

He chuckled and swatted her behind. "I'll be up in a minute, hot stuff."

"Jeez Louise." Gianna raised her eyebrows in disgust. "Do we really need to see this?"

Maria Muccio loved to be the center of attention. She blew us all another kiss before she padded up the stairs lightly in her tiny high heels. She reminded me of a Barbie doll.

Gianna downed the rest of her wine in a single gulp. "Why is it I feel like she's the child sometimes, and I'm the mother?"

Grandma Rosa grimaced as she brought her finger to her head in a circular motion. "Your mama, now, do not get me wrong. She is my daughter, and I love her like crazy, but sometimes she acts like a big child. Maybe she is going through the puberty bit again."

"More like the change," I said.

We were startled by a rap on the door. Grandma Rosa peered out the window cautiously then shook her head. "Nicoletta."

My father snorted and got to his feet. In the past couple of years, he'd grown stouter across the middle. He no longer exercised and had started going to Denny's for a Grand Slam breakfast every morning. His reasoning was that people should indulge in what they loved while allowed. You never knew when God was going to call you home.

"Crazy broad probably wants to borrow oregano at this hour. I'm going to bed. If the Gregorios need help picking out a casket, tell them to come see me. I know where they can get a heck of a deal. *Notte belle ragazze.*" He blew kisses at Gianna and me.

"Good night, Daddy." I thought it was sweet how our father always called us beautiful.

Grandma Rosa appeared in the doorway, followed by Mrs. Gavelli. She gasped when she saw me and pointed her finger. "You! Why you no in jail?" She turned to my grandmother. "Your granddaughter, she kill that nice Amanda. I call police and tell them you here." She started for the phone on the kitchen wall.

"Mrs. G, the police know where I am." I rubbed my weary eyes.

Grandma Rosa grabbed Mrs. Gavelli's arm and spoke to her angrily in Italian. Mrs. Gavelli continued her tirade while flapping her arms about and extending her hand in my direction. Gianna looked at me and rolled her eyes. We'd seen this wacky bit transpire between the two of them before.

"Get out of this house," Grandma Rosa responded, this time in English. "How dare you come in here and accuse my granddaughter of murder."

Mrs. Gavelli glared at me. "Is not right. You a bad lot."

"Out!" Grandma yelled.

"I call police from my house." Mrs. Gavelli folded her arms across her chest. "I tell everyone what you do."

My grandmother charged into the kitchen and returned with a broom, holding it over her head. "If you do not leave now, you will be sorry."

They took up their fight in Italian again, which ended with my grandmother rapping Mrs. Gavelli on the backside with the broom. Gianna and I sat motionless, waiting for the drama to end. It was useless to interfere.

Breathing heavy, Mrs. Gavelli shook her fist at my grandmother. "Crazy loon. We see how you like to visit little *monella* behind bars." She'd been calling me a brat ever since the incident with Johnny.

Without another word, she pulled at her tan-colored knee-highs, which had rolled down around her ankles, and flounced out the door.

"Gianna, you need to go to bed. Sally will help me stack the dishes." My grandmother calmly turned and started to clear the table as if nothing had happened.

Gianna and I stared at each other, confused.

"Grandma, shouldn't I help?" Gianna asked. "Sal's had kind of a rough night."

Grandmother Rosa raised an eyebrow at my sister and pointed toward the stairs. "You go to bed. Sally will be fine."

She wanted to talk to me alone.

Gianna seemed to get the message as well because she didn't argue any further. She kissed Grandma Rosa good night then threw her arms around my neck. "Don't worry. Everything will be all right."

I gave her a kiss on the cheek and gathered the rest of the dishes. I followed Grandma Rosa into the bright-yellow kitchen, where she spent most of her time. As I reached for the large cast-iron casserole dish on the stainless steel stove, which held remains of braciole and tomato sauce, she stopped me.

"Leave the braciole pan to soak. We will stack the rest of these in the dishwasher."

I nodded and did as I was told. When we'd finished stacking and Grandma had wiped down the counters, she motioned for me to sit at the round, teakwood table. She took my hands in her tiny, warm ones. Her dark eyes held years of wisdom I hoped I'd inherit someday. The wrinkles around them were fine, but her skin was still flawless, even at the age of seventy-five. Unlike my mother, Grandma Rosa didn't rely on face-lifts to look younger. She told everyone the secret to beauty was eating good Italian food and having olive skin. She said it hid your age better.

"People are going to say lots of ugly things to you now that this has happened." She frowned. "You hold your head up high. You have done nothing wrong."

My insides quaked. "Everyone's going to think I killed her, aren't they? Like Mrs. Gavelli?"

Grandma Rosa shrugged. "They might. People always like to make something out of nothing. You need to be careful. Your business may depend on this. Do not let people think you have anything to hide, or they will stay away."

"I don't have anything to hide," I answered honestly. "Pretty much everyone in town already knows about her and Colin. That's why they might think—"

My grandmother shook her head. "I never liked that boy. Too shifty. When you said you were going to marry him, I wanted to cry. You should have stayed with Mike."

"Grandma, that's ancient history." I thought of our kiss last night, and my cheeks heated.

Grandma Rosa didn't seem to notice. "He is a nice boy. Always sweet to me when I see him. Listen, my dear, you are a good girl. My old heart aches for what you have been through. I want to see you happy before I die and have great-grandchildren to hold. You are the smartest one in this family. With a little luck, you can really make something of yourself and this business."

I swelled with pride. Her opinion had always mattered so much to me. Sometimes she was the only one who ever actually listened to Gianna and me when we were growing up. "Do you really think so?"

"I know you will. Like I said, you are the smartest one in the family. Well, next to me, that is."

I laughed. "Um, Grandma, you might have forgotten Gianna is going to be a lawyer in the very near future?"

Grandma Rosa shook her head. "Your sister, she is book smart and also a good girl. You, on the other hand, have street smarts. They are more valuable. You have experienced—what do they say, the school of hard rocks?"

"Knocks." I grinned.

She shrugged. "Whatever. My point is, there will be some ugly talk about you soon. Ignore what people say, and rise above it."

"Like Mrs. Gavelli, you mean."

My grandmother made a face. "Nicoletta is a different story. She has her reasons for what she does." She paused. "But she is still a little bit loony tune."

I leaned over to give her a fierce hug. "What would we do without you?"

Grandma patted my cheek gently. "You would all be lost. Remember, though, during this difficult time, not to stoop to other people's levels. You are better than that."

"I'll remember, Grandma, I promise. You really do hold this family together."

My grandmother sighed. "Someone has to. Your mama, she acts like a little girl, and your papa lives like he has one foot in the grave. Imbeciles."

I chuckled, amused as always by her honesty.

"Do not worry, my sweet. I will always watch over you and your sister. If not here," she jerked her finger to the ceiling, "then, God willing, when I am up there."

CHAPTER SIX

"Come on, tell me what really happened, Sally. I promise not to tell anyone."

I raised an eyebrow at Wendy O'Brien, one of the most notorious gossips in Colwestern. Josie and I had graduated high school with her only son, Jake. He was my mother's latest attempt at getting me hitched again.

I shook my head as I placed six sugar cookies in a bag for her, along with a fortune cookie. "I already told you what happened. I found her lying on the porch."

Mrs. O'Brien frowned, her gray eyes appraising me with skepticism. "That's not what I heard. Everyone says you two were fighting."

My jaw almost hit the floor. I glanced sideways at Josie, involved in her own battle of wills with elderly Jeannie Peterson. The eccentric woman was quite particular about her cookies. She pointed at the glass, impatience written all over her face. "No, not that one. The one behind it. Can't you see, Josie? That one clearly has more chocolate chips."

Josie cursed under her breath. "Only one cookie, Mrs. Peterson?"

"That's all." She placed her hands on her large girth of a stomach. "And don't forget my fortune cookie either."

Josie gave me a death stare. I flinched as I handed Mrs. O'Brien her change.

"That's it?" Mrs. O'Brien frowned. "You're not going to tell me what the fight was about?"

"There was no fight, Mrs. O'Brien."

She snorted and sat down at a table. Her piercing eyes never left my face as she brought a cookie to her lips, afraid to miss any of the ongoing chatter.

"Yeah, right." Jeannie's loud cackle startled me. "I heard Amanda was taunting you about Colin. Everyone said you were ticked off and tried to rip her hair out of her head, and then you pushed her down on the porch."

I opened my mouth in astonishment. "That's ridiculous. I'd never do something like that."

"It's all over town." Mrs. Peterson nodded, as if that explained everything. She snatched her bag from Josie. "Hey, I'm not blaming you, honey. If you ask me, it's just desserts for that evil thing." She shook the bag and grinned. "No pun intended. Do you know what that rotten little snot did to me? She told me last week I couldn't have a facial at her salon because I might break the chair. Can you believe the gall of some people?"

She turned and fiddled with her umbrella as she waddled out the door, munching away on her cookie.

"Thank God she's gone." Josie slammed the register drawer shut. "Next time you get to wait on her."

Since we were children, Jeannie Peterson had managed to terrify the both of us, but Josie always maintained an extreme dislike for the woman. Jeannie was a widow with no children and mannerisms that resembled those of a witch. Gap-toothed and always dressed in black, rumor had it she also trapped and cooked small animals. As youngsters, we'd avoided her house on Halloween.

"Next." Josie motioned to a slender woman with long, dark hair.

The woman was about the same age as Josie and me. She glanced at the two little girls running around her in circles and caught each one by the hand. "Tell the lady what kind of cookies you want. One apiece."

Josie gave me another knowing look. Yes, it wasn't one of our more prosperous days.

The younger child, about age five, wore her hair in two neat blonde pigtails tied with red ribbons. She peered out at me from behind her mother, fingers in mouth. I melted at the sight of her and smiled as her enormous cornflower-blue eyes watched me with interest. She took her fingers out of her mouth and grinned, revealing a huge space where two front teeth used to be.

"Oh, Mommy, sugar cookie." She jumped up and down.

"I want the one with the jelly on top, Mommy." Her older sister had dark hair like the mother. She touched the glass with her fingertips, unable to contain her excitement.

"Paws off," Josie snapped. The little girl looked up at her, startled.

"It's all right," I reassured her while frowning at Josie. I reached for a piece of waxed paper and held out two fortune cookies. "Would you little ladies like one?"

"Yummy." The blonde licked her lips and reached for the cookie while her mother smiled at me.

"I don't know." The dark-haired girl held out her hand, but watched me thoughtfully. "I heard you made some lady eat one, and she choked to death."

"Molly." Her mother's eyes widened in alarm. "That's not true." She turned to me and blushed. "Right?"

What was with these people? "We're not sure what happened to her, but it wasn't from the cookies."

Mrs. O'Brien rose to her feet. "Sally, no one would blame you if you shoved one down her throat. Not after what she did to you."

I was mortified the children were hearing this. "Please, Mrs. O'Brien. I don't think this kind of talk is, um, appropriate right now."

She ignored me and stared down at her fortune cookie. "Well, what the heck."

"What does it say?" Josie asked. "Wait, let me guess. Don't ever assume because you'll make an ass—"

I cleared my throat loudly, and Josie closed her mouth.

Mrs. O'Brien read her fortune aloud. "Your intense personality can leave quite an impression on people."

Josie choked back a laugh then turned it into a cough.

"Well, I never." Mrs. O'Brien made a face. "That's the thanks I get for trying to defend you." She glowered at me. "Nice attitude. By the way, stop calling Jake and asking him to come for dinner."

My mouth opened in surprise. "I don't know what you're talking about. I haven't even seen Jake since I've been back." Recognition slowly dawned on me. *Uh-oh. Dear old Mom.*

"Well, then tell your mother to stop calling and pretending she's you." She held the piece of paper up. "And get some real fortunes." She pushed the door open with force, and the bells jingled merrily.

The dark-haired woman handed Josie money. "Come on girls, let's go. What do you say to the nice lady?"

"Thank you," they both chimed together.

Molly glared at Josie. "You're mean."

"I've been called worse, kid." Josie walked into the back room, unperturbed.

Molly watched her retreating figure and looked to me for assistance. "You should fire her, lady."

When I bit my lip to hide a smile, her mother met my gaze and grinned. "How many kids does she have?"

"Four," I said.

She nodded with sudden understanding. "That explains it."

"Bye!" The little blonde danced out the door while I waved at her.

"You come back whenever you want another fortune cookie, okay?" I told them.

"Bye, now!" Josie hollered from behind me.

I put my hands on my hips and turned to face her. "Would it have hurt you to be nice to those sweet, little girls?"

Josie waved a hand dismissively. "Please. The oldest one is in Danny's class at school. She's always kissing the boys on the playground. I don't trust her."

"Why, does she happen to remind you of someone?" I teased.

She tossed her hair in defiance and ignored my comment. "You're such a sucker for kids. Wait till you have some, you'll learn."

My heart ached at the words, but I said nothing. Josie sighed and put her arm around my shoulders. "I'm sorry, Sal. That was stupid of me."

"No worries."

"You never should have married that louse."

I couldn't argue with that statement. From the beginning, the one thing Colin had always been honest about with me was children. He didn't want them. Ever. Sadly, I had been young and foolish enough to think I could get him to change his mind with time.

"Live and learn, right?" My eyes were growing moist. I blinked a few times and went into the back room to check the inventory.

Josie followed. "Hey, for whatever it's worth, you don't need a husband to have one."

I held back a laugh. "Are you suggesting I visit a sperm bank or something?"

"Why not? Lots of people do it these days."

I opened the freezer to check on the pre-made dough. "Hel-lo, have you met my family? That is so not happening. My father would have a stroke."

"Oh, you Italians." Josie chuckled. "Always so old-fashioned."

The bells on the door announced we had another customer. We walked back into the storefront together, curious as to whom our next patron might be.

Josie let out a sigh. "I swear, if one more person asks about Amanda—"

"What about Amanda?" a woman asked.

My jaw dropped. Standing there, in an expensive, beige raincoat, was Amanda's mother, Kate Gregorio.

Josie's face was frozen, her eyes bugging out of her head.

"Oh, dear, look what I've done." Kate stared at the puddle on the floor and shuffled her feet. "I'm sorry to have made such a mess."

I walked toward her. "That's okay, Mrs. Gregorio. Don't worry about it." I hesitated for a minute. "What can I do for you?"

Her amber-colored eyes were full of pain. "I'd like to talk to you if you have a moment."

Oh, boy. "Of course. Please sit down." I pulled out a chair for her and sat down in one next to her.

"Thank you." She placed her Louis Vuitton handbag on the empty chair between us and removed her coat. I didn't know Mrs. Gregorio well, but from what I'd been told, she wasn't like her daughter. A wealthy woman, whose husband had died two years ago, she was always willing to lend a hand when it came time for a donation or anything else to help the town.

Josie reached for her coat. "Let me hang that up for you. Can I get you a cup of coffee?"

"That would be lovely. Do you have decaf?" Kate sat down.

I turned to my friend. "I picked up a huge box of K-cups the other day. They're in the back room, top shelf."

Josie nodded and disappeared with Kate's coat.

My hands shook so hard in my lap that I prayed she wouldn't notice. I lifted my head to meet Kate's gaze. Her black hair was perfectly coiffed and pulled back from her gaunt face. Dark circles of weariness shone under her eyes.

She sat there, her mournful face watching me until I couldn't stand it anymore. "I'm really sorry about Amanda, Mrs. Gregorio."

A lone tear rolled down her cheek. "Please call me Kate. And thank you."

Another awkward silence. I kept praying Josie would return and hoped she wasn't staying away on purpose.

Kate cleared her throat. "Sally, I know you and Amanda weren't friends. I also know about the incident with your husband. I mean, ex-husband."

"Mrs. Gregorio, er, Kate." I clasped my hands together. "I didn't have anything to do with Amanda's death. I hope you'll believe me."

She reached out to grab my hand in between her two fragile, ice cold ones. "I didn't come here to accuse you. I thought maybe you might remember something about that night. Anything at all would help."

I was ashamed my first thought had been about protecting my own hide. "I don't know what would help. Amanda came in, bought some cookies, then went outside to eat them. I closed the shop, went upstairs for a few minutes, came downstairs, and found—her."

Kate sighed. "Yes. Officer Jenkins has been to my house twice already about the investigation. I hoped there was something you might have forgotten. You know, that might help the police catch the person."

I looked up to see Josie standing beside Kate, placing coffee and a small pitcher of cream in front of her. Alarm registered in her blue eyes.

Confused, I stared at Kate. "Catch them? I don't understand. Do you know what caused her death?"

"Amanda was highly allergic to bees. Her lips and eyes were swollen, along with her tongue. The doctor said all signs of death pointed to an anaphylactic reaction." She hesitated. "But—"

Josie's nostrils flared. "You think it was something else?"

Kate exhaled sharply. "A lot of things just don't add up. They could find no visible signs of a bee sting on Amanda. Also, she carried an EpiPen everywhere she went, but there wasn't one in her purse. The police said the contents were spilled out all over your porch, as if she might have been searching for it."

I nodded. "I noticed that too."

Her mouth tightened into a thin, hard line. "I believe someone is responsible for my daughter's death."

Sheer panic spread through my body. "I swear to you, there was nothing wrong with the cookies she ate."

Kate's eyes filled with unshed tears, and she dabbed at them with her napkin. "I'm sorry. I didn't come here to upset you."

"So if it wasn't an actual bee sting, how did she die?" Josie asked.

Kate twisted her napkin between her hands. "The doctor said it's possible she ingested bee venom somehow."

"Do you know what else she had to eat before she came here?" I asked.

Amanda's mother released my hand and reached into the center of the table for a packet of Equal. She poured it into her cup and added a drop of cream. "That's the strange part. Amanda had an upset stomach earlier that day and told me she hadn't eaten anything. When I spoke to her on the phone, she said she had a craving for cookies and was going to stop by your shop."

This was getting worse by the minute, and I struggled to make sense of it all. "She had to have eaten something else."

Kate shrugged. "I don't know. I've been thinking about this over and over. She was at my house earlier in the day and didn't eat then. About four o'clock, Amanda announced she was going over to her apartment to change. She called me a little while later. It was right before she left for your shop." She paused. "Amanda almost died once before from a bee sting, you know."

My stomach lurched. "I didn't know. What happened?"

"A pool party two summers ago." Kate stirred her coffee in an absentminded way. "She got stung and immediately went into shock. Fortunately, one of the hosts located the EpiPen in her purse and applied it." She looked at me sorrowfully.

Guilt crept over me. If I'd stayed downstairs, I would have heard the commotion on the porch. Perhaps Amanda had banged on my door repeatedly, but I never heard anything since I was in the shower. I shut my eyes tight. How helpless and frightened she must have felt when she went to search for her EpiPen and didn't find it. And then to die all alone like that. "If only I'd never gone upstairs to change."

I didn't realize I'd spoken the words aloud, until Kate patted my hand. "I'm sure you would have done your best to help her."

Josie paced back and forth in front of our table. "You really think someone might have done this deliberately?"

I held my breath and waited.

She paused a long moment before answering. "Yes. I think someone wanted Amanda dead."

A shiver crept down my spine.

Kate took a sip of her coffee. "Let's be honest, shall we? God knows I loved my daughter more than anything, but there were many people who didn't. She said and did hurtful things." Her eyes were full of pity as she looked at me, and I flinched. "I once overheard her telling Charlotte about your ex-husband. She sounded as if she was proud of wrecking your marriage. I'm sorry for all the pain she caused you."

As much as I appreciated her apology, I felt I had to be

fair about the situation. "She didn't wreck it by herself. Colin had a little something to do with it as well."

She sighed. "I'm afraid my daughter made many enemies during her short life. We spoiled her terribly. You see, we couldn't have children. When Amanda's father and I adopted her at the age of four, she brought us such joy."

This was news to me and apparently to Josie as well who stood there, her mouth hanging wide open.

I shifted in my seat. "I didn't know Amanda was adopted."

"I think we tried to prove our love for her by giving her material things." Kate sighed. "What a mistake that was. We certainly didn't do her any favors. I did so hope that you could help me."

"I'll do whatever I can," I volunteered.

She hesitated as she glanced at both of us. "Amanda didn't have many friends. I was wondering if the two of you might consider coming to the wake Sunday afternoon. It's being held at Phibbins Mortuary."

"Of course." My insides filled with dread as I worried about the attention my presence would attract. Almost everyone in our gossip-rampant town knew about her and Colin. "We'd be glad to go." When Josie raised her eyebrows at me, I ignored her silent protest. "You're sure she had nothing to eat or drink before she came here?"

"The only thing she might have had was a fruit smoothie they stock in the waiting room of her spa. She told me they helped settle her stomach." Kate paused. "Have either of you been there?"

Josie and I both shook our heads.

"Amanda kept a supply in her fridge at home. She was crazy about them and sometimes brought one along in her car too." A sudden gleam came into her eyes, and her mouth dropped open. "Dear God, do you think someone could have put something in her drink?"

I pursed my lips. "I guess it's possible. Smoothies are thick, and she might not have noticed a difference in the taste right away."

"Oh, how stupid of me. Why didn't I tell the police about

it when they asked if she'd eaten anything else?" Kate's lower lip trembled.

"I'm sure it just slipped your mind. I'd like to help you find out who did this." What I didn't add out loud was that until the person responsible was found, it was likely people would believe I had something to do with Amanda's death. My nemesis just happens to drop dead outside my cookie shop? *Yeah, Sal, nothing to worry about there.* A light bulb went on in my head. "I could call Officer Jenkins and tell him about the smoothie, if you want. Maybe they found one in her car." I tried to remember if there'd been a cup on the porch, but I was drawing a blank.

Relief filled Kate's voice. "That would be wonderful. He also has a key to Amanda's apartment if they need to search it again. I have relatives coming from out of town for the service, and I really must get home." She stood and handed me a business card, then smiled at the both of us. "Thank you for the coffee. If you happen to think of anything else, please call me, day or night."

"Of course." I nodded as Josie went to retrieve her coat.

Kate's somber eyes rested on my face. "Amanda used to come over and spend the night a couple of times a week. We were so close. Thank goodness I still have Charlotte living there, but it's lonely for me without my baby."

The bells over the door chimed, and we watched her depart, shoulders hunched forward as the rain continued to cascade around her retreating figure.

There was a lump in my throat. "I feel so sorry for her."

"I know." Josie stared out the window. "She's such a sweet thing. We should have guessed about Amanda being adopted. She was nothing like Kate."

"Uh-huh." I was barely listening.

She frowned. "You've got something brewing. Out with it."

I tapped the card in my hand. "If we could find proof Amanda ate or drank something else besides the cookies, it may clear me and the shop. Maybe we could even find the killer, too." Excited, I opened the cash register and removed the drawer.

"What are you doing?"

I lifted out another business card. "Brian's card. I'm

going to call and tell him about Kate's visit and ask if they might have found the container the smoothie was in."

"He doesn't have to tell you anything, you know." Josie threw Kate's Styrofoam cup in the trash.

I gave her a saucy smile. "I think he will, though."

Josie grinned in return. "Oh, do you, now? Sal, fess up. You like him."

"Don't be silly. I just met him."

"Liar, liar." She stuck her tongue out at me in a childish manner and walked into the back room.

I sat back down at the table and entered his number into my phone. Nervous flutters danced in my stomach while I waited.

Brian answered on the second ring. "Officer Jenkins speaking."

Heat crept up my neck. "Hi, Officer, er, Brian. This is Sally Muccio."

There was a brief silence on the other end, and then Brian's voice oozed forth with warmth. "Hello, Sally. I was just thinking about you."

CHAPTER SEVEN

———

Our steady stream of curious customers had finally ceased for the day, along with the rain outside. Fog settled in as the sun began its rapid descent in the sky. I redirected my gaze from the window and tried to concentrate on calculating today's sales receipts. It had been a long afternoon, and we didn't have much to show for it.

Josie was sweeping the vinyl floor around me. She leaned on the broom and glanced over my shoulder. "Please tell me my eyes are playing tricks on me."

I sighed and shook my head. "I wish."

"That's *all* we did today?"

"Maybe tomorrow will be better." I pressed my fingers against my temples in a vain attempt to relieve my stress.

"I sure as hell hope so." Josie emptied the dustpan into the garbage can with a vengeance. "I wish she could have picked somewhere else to die."

My mouth opened in astonishment. "Josephine Sullivan!"

There was a long silence while she slanted the broom against the counter. "I'm sorry. I mean, I'm sorry she's dead. I'm also sorry she had to die here. What are we going to do?"

I folded my arms on the table and leaned my head on top. "I don't know. I'd hoped after the autopsy came back, the shop would be cleared. Maybe if they find a smoothie and test it—"

"Are you kidding?" Josie snorted in disgust. "If something shows up in the drink, people might think you put it there. It's not going to get better, only worse."

I tried to remain calm. "Okay, let's stay positive here."

"What happens if they make us close the shop? For good?" Josie sat next to me and clutched my arm. "I need this to work, Sal. We can't get by on Rob's salary alone."

I nodded. "I know. I'm in the same boat as you. If the shop goes belly up, I'll have to move back in with my parents. I don't think I could survive that."

"At least your parents are willing to help. My mother's never thought about anyone but herself." Her lower lip started to tremble. She pushed back her chair and walked rapidly into the back room.

Something was definitely wrong. Confused, I got to my feet and followed her. She was clutching the block table, hands shaking.

"Hey." When I touched her shoulder, she collapsed into tears. Mystified, I put my arms around her. "What is it?"

She drew back and grabbed a paper towel to wipe her eyes. "I'm sorry."

"What's wrong? You haven't been acting like yourself all day."

She brought her eyes level with mine, and her cheeks reddened. "I didn't want to tell you—"

Now I understood her hesitation. "Do you need money?"

She nodded, glancing at the floor. "How did you know?"

I gave her hand a reassuring squeeze while I reached for my purse on a nearby shelf. I drew out my leather checkbook and a pen. "We've been friends for twenty years. Give me a little credit, will you. Is three hundred enough?"

Josie's jaw dropped. "I don't know when I can pay it back. You can take some out of my salary each week."

"You're not going to pay me back." I signed the check and put it in her apron pocket. "This place wouldn't be possible without you."

"Sal." Her voice trembled as she hugged me. "You've been so good to me. And you're great to my boys, always buying clothes and toys for them. I don't want you to think this is for something frivolous. Danny needs glasses, and Rob's insurance won't cover it."

My heart went out to her. "I wish I could afford to purchase health insurance for you. Maybe someday—"

Josie held up her hand. "That's not what I was implying. I appreciate this more than you'll ever know."

I cleared my throat, afraid I might cry too, and glanced at the clock. Six thirty. "What do you say we close up a half hour early? I doubt we'll get any big orders."

She nodded and exhaled a long breath. "Okay."

I turned the sign to *Closed* on the front door and locked it.

Josie grinned. "What time are you meeting charming Officer Jenkins?"

"Seven." I wanted to take a hot shower, but there wasn't enough time.

"Oh, now I understand." Her eyes gleamed. "Why didn't you ask me to close up, silly? Go upstairs and start primping."

I waved my hand dismissively. "We're only meeting for coffee at South Street Diner. It's not a big deal, trust me."

"I see." Josie started to wipe the tables down. "And was this little rendezvous his idea or yours?"

Her eyes shone, and I was pleased my gift had made a difference. There was no need to tell her how worried I was about the shop's livelihood or that three hundred dollars could have paid my rent for another week. Josie's life had never been easy. She'd grown up in poverty, a house overcrowded with too many siblings. She was the child her parents managed to forget about and had eaten more meals at my home than her own. Josie swore her children were going to have a better life, no matter what she had to do. The problem was that as soon as she and Rob started to get a little ahead, another minor catastrophe would befall them.

"It was Brian's idea. Hardly a rendezvous. I told him about the smoothie, and he suggested we meet."

She shook her head. "I think you're wasting your time. He's a policeman. He's not going to tell you what they found."

I shrugged. "We'll see."

"Hmm." Josie peered closer at me. "Perhaps it isn't a waste of time."

She was impossible. "What are you talking about?"

Josie's smile was wicked. "Hallelujah. This might be exactly what the doctor ordered."

I made a face. "I'm not looking for a new boyfriend. I want to find out who's responsible for Amanda's death. That's all."

"Whatever you say." Josie gave me a thumbs-up.

* * *

At 7:15, there was still no sign of Brian. I sat in the booth of the old-fashioned, fifties-themed diner. Should I call him? Had he stood me up? And why was I even using that phrase? *It's not a date, Sal.*

I sat brooding over my cup of coffee, unsure of what to do next. Someone dropped a red rose on the table in front of me. When I looked up, Brian was standing next to the booth, grinning at me.

"Sorry I'm late." He slid into the seat across from me and nodded at the rose. "I was passing the florist and figured you might need some cheering up after the last couple of days."

I sniffed at the flower, inhaling the fragrant smell. It had been a long time since a man had done something nice for me. "Thank you. It's beautiful."

He started to say something then colored up. A waitress appeared, and he glanced quickly at the menu. "Would you like something to eat?"

"No, thanks."

Brian ordered coffee and a grilled cheese sandwich. After the waitress left, he crossed his arms on the table and leaned forward, his gaze level with mine. He wasn't wearing his uniform. Instead, he was dressed in jeans, sneakers, and a white Yankees T-shirt, which revealed his muscular arms. I wiped my sweaty palms on my jeans.

"Did you go home to change first?" I asked.

He shook his head. "I had the day off, but I've been busy doing some work on the investigation. Your theory was correct. We did find a plastic cup in Amanda's car yesterday containing a smoothie. It was almost full, like she'd only taken a couple of sips at most. Very good detective work on your part, even though we beat you to it." He smiled.

"Well, like I said, I happened to be with Kate when she

mentioned the drink and wanted to tell you. Let's be honest. I need to clear my name from this entire situation."

The waitress reappeared with Brian's sandwich and coffee.

"I understand completely. I haven't had a chance to tell Kate yet. Plus, it only went to the lab for testing this morning. I've asked them to put a rush on it. We'll be able to get it analyzed to see if anything suspicious shows up."

Brian shoveled the sandwich into his mouth, and I tried not to laugh.

"What?" he asked.

"You remind me of the little kids that come into my shop and can't stop eating cookies."

Brian nodded. "I know. I'm terrible when it comes to eating healthy. I do try to stay in shape though. I have to for my job. I go to the gym four or five times a week."

Oh, believe me, it shows.

"Speaking of cookies…" I tossed a white bag onto the table. "These are for you. A dozen chocolate chip. Josie said they were your favorite."

"That's really nice of you." His eyes twinkled at me as he took a cookie out of the bag. When he bit into it, crumbs fell onto his baseball shirt. "Mm."

I shook my head. "You're from Boston and wearing a Yankees shirt?"

"Well, I can't wear it back home. I'd have to take my gun everywhere for protection." Brian winked. "How about you? Do you like baseball?"

"I love it."

"Yankees fan?" he asked, hopeful.

I smirked at him. "Sorry, I was brought up on the Sox. My grandmother's team."

He smiled and groaned as he bit into the cookie again. "And you're a New Yorker!"

"Okay, I get your point." *God, he is so adorable.*

"Maybe we could take in a game sometime." He finished the cookie and gave a low moan. "That was great."

I fanned myself with a napkin, finding it suddenly very warm in the booth. "I should have brought you more. We didn't sell much merchandise today."

He pursed his lips. "Are people staying away because of Amanda?"

"Actually, it's the opposite. We've had quite a few people coming in. But they're asking questions and not really buying much. We even caught one guy taking pictures on my front porch this morning. Josie chased him away with a broom."

"Morbid curiosity." Brian shook his head in disgust.

I sighed and fiddled with my spoon. "Something like that, I guess."

"I'm sorry you have to go through this. Hopefully things will get back to normal soon." His eyes searched mine, and he hesitated for a moment. "Can I ask you a personal question?"

My insides quivered like jelly. "Of course."

"How long were you married?"

"About five years." This wasn't the question I'd been expecting.

Brian took a sip of his coffee. "What was your married name?"

"Brown." I shifted in my seat and really hoped this would be the end of such an unpleasant subject.

Recognition dawned on his face. "Wait, Sally Brown? Like, as in, Charlie's sister?"

I rolled my eyes. "Another reason why I decided not to keep it after the divorce."

His grin lit up the entire room as he laughed. "So while we're on the subject of names, how'd you wind up with Sally? It doesn't sound very Italian. Is it a family name?"

I heard this all the time. "I'm the eldest in a Sicilian family. My dad desperately wanted a son. He was going to name him Salvatore after his father. I kind of screwed that up for him."

"Okay, that makes sense now." He was reaching across the table to take my hand when his cell phone rang. He looked at the screen, and a muscle ticked in his jaw. "Excuse me for a moment, Sally." His tone changed quickly from gentle to brisk. "Officer Jenkins. How can I help you?"

I tried not to eavesdrop, but being curious by nature it was impossible, especially when I caught wind of who the conversation concerned. Amanda.

"I see." Brian frowned. "I appreciate you putting a rush on it. Yes, this does change things. Thanks, Pete." He clicked off and looked at me with concern.

"What's wrong?"

He hesitated while he glanced around the room. "This is confidential."

My stomach lurched. "Brian, please tell me what's going on."

He lowered his voice. "That was the lab. There were traces of bee venom found in Amanda's smoothie."

"Oh my God." I struggled to breathe normally. "So someone did kill her."

"It looks that way. She might have had a sip or two from the drink on the way over to your shop, and then—" His face was a mask of worry. "Do you know what this means?"

"Maybe that people will stop looking at me like I'm a murderer, I hope."

Brian took a sip of his coffee. "This means someone might have been trying to frame you for her murder. Maybe the killer knew she was coming to your shop and wanted everyone to think you'd given her a tainted cookie. Or they hoped she'd bring the drink into your shop and people would think you tampered with it. This also means the killer was in her apartment that day and knew about her allergy."

My head was spinning. This was too much to take in all at once. "Does this narrow down the suspects then?"

Brian shrugged. "Not really. According to Kate Gregorio, many people were aware she had an allergy. Family, friends. I'm sure her employees must have known, too. I've questioned a couple of them already. There was an incident when she was stung and almost died a couple of years ago too. And you know how people like to talk in this town."

Yes. That much I did know.

"You need to be careful. Someone might be trying to make trouble for you." He frowned.

"Do you think my shop will get back to normal now?" I asked.

"I can't answer that. I'll call Kate and let her know the results, but it's important you don't say anything about this."

"Could I at least tell Josie?" I drained my cup.

"On two conditions." Brian reached across the table to take my hand in his strong, cool one, and a delicious shiver wafted up my spine.

"The first is, she can't tell anyone. Like I said, we're not making this public knowledge yet. I shouldn't have even told you. If more people know the situation, it might be tougher to catch the perpetrator."

I hadn't thought of that. "I'll make sure Josie understands. I want to help too."

Brian shook his head. "Absolutely not. This may be dangerous. I can't stand the thought of you getting hurt."

"My business and reputation are on the line until I find out who did this. Kate came to the shop to ask for my help, you know."

"Yes, you told me on the phone." Brian's voice was gentle as he kept a firm grip on my hand. "Let the police handle this. It's what we're here for."

"Will you be at the wake Sunday afternoon?"

He nodded. "I hope to. If not, another officer will be there. I have to drive to Boston tomorrow, and I'm staying over. It's my parent's fortieth anniversary."

"Oh, that's lovely." What a wonderful son to drive all that way to be with his parents on their special day. "Will someone else be working on the case while you're away?"

"Of course. I'm not the only one investigating. Like I said, I'll be back on Sunday. I need to notify Kate of the findings as well. I'll call her when I get home tonight." He finished his coffee as the waitress approached us with the check. He waited for her to depart. "I really want to be at the wake. Sometimes the killer shows up there, so they can get an idea of what everyone else knows."

I raised my eyebrows. I'd definitely be there then.

"In the meantime, I want you to be good while I'm away. Which brings me to the other condition."

I was afraid my hand was getting sweaty. If so, he didn't appear to notice. Or care. "Okay, I can't tell anyone beside Josie. So what's the other?"

He gazed into my eyes and smiled. "I want you to

promise you'll have dinner with me sometime next week, after I get back."

The butterflies in my stomach were back full force. I knew I should refuse, but my head started swinging back and forth like a bobblehead before I could stop it. "I'd like that."

"Good." Brian spoke in a low, smooth voice. "I can't wait."

When a man stopped beside the table and cleared his throat loudly, I looked up and froze.

Mike returned my gaze with one of surprise. He stared at Brian's hand on top of mine, and his face reddened. Embarrassed, I slowly released my hand and took a hasty sip of water. I opened my mouth to say something, but the words stuck in my throat.

"How's it going, Mike?" Brian asked.

Mike tore his eyes away from me to give Brian a surly look. "Fine, thanks. And you, officer?"

"Never better." Brian gestured at the takeout container in Mike's hand. "Dinner on the run?"

"I'm installing a main beam in a two-family. Looks like I'll be tied up pretty late tonight."

Heat rose through my face like a sauna as both men watched me. I took another sip of water in a vain attempt to cool myself and stall.

"Do you know Sally?" Brian asked.

Mike's eyes locked on mine, and his sour look turned into a smirk. "Oh, yeah. We've met a few times." His face took on a strange expression similar to one I'd seen before when he'd tried to mask his true feelings. Pain? No. More likely anger this time. "Glad to see you're feeling better."

"Um," I began, "about the shoes—"

Mike nodded at Brian. "Nice seeing you, officer. Take care." After one more lingering glance at me, he opened the glass door and disappeared into the night.

Brian drummed his fingers on the table. "Let me guess. You guys dated once?"

My mouth fell open. "How'd you know?"

"It wasn't hard to surmise from the way he was staring at you. He also seemed pretty pissed off I was holding your hand."

"It was a long time ago. We've gone our separate ways."

Brian appeared doubtful. "It didn't seem so from his expression."

"He has no designs on me. Only another guy who did me wrong." I clapped a hand over my mouth. *Great.* I sounded like a bad country song.

"We're not all like that, you know." He watched me soberly.

My heart softened as I stared into those enormous, green eyes. "I believe you."

Brian was silent for a few seconds. "I have no right to tell you what to do, but it might be best for you to stay away from him."

I laughed. "I told you, there's nothing between us anymore."

"That's not what I meant. He could be dangerous." Brian lowered his voice. "Mike Donovan is on my list of people to question."

"That's ridiculous. Mike's harmless. I mean, he's had some family issues in the past. When we dated, he was jealous every time I even talked to a member of the opposite sex. Other than that, he's a decent guy." *Why do I insist on defending a man who broke my heart?*

"What sort of family issues?"

"His mom was an alcoholic. She died a couple years ago. His father took off when he was five, and his stepfather used him like a punching bag. He's been through a lot," I said quietly.

"You act like you still have feelings for the guy." It sounded more like an accusation than a statement.

I shook my head vehemently. "Why would you be questioning him? He and Amanda weren't friendly."

Brian's eyes darkened. "Don't be too sure."

"What's that supposed to mean?"

He hesitated. "A neighbor spotted him going into Amanda's apartment the same day she died. No matter what you say, he's a suspect, Sally."\

CHAPTER EIGHT

———

Josie cast a sideways glance at me from the passenger seat of my car. "Okay, since you wouldn't tell me anything on the phone, can you please enlighten me now as to where we're going?"

When the light turned green, I plowed ahead in my old, reliable Corolla. "You and I are going to visit Mrs. Gregorio, I mean Kate. I want to ask her if she has any idea who might have been in Amanda's apartment lately. It's okay—she knows we're coming."

Josie leaned over and turned the radio on. "I thought Brian told you to stay out of this. Speaking of which, you never did tell me how the rest of your date went with him tonight."

Carrie Underwood's voice resonated through my speakers with the opening lyrics of "Before He Cheats." I winced and pushed the off button. "It wasn't a date. We were only together for forty-five minutes. We had coffee. That's all."

"And?" My best friend prompted.

I concentrated on the winding road ahead of me. "He's leaving early tomorrow morning for Boston, so we wrapped things up pretty quick. He'll be back sometime on Sunday." I paused for a moment. "He wants me to have dinner with him next week."

"I knew it!" Josie clapped her hands. "And he's so hot. But he's not going to like you coming out here to question Kate."

"He doesn't have to know. And she did ask for our help, remember. We need to get our sales back up. We can't afford to have many more days like today."

"Don't I know it," Josie groaned. "Did he tell you if they have any potential suspects?"

Might as well get it over with. "He said Mike was seen at

Amanda's apartment the same day she died."

She gasped. "I don't believe it. He'd never hook up with the likes of her."

"Who knows?" I remembered the displeasure on his face when he spotted me with Brian earlier. I was certain Mike would never harm Amanda, but the thought of him possibly sleeping with her was enough to make the bile start to rise in my throat. "By the way, he was there."

"Who was where?"

"Brian and I saw Mike at the diner."

"Get out! What happened? Were you two making out?"

I snorted in disbelief. "Give me a break. In the diner? When are you going to stop reading those silly romance novels?"

"Hey, don't knock 'em till you've tried 'em." Josie chuckled in the darkness. "I can't believe this. You've only been divorced a couple of weeks, and two gorgeous guys are already fighting over you. You're my idol."

"Oh, please. It isn't like that at all."

I took a left onto secluded Firetower Road where Kate's mansion was located. I'd been there once before, but never inside. One time after school, Mike had stopped to pick up a check from Kate for work his stepfather had done on the property while I'd waited in the car. I still remembered how his blue eyes had flashed with excitement afterward. "Sal, it's like freaking Buckingham Palace in there!"

A wrought iron gate was stretched across the bottom of the driveway. Stationed to my left was a portable security booth occupied by an elderly man who watched my car approach with interest. He slid the window open and nodded, a displeased expression upon his well-weathered face. Maybe we'd interrupted his nap. "May I help you, ladies?"

"Hi." I smiled. "Sally Muccio and Josie Sullivan to see Mrs. Gregorio, please. She's expecting us."

The guard frowned as he shut the window. He picked up a phone, and we could see his mouth moving at a rapid pace through the glass. After a few seconds, he replaced the receiver. I waited for further instructions from him, but he only stared back at me.

"Sal," Josie said. "We can go now."

I turned my head and noticed the gate had opened, beckoning our arrival. I gave the man a little finger wave of thanks, which he answered with a sour expression.

Josie's mouth fell open. "Holy cow."

Even at night, the Victorian mansion with its ivy façade was quite a glorious affair to behold. There was enough outside lighting to blind onlookers and reminded me of Yankee Stadium on game night. The lawn was manicured to perfection with rose and azalea bushes everywhere. A large, bronze statue of Anthony Gregorio, Kate's husband and Amanda's father, stared down at us from beside a stone water fountain.

Josie stared at the statue as if it were alive. "Kind of creepy to put it in front of the house, don't you think?"

Several cars were parked around us. "Shoot. I forgot Kate has family here. I shouldn't have bothered her."

"If she hadn't wanted you to come, she would have said so."

I stepped onto the front porch and rapped the brass knocker on the heavy mahogany door. A man I assumed was her butler answered.

"Hi. Sally Muccio and Josie Sullivan to see Mrs. Gregorio, please."

The man nodded and ushered us in. "May I take your wraps?"

"I'm a bit chilly. I think I'll keep mine." Josie pulled her sweater tightly around her shoulders.

He pursed his lips. "Very well. Please accompany me to the library. Mrs. Gregorio requested you wait for her there."

We silently followed the man down a long, sterile hallway, past a winding mahogany staircase, a studio, and a conservatory. He stopped in front of a room with a stone fireplace the size of an entire wall. Across from it were several wingback chairs and a Tommy Bahama coffee table that held a silver tea service and gooey pastries. The other walls contained built-in bookshelves with a vast range of leather-bound novels. By glancing at them, I could tell several were antiques.

"Mrs. Gregorio will be in shortly." The butler bowed slightly then left us to our own devices.

"I'm surprised he didn't tell us not to touch anything."

Josie's eyes darted around the room. "My God. I knew they were wealthy but had no idea the house was this ritzy. Did you?"

"Yes. Mike used to come here to collect payments for his stepdad's business." I smiled to myself, remembering the tender look in Mike's eyes when he'd kissed me in his car and said he wanted to build me a mansion like Kate's someday. We'd been so happy then. *Ugh, I'm doing it again.*

High heels clicked on the terrazzo flooring in the hall seconds before Kate appeared, wearing a navy, silk dress and a diamond necklace with enough bling to light the room by itself. She gestured for us to sit and started to pour from the silver teapot.

"Mrs. Gregorio," I said.

"Kate," she reminded me.

"Kate, I apologize. I'd forgotten you were having company this evening. And it's so late." I glanced at the grandfather clock, which read 9:05. "We don't want to take up any more of your time than necessary."

"Nonsense. I'm pleased you called." She poured tea for each of us and then a cup for herself. "Help yourself to the cream and sugar and pastries. Now, what can I do for you? You said it was regarding Amanda's possible—" she hesitated, "murder."

I nodded. "Yes. Did Officer Jenkins call you?"

"He told me about the bee venom in the smoothie." She stared at us, tears glistening in her eyes. "Who would do such a thing?"

Josie reached for a cheese-filled pastry. "That's what we want to know, too."

"Can you give us any idea of who might have been in her apartment the last few days? Did she have a security camera?" I leaned forward, hopeful.

Kate shook her head. "I'm afraid not. I suggested it once, but she thought the idea was ridiculous. Of course, it was a very safe neighborhood, so I didn't press. I wish I had now."

"Officer Jenkins said Mike Donovan was spotted at her apartment the other day. Do you know why he might have been there?" I held my breath, afraid for the answer.

"You mean Ray's stepson? No, I don't know why he'd be there." Recognition dawned on her face. "Isn't he the boy you used to date?"

Embarrassed, I plodded on. "That's not why I'm asking. I guess he's now being considered a suspect."

To my amazement, Kate didn't act surprised. "Well, why wouldn't he be? Ray was a great carpenter, but I'd heard rumors he and his wife were abusive. Those things do tend to run in a family, you know."

"Well, I don't believe Mike would ever intentionally hurt anyone." She could say what she wanted, but I knew in my heart he wasn't at fault. Even during our worst blowouts, he'd never laid a finger on me.

"I'm sorry, Sally." Kate sighed. "Since these new findings, I wonder if there's anyone I can trust."

Uh-oh. Josie and I exchanged glances. Perhaps Kate was starting to suspect us as well.

"It's okay." I fought the urge to chew on my fingernails. "You're going through a terrible ordeal. I was wondering if you might know of anyone else who'd been in Amanda's home recently."

Kate shook her head and reached for a phone on the table. "Let me ask Charlotte to come in here. She might have answers. Those two were always together." She pressed a number and then waited. "Yes, Harper, please ask Charlotte to come into the library. Thank you." She replaced the receiver and took a sip of her tea. "So you believe whoever was in her apartment the last day might have slipped the venom in her smoothie?"

I looked at Josie. "Well, it would make sense."

"And her EpiPen? The police never found it. Do you think whoever killed her took that as well?"

"Yes, if they didn't want her to survive." The words sounded harsh to my own ears.

"If only Amanda had checked her bag before she left the house." Kate sighed and put her head in her hands.

Charlotte stood in the doorway. She was wearing a black, shapeless dress that came down to her ankles, way too long for her short stature. Her dark, straggly hair was held back from her face in an outdated banana clip. She glanced from me to Josie, bewildered.

"Hi, Charlotte." I smiled.

She frowned behind her glasses. "Sally, Josie. What are you guys doing here?"

"Charlotte, sit down please." Kate patted the chair next to hers, and Charlotte immediately went to her aunt's side. "Sally and Josie are trying to help us find the killer."

Charlotte's already pale face became a more pasty shade. "Then it wasn't an accident. Amanda was murdered?"

Kate nodded soberly. "Yes, it appears that way."

"Oh my God." Charlotte let out a whimper and clutched at Kate's arm. Kate reached her other arm around to hug her tightly.

Josie cleared her throat. "Kate, I don't think the police want too many people to know about this yet."

"Nonsense." Kate waved her hand in an impatient gesture. "Charlotte's like a daughter to me. I'm not going to hide the truth from her."

This was becoming a mess. "Charlotte, you spent a lot of time with Amanda. Do you have any idea who was at her house the day she—she died?"

Charlotte wiped her eyes and met my gaze but remained silent.

"Dear, this is important," Kate said. "You were over there almost every day. Did you notice anyone?"

Charlotte glared at me and Josie. "Why should I tell you anything? You both were threatening her the other day when we came to your shop."

Oh, no.

Kate watched us, horrified. "I don't understand. You threatened my daughter?"

Josie's cheeks turned the color of her hair. "Kate, it wasn't like that. Amanda said some things to Sally about Colin, and we made a joke back. We didn't mean anything by it. Honest."

"I see." Kate's tone was stiff as she watched her niece. "Charlotte, if you saw anyone at Amanda's, we need to know."

Charlotte's eyes never left my face. My palms were getting moist as I waited for her answer.

"Please." Kate's voice trembled.

Charlotte turned to face her aunt. "A lot of people would come by, me included. The girls from the spa would stop over to get their checks sometimes, if Amanda didn't come in on payday." She let out a long sigh. "She could be selfish that way."

Kate frowned. "Anyone else?"

Charlotte hesitated while she wiped at her eyes. "There was usually a guy or two over every night." She bit her lip as she watched Kate lower her eyes. "I'm sorry, Auntie Kate. I didn't want to tell you."

"Did you know them?" I asked eagerly.

Charlotte's face twisted into an ugly expression. "Well, one was your ex-boyfriend Mike. He was there at least twice this past week."

Josie wrinkled her nose as if she smelled something repulsive. "Mike would never sink that low."

Kate shot her a death stare as I winced. Good grief. My best friend had a mouth larger than her minivan.

Red-faced, Josie continued on. "I mean, er, Mike was kind of slow. Um, anyone else you can think of?"

Charlotte started weeping. "I promised I wouldn't tell anyone about him."

"Oh, dear Lord." Kate's voice quivered as tears gushed over her cheeks. "Amanda is gone, Charlotte. She's dead. Don't you want to help catch the killer?"

"Of course I do, but he—" Charlotte cried.

Kate was losing patience. "Then out with it. Who was she seeing?"

"He was there every night. I think she really liked him. I've no idea what the attraction was when she could have had any guy she wanted. And clearly did." Charlotte spoke with triumph in her voice as she lifted her eyes to meet mine.

It was as if someone had twisted a knife in my back. The pain was intense.

"You bitch." Josie gritted her teeth.

Kate stared at Josie in surprise then turned back to her niece. "Tell me. Who is this man?"

Charlotte wiped her eyes with a napkin. "Vido Falzo."

CHAPTER NINE

––––––

"Dang," Josie breathed. "So it *is* true. Vido and Amanda—how freaky is that?"

I nodded my head absently as I descended the slick marble driveway. Fortunately, the gate was wide open, so no need for me to stop. Kate had probably called ahead and told Mr. Personality Guard she wanted us off the property as soon as possible.

I couldn't stop thinking about Mike. What was he doing at Amanda's apartment? And why did I even care?

"Hel-lo, Sal?" Josie waved her hand at me.

"Oh, sorry." I chewed on my lower lip. "My mind must have been somewhere else."

She looked at me sideways. "Uh-huh. I know where your mind is."

"What are you talking about?"

"Hey, I don't care what geeky Charlotte says. There's no way Mike would have been dating Amanda."

I turned onto the main road as my phone pinged from the backseat. "Someone texted me. Can you grab my cell and see who it is?"

Josie reached into the backseat for my purse. "Ooh, maybe it's Mr. Hottie Policeman. He's missing you already."

I laughed. "Yeah, right. Brian's leaving at four in the morning. I'm guessing he's in dreamland right about now."

"Dreaming of you, I'm sure." Josie teased as she studied my phone. "Oh boy. It's from Gianna."

"What's wrong?"

Josie read aloud. "Where are you? Stop by the house. Dad thinks his time has come. About to go out of my mind. I'm moving in with you."

I groaned as I switched lanes. "You see? If the shop doesn't make it, I think I'd rather be a homeless person than move back there. Send her a text, and tell her I'm on my way, please. Do you want to come along?"

Josie's fingers moved swiftly on my phone. "Hell, no. I'll take a house full of screaming kids over that drama any day." She put the phone back in my purse. "Okay, so we need to figure out our next move."

"What next move?" I asked.

"We have to think about who might have done this. So far we have Vido, Mike, the girls at the spa—"

I frowned. "Take Mike off that list. I know he didn't kill her."

"You don't know anything. People change. Maybe she was blackmailing him."

I burst out laughing. "But she's the one who had all the money."

"There are lots of other reasons to blackmail people, silly. Why don't you ask him yourself?"

I stopped for a red light and turned to face her. "Are you nuts? What on earth would I say?"

"Did I say talking had to be involved?" Josie smiled.

"Look, I was drunk the other night. That will never happen again."

She ignored me. "And we'll have to talk to Vido. Maybe tomorrow morning when he comes by to get the cookies for the baby shower." Josie snapped her fingers. "I've got it. Afterward, you and I will visit Amanda's spa. I could use a massage, and the birthday cake I sold to Mrs. O'Brien should pay for it."

"I don't think Brian will like us going around questioning everyone."

"Brian can take over when he gets back from his trip. We don't have time to fool around here. Sure, we've got people coming in to the store, but they're not buying much. I'd better cut back on making cookies for a while. Look at all the ones we didn't sell the last few days."

I sighed. "I'll take them to the homeless shelter tomorrow. Why not make someone else's life better if we can?"

"I don't have a problem with that. What bothers me is the money we're losing. I've got four kids to feed."

"If something happens, I'll find a way to help you. I promise."

Josie squeezed my arm. "You've already done more than enough. I don't want to be a charity case."

"It's not charity. It's a friend helping out another friend." I stared sideways at her, a lump in my throat. "There's nothing I wouldn't do for you. I hope you know that."

Josie wiped at her eyes. "Same here. Stop getting all sentimental on me."

"Remember how you jumped in and saved me at the lake when I couldn't swim?"

She chuckled. "Yeah. And remember how I was the one who pushed you in?"

We laughed, recalling one of the rare fights we'd had growing up. Josie had been so jealous in fifth grade when Jimmy Caruthers revealed he wanted to ask me to the spring dance instead of her.

I pulled into Josie's driveway. The cozy, beige bungalow was awash with light and looked inviting.

"So we'll do it? Visit the spa tomorrow, I mean?" Josie raised her eyebrows at me.

I nodded. "I'll ask Gianna if she can watch the shop for a couple of hours."

"Perfect." Josie reached for her handbag. "I'll open the shop at nine, then call and schedule some appointments for us at the spa. Want to come in and say hi to the kids? I asked Rob to keep them up until I got home."

As she spoke, the front door opened, and two little figures appeared in the doorway, both in footie pajamas, one holding onto a blanket. Another little boy peered out at us from a window. He spotted Josie and waved. The two in the doorway cried "Mommy" simultaneously.

I smiled. "No, I'd better get over to the house before Gianna has a stroke."

"Okay." Josie reached back into the car to give me a squeeze. "See you tomorrow, partner."

She ran toward the house, where she was instantly

enveloped in hugs. With my car window down, shrieks of laughter filled my ears. Rob met Josie at the door and kissed her as she took the baby from his arms. They all waved to me then the door closed behind them.

There were tears in my eyes as I drove away.

* * *

Gianna met me at the front door. She looked tired and drawn. "I haven't been feeling well all day. I've gotten no studying done, and now this. I hope you brought liquor."

I hugged her and walked into the house. "Where is he?"

Before Gianna could reply, my father's voice boomed from the living room. "Is that my baby girl? Come say good-bye to your father."

Grandma Rosa was in the foyer, shaking her head. "Crazier than a loon. He went to the doctor today."

Panicked, I looked from Gianna to my grandmother. "You didn't tell me that part. What happened?"

Grandma made a face. "Nothing. They told him he is in perfect health."

"Gianna," my father yelled. "Bring me the tape measure. I don't know which one of these coffins I can fit in."

My sister clenched her jaw. "That's it. I'm going to bed. I can't take any more."

"Have you eaten?" Grandma Rosa asked me.

"I'm fine. Don't go to any trouble on my account."

"You need dinner. Look at how skinny you are." She poked at my ribs.

I rubbed my eyes. "It's a little late for dinner."

"Nonsense," my grandmother scoffed. "In an Italian family, it is never too late for dinner."

"Stay the night," Gianna pleaded. "I need someone sane here. Besides Grandma, that is."

Normally, I would have said no, but after witnessing the heartwarming scene at Josie's house, a sensation of loneliness had settled over me. I didn't want to go home to my empty apartment. "Okay, on one condition."

Gianna shook her head. "I'm not measuring him for his

coffin. I did it last week."

My sister and grandmother followed me into the kitchen as I grabbed the tape measure out of the junk drawer. "I need you to watch the shop for me tomorrow afternoon."

"I've got to study," Gianna objected. "I'm way behind."

I sat down at the table and stifled a yawn. "Please? It won't be so bad. Most people are coming in out of curiosity, so there won't be much to do." I wanted to bite my tongue off as soon as I said the words. If my grandmother knew things were getting bad, she'd whip out her checkbook, and I didn't want that.

"So you're not making any sales?"

"We're making sales. It could be a little better though." That was the understatement of the year.

Gianna reached over and patted my hand. "As soon as the situation blows over with Amanda, things will get better. I'll come over. Let me know what time you need me."

My father roared. "Hey, I'm dying in here. Doesn't anyone care?"

"Stupido," Grandma yelled. "Keep your pants on."

"Where's Mom?" I asked.

Grandma Rosa grunted while she made the sign of the cross. "She is off with those flighty real estate friends of hers at some awards banquet. God knows what she is doing."

"Awards banquet? But she hasn't sold anything." I was confused.

My grandmother waved her hand in an annoyed gesture. "Your mama—she is what they call a nutsy cookie."

I chuckled. "That's nutsy cuckoo, Grandma."

She grunted while she hunted around in the cabinet for something. "That works too."

Gianna raised her eyebrows at me. "They're both driving Grandma and me bonkers. I think *we* should get awards."

Grandma Rosa slammed a bottle of amaretto on the table and reached back into the cabinet for three shot glasses.

I raised my hand. "None for me."

"I think there is beer in the fridge." Grandma downed her drink in record time.

I shook my head, remembering the other night with embarrassment. "Thanks, but I'm done with beer."

Gianna grinned. "Oh, that's right. I want all the juicy details."

I feared the expression on my face might give me away. "What are you talking about?"

"Josie said he kissed you."

My cheeks grew hot. "I was drunk. He was all over me."

"Mike? I'll bet." Gianna winked.

Grandma Rosa's eyes widened, and she refilled her glass.

My father's voice shook the room. "Nobody cares about the breadwinner. Well, you'll care when there's no one to pay the bills around here."

I sighed and rose from the table.

"No." Grandma gestured to my sister. "You go. I must talk to Sally."

Gianna groaned. "Oh, come on, Grandma."

My grandmother yelled something at her in Italian that we didn't understand and pointed to the living room. Gianna grabbed the tape measure and slunk out of the kitchen without another word.

"So what is this about you and the police officer?"

I was thunderstruck. "Where did you hear that?"

My grandmother reached into the fridge to get me a ginger ale. "Mrs. O'Brien saw you two having dinner earlier tonight. I guess that is why you are not hungry." She rolled her eyes at me.

I bit my lip so I wouldn't laugh. "It wasn't like that, Grandma. We were talking about Amanda."

"I hear he is a nice-looking boy."

"Yes, he's handsome."

"Mike is a nice boy too. Handsome. He took good care of his mama when she was dying, and Lord knows she did not deserve it. The way she and that husband of hers used to smack him around all the time. Absolutely shameful."

I nodded sadly. Mike had told me several times how empty his life had been until he had found me. It still hurt to think about.

"You should not have broken up with him." Grandma shook her head. "You never gave him a chance to explain. He should have been your husband, not that—that clown in Florida."

I choked on the soda I was swallowing then wiped my mouth with the back of my hand while I thought about how to respond. "It never would have worked, believe me."

"A nice boy," Grandma repeated. "If he sees me at the store, he carries my groceries to the car. What man does that these days?" She pointed her finger. "He still loves you."

"He's a suspect."

She frowned, the lines in her face deepening further. "A suspect? For Amanda's death?"

"I'm afraid so."

I expected my grandmother to cry out in alarm, but she kept her calm gaze fixed on me. "Baloney. Everyone she knew is a suspect, even me. I wanted to kill her myself after what she did to you."

I was shocked. "Grandma!"

Without further comment, she reached back into the fridge and produced a piece of her famous homemade cheesecake for me. I licked my lips, and my stomach growled. I'd been too nervous to eat at the diner, but I was starving now.

Grandma beamed. "Your favorite. I made it especially for you."

I closed my eyes and savored the first bite, letting the rich taste of sweet ricotta roll over my tongue. With a moan, I reached over to hug her. "Yum. You're the best."

She folded her hands on the table while she watched me eat. "Mike would not have done that, and you know it."

I sighed, resigned to following my gut intuition. "Yeah, I do."

"You will have to make a choice soon."

She wasn't making any sense. "What choice?"

Gianna came back in the room and tossed the tape measure on the table. "He's freaking out. He thinks he shrunk half a foot since last week."

"I need to sleep. The crazies get up early around here." Grandma stood then kissed us each on the cheek. "Pleasant dreams."

"Grandma," I called after her. "What choice?"

She smiled, but didn't answer.

CHAPTER TEN

———

Josie tied a silver, curly ribbon around the pink plastic wrap that adorned the cookie tray. She stepped back to survey her masterpiece one last time. "What do you think?"

I looked over her shoulder. "They look great, as always. And I adore the baby carriages. They're my favorite."

"Thanks. Where the heck is Vido? These cookies have to be delivered by noon sharp."

I glanced at the clock. Eleven thirty. "Stay calm. He'll be here."

"There's a ton of that strawberry frosting left. Do you want me to freeze it?"

I thought for a moment. "No, leave it in the fridge. If we don't use it by Monday, we'll freeze it then." The bells announced we had a customer, and I patted Josie's arm. "You relax. I'll see who it is."

Josie snorted and leaned against the prep table. "I don't know who could be left. We've had everyone in here this morning except a reporter from the *National Enquirer*."

I actually wouldn't have minded a reporter if he ended up buying something. I couldn't run a business like this, selling a cookie here and there. These people were more interested in Amanda than my products. I had to get to the bottom of this before my business suffered any further.

Gianna was seated by the window, texting. Two black, leather-bound law books the size of massive dictionaries were perched on the table in front of her. She put her phone down and got to her feet when she saw me.

"I need chocolate. *Bad.* Have you got any of the Chocolate Glazed Donut coffees? And I want Dutch cocoa cookies, too."

Josie appeared from the back room. "Thank God it's you. I never thought I'd say this, but I don't want to see any more customers today."

Gianna made a face and sat back down. "I know. Frank just texted me and said plenty of customers have been coming into the sub shop, asking him what he knows about Amanda."

"Don't they have anything better to do?" Josie grumbled as she grabbed a paper plate and placed three chocolate cookies on it.

"It's crazy." Gianna shot me a worried look. "People keep asking Frank if she was murdered."

I heaved a huge sigh. "Perfect. Another rumor that will be great for business." I hunted through the wicker basket filled with K-cups to distract myself. "Let's see, Hot Cocoa, Breakfast Blend, Caramel, aha! Found one." I waved the cup triumphantly in the air while Gianna clapped her hands.

"PMS or parents?" Josie asked.

"Both," Gianna and I replied in unison.

"Well, people do say we're like twins." I placed the K-cup in my Keurig machine.

Gianna leaned her head back as she munched on a cookie. "Oh, this is delish. So what are you guys having done at the spa?"

"I booked a massage for me and a facial for your sister." Josie turned to me. "Hope that's okay. I know how much you love them."

I closed my eyes for a second, imagining the steam on my face with waterfall music playing in the background. "Sounds like heaven. I haven't had one of those in ages. I may curl up and fall asleep."

"There won't be time for that." Josie shook her finger at me in an admonishing way. "We're going there on business, remember? Plus, I asked for their special double room, so we can be in there together. The two of us will be able to observe the techs' behaviors more closely."

I placed the coffee in front of Gianna. "Well, it'll still feel good, no matter what."

A rap sounded on the back door.

"Thank goodness. He's got a twenty minute drive ahead of him." Josie grumbled as she headed toward the back room, with me at her heels.

Josie opened the door. Vido leaned against the doorjamb, a cigarette dangling out of the side of his mouth. He was dressed in his usual outfit of hole-riddled jeans and a dirty, white T-shirt.

"Hello, ladies." He bowed from the waist.

Josie wrinkled her nose in disgust. "Do you think you could wear a jacket when you get there? It doesn't look professional to have a man with a stained T-shirt delivering cookies to a baby shower."

"Josie," I warned. I didn't want to make him angry.

Vido glanced at both of us, his smirk becoming an evil-looking smile. "Whatever you say, my lovely." He tossed his cigarette butt into the alley.

Josie moved aside to let him enter. We each picked up a tray and placed them in the trunk of Vido's car.

"Do I gotta collect money from them?" He lit another cigarette.

"No, they paid when they placed the order, so you're all set." I handed him two twenty-dollar bills, which he stuffed into his back pocket.

"I've been meaning to tell you girls something." Vido exhaled a cloud of smoke in my direction as he leaned against his car.

I coughed and rubbed my eyes. "What?"

"My rate is gonna have to go up." Vido spoke in a matter-of-fact tone. "Fifty dollars a delivery now."

My jaw dropped. "Fifty. That's a lot."

"Too bad, so sad." He laughed. "I got bills to pay like everybody else."

"Okay," I nodded. "We'll agree to it, on one condition."

He shook his head. "Vido don't like no conditions."

I held my thumb and forefinger together. "It's a teeny little condition."

"It's about you and Amanda," Josie said.

The smile left Vido's face, and his eyes glittered. Josie and I each took a step back.

"What're you saying?" He took another drag of his cigarette.

Josie turned to me for help, and I sighed in resignation. "Um, we kind of heard that you and Amanda, well, you know. You liked to spend time together."

Vido grinned maliciously. "Is that so?" He folded his arms across his chest. "Why do you wanna know?"

Josie gave a nervous laugh. "We're fond of you, and you're a great delivery guy. We're afraid the police might think you had something to do with Amanda's—"

"Murder?" he asked.

"What makes you think it was murder?" I feigned innocence.

"Amanda and I had—what you might call, an arrangement. We knew each other pretty well." Vido winked at me. "You know what I mean?"

Boy, did I ever.

"It's all over the town. Everybody knows she was killed. And Amanda was afraid someone was out to get her."

My jaw dropped. "You mean, she thought her life might be in jeopardy?"

"Why should I tell you anything?" Vido snapped. "What's in it for me?"

"What do you want?" Josie asked. When he leered at her, she shook her head. "No way. Almost anything but that."

Vido licked his lips and turned in my direction. "Forget about it," I said.

He rubbed his hands together thoughtfully. "Well then, I think I'd like to learn how to make cookies."

I blinked, not sure I'd heard him right. "Excuse me?"

"Yeah." Vido ran his hands carefully over the pink wrap of the tray. "Yeah, that'd be good. I really like cookies."

Who would have thought? "That's it? No cash?"

"Of course I want cash." He laughed. "What kind of an idiot do you think I am?"

Josie held up a hand. "I refuse to answer that. How will we know you're not making something up?"

"Vido don't operate like that. Look at this face. Honest as your mother's."

I sincerely doubted it. "Look, if you know anything about who really killed her, you should go straight to the police."

Vido slammed the hatchback of his car down with such a vengeance that Josie and I both jumped about ten feet in the air. The entire vehicle shook. "I don't lie about this stuff—you know what I mean? And I hate dealing with those pigs. I think I know who it was."

I tried to conceal the excitement in my voice. "The killer?"

"Yeah. Amanda liked to confide in me. There were these times when we'd be at her place and she'd hug me and—"

"Ew, no." Josie made a face.

I coughed when he blew smoke at me again. "Josie will give you personalized baking lessons for two hours one day next week."

Vido took the cigarette butt out of his mouth and extinguished it on the ground right in front of Josie. "That gets me excited."

I hate you, Josie mouthed.

"And I'll get you some cash. How much do you want?"

Vido didn't hesitate. "I need a thousand."

My eyes opened wide in astonishment. He might as well have asked for a million. This would definitely put me a few steps closer to bunking at my mom and dad's on a permanent basis. No way was I giving him that much.

"I can get you five hundred. I don't have much cash handy."

Vido scoffed. "You're a liar. You can get the money out of your business."

I gritted my teeth. "Five hundred. Take it or leave it. My business isn't exactly booming right now."

"Fine." Vido nodded in agreement. "That's still enough to get me a forty-two inch. Maybe a new DVR and some pornos too."

Josie rolled her eyes at me in disgust.

"When can you get it?" Vido asked.

The banks closed at noon on Saturday. "Well, I guess it's going to have to be Monday now."

"Okay."

Darn. I hated to wait that long. My shop would continue to suffer in the meantime. More customers asking questions. If only I could get him the money sooner.

Josie must have guessed what I was thinking. "Can't you take it out on a debit card?"

"Yes, but I have a three hundred dollar limit withdrawal for each day. I suppose I could do a withdrawal today and one on Sunday. Can we meet tomorrow?"

"The wake's at one," Vido said.

"Well, maybe you could meet us here beforehand, say at noon?" I asked. "I'll give you the money then."

Vido tugged at his beard. "Yeah. I guess that'll be okay." He sauntered back into the shop, and we followed him, mystified. "I'll take a dozen of those cookies with the jelly. On the house, of course." He pointed at the glass. "And I gotta have some fortune cookies. Give me a dozen of those too."

I clenched my fists at my sides and, without another word, grabbed a piece of waxed paper and placed the cookies into one of my little, pink boxes. I handed the box to Vido, but it took every effort of my being to keep from throwing it at him. I didn't like being blackmailed. If Brian knew what I was up to, he'd read me the riot act and probably never speak to me again. Still, there was no time to waste. I had to find Amanda's killer so that my shop could return to normal.

Vido sauntered over to Gianna's side. She glanced up from her book with apprehension. He nodded and reached into the box, cracking a fortune cookie open with his teeth. He pulled the strip of paper from his mouth while she continued to watch in horror.

He held the other half out to her. "Fortune cookie, babe?"

Gianna wrinkled her nose. "Um, no thanks. I think I lost my appetite…forever."

Vido stared at the piece of paper. "What's this mean?"

"Why, Vido," Josie grinned. "I always thought you knew how to read."

He shot her a dirty look. "You ain't funny, Josie. No, I don't get this." He read aloud. "*Your problem just got bigger. What have you done?*"

Josie snorted. "Extortion. How fitting."

The tinkling of bells sounded, and Ellen walked in.

"Hey, girlfriend." Josie leaned against the counter. "What's going on?"

Ellen looked like she needed a good night's sleep. "Not much. Dad was craving something sweet." She stared at Vido, her eyes full of wonder.

"I'll see you ladies tomorrow." Vido winked at Josie, then gave Ellen, in her jeans and sweater, an appraising look.

She stepped away from him, disgust written all over her face.

He reached into the box again and produced a jelly-filled cookie. He bit into it and smacked his lips, eyes lingering on my chest. I crossed my arms in defense and glared back at him.

"Don't worry. I'm going. Wouldn't want to keep your customers from coming in." He laughed. "Until tomorrow, girls."

Josie watched him leave then turned to me. "I swear to God, if I had the money, you'd be the one making cookies while he slobbers all over you."

"You're the one who said he was harmless." I reached under the counter to get a box ready for Ellen's order.

"He's getting worse with age." Josie shook her head. "Maybe he misses all those things he and Amanda used to do together."

The picture in my mind was unsettling. "Okay, I think I just threw up a little."

"What's going on?" Ellen's face was puzzled.

Josie turned her attention back to her friend. "I'm sorry, hun, what kind of cookies would you like?"

Ellen turned her attention back to the display case. "Let's see. How about two of the fudgy delights, two biscotti, six of the jelly, and two raspberry cheesecake."

"Twelve dollars," Josie said. "Nice to have someone buying more than one cookie for a change."

Ellen handed Josie the money. "Is it really that bad?"

"Things could be better." I sighed. "If Josie and I have anything to say about it, business will be back to normal next week."

"Why? What have you guys got planned?"

"You two better get a move on, or you won't make it in time." Gianna didn't even glance up from her book.

Josie started up the staircase. "I'm going to freshen up. Be down in a minute."

"Hurry up. We don't want to be late." I bent down to straighten the tray of fortune cookies.

Ellen clutched the box between her hands. "Where are you guys going?"

"To Amanda's Retreat for a massage and facial." I grabbed my purse behind the counter.

Ellen made a face. "Do you think it's a good idea for you to go there? I mean, when people think you might have had something to do with her death?"

"I need to find a way to clear my name from all of this. Maybe it will help." I removed my compact mirror from my purse and tried to smooth down some curls. Since the heat had broken, at least my hair wasn't as frizzy. I smiled at Gianna, poring over her books. "Thank you so much for watching the store."

She nodded absently, already engrossed in her studies.

Josie descended the staircase and slung her purse over her shoulder. "All set?"

Ellen clucked her tongue. "Well, I hope you have a relaxing time. I need to get home. Pop will be wondering what happened to me." She started for the door. "Are you guys going to the wake tomorrow?"

"Yeah, we told Kate we'd be there," Josie said. "How about you?"

Ellen frowned. "I'll see how Pop is first. Let's be honest. I wasn't fond of her and don't think people should be hypocrites about such things." She stared at both of us pointedly and then pushed her way out the front door in a huff.

"Wow." My mouth fell open. "What the heck did we do?"

Josie shrugged. "Who knows? She gets in these weird, self-righteous moods all the time. She really needs a social life. What's going to happen when her father dies?"

"Maybe she'll find a guy and fall in love." I hoped so, for her sake. She seemed lonely, and I could definitely relate.

Josie pondered this for a moment. "I don't remember the last time Ellen even talked about a date. I know she went to the prom with Billy Dunsbach, and I think they dated for a while, but I can't for the life of me remember any other guy."

My thoughts turned to Mike and Colin. "Well, at least she's been spared a lot of drama."

Josie grinned. "I love drama. If there's no drama in your life, something's wrong."

Apparently, I was doing something right then.

CHAPTER ELEVEN

———

Amanda's Retreat was known as a luxury spa for the rich and beautiful, but I still wasn't prepared for all the grandeur. A receptionist behind the black marble counter invited us to take a seat in the adjoining sitting room while our technicians finished up with their previous clients.

The high-back, Victorian chairs were plush and comfortable. A fire roared in the fireplace, despite the seventy-degree day outside. Perhaps the only thing unsettling about the place was a huge oil painting of Amanda over the fireplace.

Josie helped herself to a muffin from the coffee bar in the corner and settled next to me on the couch. "I know it's wrong to speak ill of the dead, but it takes a real shallow person to do that." She pointed at the picture.

I wandered over to the coffee bar for a drink. A middle-aged, Asian woman was behind the counter, pouring iced tea into tall, crystal glasses. She smiled. "Lemon or sugar? Or perhaps you'd rather have one of our delicious smoothies?" She motioned to the blender in front of her. "Fresh blueberries and strawberries with low fat milk and vanilla."

I stared in fascination at what I assumed had been Amanda's deadly drink, and a chill ran down my spine. "Um, no thanks. The tea will be great. With lemon, please."

She reached inside a small fridge behind the counter and produced sliced lemon, which she dropped into my glass with a pair of tongs.

"Thank you." I smiled, and the woman nodded in return.

Besides Josie and me, two other women were waiting. One was reading a magazine while the other liberally helped herself to chocolates from a tray on a nearby coffee table.

Polished hardwood floors were covered with antique, Oriental rugs. I couldn't fathom how much a business like this cost to run. It was open every day, except for Sunday.

I sat next to Josie. "I wonder how much Amanda's father left her in his will."

"Millions." Josie practically spat the word out. "He was an investment banker and partner. My mother told me. He died right before Amanda turned twenty-five. There were stipulations in his will that she'd receive her trust fund at that age. It was for at least ten million dollars."

I gasped. "Dang. But what about Kate?"

Josie wiped her mouth with a napkin. "Does she look like she's suffering? There's plenty more where that came from, honey. Amanda's wealth would have tripled if she'd survived her mother."

"Sally?" A slender, young woman with bright-red cheeks and shoulder-length, blonde hair stood in the doorway. She smiled when her eyes came to rest on me.

I waved my hand and got to my feet, placing my glass on the table.

"Hi, I'm Zoe."

"Josie?" A woman of about forty in a black T-shirt pushed her way past the younger girl. She had short, dark hair and was heavyset, her arms resembling tree trunks. I turned to Josie and rolled my eyes.

"Here." Josie moved forward with trepidation.

"I'm Liza." She pursed her lips. "You girls are in the same double room?" She pointed a finger at Josie. "I have you down for a Swedish massage? And you," the finger made its way over to me. "Zoe will be giving you a facial."

"That's right," I said.

"Stairs or elevator?" Liza asked.

"Stairs are fine," Josie assured her with a nod.

Zoe didn't look much older than a teenager. She gestured to the staircase at the right of the reception counter and Liza sidled past, with Josie and me following. "Is this your first time here?"

My sandal clipped the stairs, and I grabbed the railing for support. "Yes. I've been told such wonderful things about this place and the owner."

Liza snorted. She had the mannerisms of a drill sergeant. "Guess you've come to the wrong place then." She flung open a door and ushered us into a hallway. "Second room on the left."

I said a silent prayer of thanks that she wasn't working on me.

We walked into a large room with vinyl walls the color of sandstone with a marble finish. The pleasant scent of eucalyptus surrounded us. Dimmed, recessed lighting gave the room an overall relaxed atmosphere. A hydraulic chair and massage table were spaced about ten feet apart from each other and against opposite walls. There was an overstuffed armchair next to each one with bubbling footbaths that looked inviting. Rainforest music played softly in the background.

"Both of you undress," Liza ordered. "You." She pointed at me. "From the waist up." She picked up the beige, terry cloth wraparound towel lying on the chair with the name "Amanda's" written in cursive letters. "Then, put this on."

"And as for you." She turned to Josie, who jumped at the sound of her voice. "You completely undress before you put your towel on. Take off all jewelry, and soak your feet. We'll be back in five."

She walked out of the room, and Zoe followed, after a shy smile to us.

I removed my blouse and bra and set them on a small table next to the chair. "Why do I feel like I joined the army?"

Josie undressed quickly and wrapped herself in the towel. "I'll give you twenty bucks if you trade technicians. I'm afraid she's going to hurt me."

I placed my feet in the footbath. "I've been looking forward to this all morning. I'm starting to think it's not going to be quite as relaxing as I'd hoped."

"Remember." She glanced toward the door. "We're here to find out whatever information we can about Amanda and what they thought of her."

There was a knock, and I called, "Come in."

Zoe and Lisa both wore pink smocks with a golden "A" embroidered on the lapels. They reached down simultaneously to dry our feet with soft, white towels. Then Liza jerked her thumb toward the massage table and glared at Josie. "On your stomach."

Zoe was more patient with me. "You can lie back in the chair now. Do you have any allergies?"

"None." Amanda came to mind again.

I settled into the comfortable, well-padded chair, which Zoe reclined back slightly. She tucked a plush blanket under my arms and shone a magnifying lamp over my face. "You have very nice skin. Did you want a regular facial, the anti-aging, or a champagne one?"

I tried to crack the ice. "Is it cheap champagne or the expensive kind?"

Josie laughed with me. Neither technician responded, so we stopped.

After a minute, Zoe giggled. "Oh, I get it. That's funny."

"Hilarious." Liza landed a whack to Josie's back.

"Oomph." Josie grunted in pain.

Well, I *was* pushing thirty. "The anti-aging one sounds good, thank you."

Zoe rubbed cream into my cheeks, and the scent of honey penetrated my nostrils. She reached for a hot washcloth and gently draped it over my face. "Okey-dokey."

I closed my eyes and listened to the soothing sounds of waterfalls playing on the CD in the background. I was sorely tempted to let myself fall asleep. There was work to be done though. Zoe removed the cloth, and I forced my eyes open, curious to see her reaction to the upcoming questions I planned to ask. "How long have you worked here?"

She turned on the steam machine, and the mist began to permeate the air. "I've been here about a year. Liza's been here, what, two years?"

"Since the place opened." Liza leaned over Josie's shoulders with a determined look on her face. "Already too long."

Ow, Josie mouthed, a pleading look on her face.

"I was sorry to hear about your boss." My remark seemed like a bad idea when I noticed it cost Josie another whack to her back.

"That lying little slut." The lines around Liza's mouth

hardened, and she began to breathe heavy.

Zoe glanced at Liza with surprise then smiled hesitantly. "Liza and Amanda didn't always see eye to eye."

"No one saw eye to eye with that wench." Liza's eyes glittered. "She didn't give a damn about any of us. Remember last year, how she promised us all Christmas bonuses?"

Zoe nodded.

Liza started working on the neck area vehemently. A small, strangled cry escaped from Josie.

"You want to know what we got, what the fabulous bonus turned out to be?"

"Um, sure." Josie's answer came out muffled.

Liza stopped for a minute to rub more oil on Josie's back. "We each got a gift certificate for a free manicure. Can you believe it? All the money that little tramp had, and she gives out manicure coupons. Like we don't spend enough time here already."

"I'd been hoping for some cash." A wistful look crossed Zoe's face.

"We all wanted cash." Liza glared at her.

Josie waved her arms in a panic, but Liza appeared not to notice. I winced as I watched her.

"Can you breathe?" I asked.

"She's fine," Liza grunted. "Aren't you?" It sounded more like a threat than a question of concern.

"Um, yeah." Josie's voice sounded far away. "Fine."

"Anyhow, I went to her a couple of weeks ago to ask for a loan. She pretty much laughed in my face." Liza did a karate chop to Josie's neck, which made Josie cry out. "No one laughs in my face."

"Nobody," Josie croaked.

"We only make minimum wage here." Zoe lowered her voice. "We really depend on our tips. I need them to survive."

I could take a hint.

"There's a rumor going around she might have been k-killed." Josie managed to squeak out.

"Good," Liza mumbled under her breath. "Karma's a bitch, and so was she."

"Who'll run the business now that she's—you know,

gone?" I asked.

Zoe finished massaging my hands with cream and placed them inside heated mitts. "I guess her cousin, Charlotte, will take over. I hope they don't decide to close it. I don't know what I'd do then."

"Run the business?" Liza repeated. "That squeaky little thing? Charlotte's another one like Amanda. Shows up when she feels like it and pretends to take care of the books. What a joke. At least Amanda had some business sense. That mouse is a waste of precious air."

Zoe shrugged. "I haven't even seen her since Tuesday."

"Yeah. Payday. That's the only time you ever see her. She handed out checks, helped herself to some cash, and left."

"Right after she and Amanda had that argument." Zoe slathered more cream on my face.

My ears pricked up. "What kind of an argument?"

Liza shot Zoe a dirty look. "It was nothing. They were always bickering. Or shall I say, Amanda was always ordering her around. And Charlotte was stupid enough to take it." Her eyes darkened as she ground her hands into Josie's back.

Help me, Josie mouthed.

"Um, Liza, Josie had a baby recently," I said. "Can you take it a little easy on her?"

"I thought you wanted to relax?" Liza frowned as she pounded on Josie's back like she was beating a drum. "You're going to feel like a whole different person when I'm through with you."

"That's what I'm afraid of." Josie shut her eyes.

Zoe started to do some extractions on my face. "They started arguing right after that really hot-looking guy showed up."

She had my full attention. "Do you get a lot of male customers?"

"Not any like him." Zoe laughed. "He was fine."

Josie lifted her shoulders off the table. "What'd he look like?"

"Tall, dark, and handsome." Liza pushed her back down.

Zoe gently massaged my neck. "Tall, black curly hair,

bulging muscles, and the most gorgeous blue eyes I've ever seen. Amanda called him Mike."

My heart lurched as Josie managed to turn her head enough to meet my gaze. The blood pounded into my face.

"Do you think they were dating?" Josie asked Zoe.

I was relieved she asked the question, not positive I could get the words to come out.

"I don't know." Zoe removed my mitts. "I tell you, I wouldn't have minded dating that hottie. He didn't seem to like it when Amanda touched him though. Then they went in her office and came out when I finished giving someone a facial."

Liza's face turned crimson while she beat on Josie's back again. "Doesn't take much guessing to know what they were doing in there. Amanda was always using her office for some not-so-secret rendezvous. Cheap slut." She gave Josie's back one final whack. "There. All done."

A groan escaped Josie. "I can't move."

"Good." Liza's tone was pleased. "That means you got everything out of the massage you were supposed to. And you were wound tight, believe me. I didn't think you'd ever unravel." She wiped her hands on a towel. "We'll wait outside while you both change." She motioned to Zoe, who followed her like an obedient little dog.

"Thank you." I smiled at Zoe. "The facial was great."

She beamed. "I'm so pleased you like it. Like Liza said, we'll wait in the hallway." She hesitated for a moment. "That's when our patrons tip us. Well, if they choose to, that is."

Liza's voice boomed. "Zoe, stop begging. Let's go."

After they shut the door, I walked over to Josie, who still lay motionless on the table. I rubbed her head like she was an ailing child.

"Are you okay?"

She whimpered. "If you think I'm going to tip that monster for breaking my back, you're crazy."

"I'll give her something, don't worry. If I don't, she might throw us both down the stairs. Can you move at all?"

Josie grabbed my hand and, with assistance, slowly raised herself up from the table. She placed a foot onto the floor and grimaced, while the other slowly followed. "We may need to get me a brace on the way home. I don't think I can go back to work today. Time for me to go home, curl up, and die."

"Don't worry about the shop. Maybe it's only a temporary stiffness, and you'll feel better tomorrow."

"Crippled is more like it." Josie started to put her clothes on, with my help. "Can you believe that broad? All the things she said about Amanda. I mean, come on, tell us how you really feel, babe."

I shook my head. "Amanda didn't have many fans." I definitely knew all about that.

"Sal." Josie leaned forward and whispered. "Liza could have done it."

"No, I don't think so." My voice sounded unconvincing, even to myself.

Josie looked as if she might explode. "Are you kidding? She almost killed me, and we just met!"

There was a tap on the door. "Ladies, whenever you're ready."

Josie clenched her teeth. "Oh, yes. Let's not keep Godzilla waiting any longer."

"Quiet. She'll hear you." I projected my voice in the direction of the door. "We'll be right out." I threw my clothes on and grabbed my purse, producing two ten-dollar bills from my wallet. "This will have to do. I can't wait to see what the rest will cost us."

"Tell me about it. On the bright side, we learned some valuable information." Josie hobbled toward the door. "No great loss without some small pain."

"You mean gain," I corrected her.

"Not in this case." Josie winced as she reached over to open the door.

Zoe stood in the hallway, a meek expression on her face.

Liza stood next to her, arms folded across her rounded stomach, glaring at both of us. "Well, you two certainly took your time."

I handed each woman a ten-dollar bill. "Thank you both very much for a—an interesting experience."

"It was our pleasure." Liza seemed to soften a little at the sight of the money. She led the way toward the stairs, and we followed, Josie leaning on me for support. "Come back any time."

I touched my face gingerly. "I love the honey smell in the facial."

Zoe giggled. "Isn't it great? We sell the mask here, if you'd like to purchase a jar. We even mix the ingredients for it ourselves. Amanda, rest her soul, kept up on all the newest trends. Bee venom facials are very popular at salons in New York City, and they've done well for us too."

"Did you say bee venom?" I almost choked on the words.

"Yes. That's the active ingredient in the anti-aging facial, along with manuka honey and natural botanical oils. They stimulate, nourish, and moisturize the skin. I guess it's kind of funny that Amanda would even want to feature it at her salon, what with her allergy to bees and all."

"Bee venom?" Josie repeated. Her face was whiter than flour.

We had reached the reception desk.

Liza had a sly smile on her lips. "Even if you're allergic, the stuff can't hurt you unless it's ingested somehow. Still, Amanda never went near it."

Her eyes glittered while Josie and I retreated a hasty step backward.

"And to think, I could have ended all of my problems sooner. How unfortunate." She clucked her tongue at both of us and then disappeared back up the stairs without another word.

CHAPTER TWELVE

———

"Oh, my God." Josie's eyes widened in alarm.

The receptionist looked puzzled. "Was something wrong with your service, ladies?"

"Um, no, of course not." My heartbeat was racing a mile a minute. I took a deep calming breath and reached for my wallet. "How much was the facial?"

"Let's see, one hundred and fifty dollars." The receptionist stared at the computer screen in front of her. "And the massage was one hundred."

Josie's eyes flashed with surprise. "A hundred? The girl on the phone told me fifty."

"I'm so sorry. Perhaps she misunderstood. Cash or credit?" The receptionist held out her hand.

"But I can't even freaking move! I want—"

I pinched Josie's arm in warning. "She went to the gym this morning. I kept telling her not to overdo it. Put both services on my card, please."

Josie cursed under her breath. "Sal, I'm not going to let you do this."

I signed the slip while ignoring her protest. Trying to find a killer was proving to be costly.

The receptionist handed me a receipt. "Thanks again. By the way, we welcome reviews on our website. Here's the address." She pushed a business card across the counter at each of us.

"Now you're talking." Josie reached out to grab the card.

I snatched it from Josie's hand and escorted her out the front door. "Bye now!"

The receptionist stared at us in confusion.

"I'll give her a review." Josie's face was bright red as I unlocked the car. She groaned and crawled into the front passenger seat. "Thank God you drove. We'd crash and burn if I had to maneuver this car right now."

"Bee venom." A shiver went down my spine. "You know what this means? What if one of them was at her apartment that day and slipped it in her drink? Charlotte said the employees went there sometimes."

"I can picture Liza killing someone." Josie massaged the back of her neck and winced. "She hated Amanda. Plus, she's nuts. Double motive right there."

"Yeah." I fell silent as Mike came to mind again. What had he been doing at the spa? And more specifically, in Amanda's office?

I remembered Zoe's reference to Amanda touching him, and heat crept into my face. Why did this bother me so much? I had no claim to him anymore. Amanda had burned me badly, but she was dead now. Yet, I still couldn't seem to let it go.

"Hel-lo, Sal?" Josie clapped her hands. "I'm in agony, and you're tuning me out. Where'd you go?"

"Sorry. I guess I was daydreaming."

"Uh-huh. Come on, I know you. You were thinking about what Zoe said. When she mentioned Mike coming to see Amanda."

"No, I wasn't."

"Then why are you blushing?"

"Look, it doesn't matter if they were seeing each other. That's his business. I think I need to pay him a little visit though."

"Do you now?" Josie's smile was wicked.

I brought my car to a stop in the alley behind the bakery. "If he was seeing Amanda, he might have some idea of who was trying to kill her."

"Do you think he'll tell you the truth? I mean, about their relationship?"

"That isn't important right now." I opened the car door. "I'm only interested in finding out who killed Amanda."

"Right." Josie gave me a doubtful look.

With the exception of my sister, the shop was empty.

Gianna sat in the exact same spot we'd left her in, still poring over law books. Three empty coffee cups were stacked next to her.

"How'd everything go?" I asked. "Did you get a lot of customers?"

Gianna stood and stretched. "Probably about twenty or so, I'd say."

"Awesome." I grabbed the back of a chair with both hands. "Did they buy much?"

"A few." Gianna shut her book. "One woman bought a dozen chocolate chips. Then Mrs. Gavelli came in and asked for a single butter cookie."

Josie made a face. "Did you tell her what she could do with it?"

"Be nice now." I turned back to Gianna. "Did she ask if I was arrested yet?"

Gianna's lips curved upward slightly. "Well, she did wonder why you weren't here. She hoped they'd finally come to their senses and hauled you off to prison. Said it might be your only salvation."

"Great." *Why did the woman hate me so much?*

"Oh, and she asked for two fortune cookies. No, wait, that's not strong enough. She *demanded* them. People were staring, and I didn't have the strength to argue with her. I hope that's okay."

I nodded. "No problem."

"What'd the fortunes say?" Josie asked. "Did they tell her to pull the knife out of your sister's back?"

"She didn't read them out loud. After she opened the first one, she threw it on the floor and left in a huff." Gianna's eyes filled with mirth. "It said, 'Life is too short for cheapskates.'"

We all laughed.

I dumped Gianna's coffee cups in the trash. "I guess she won't be back for a while."

Gianna gathered her books in her arms. "You said you're going to the wake tomorrow, right?"

"Are you going?" I cocked one eyebrow.

"I'm not sure. I mean, I'm sorry she's dead, but I have no desire to go to a wake for a woman who caused you so much pain," my sister said. "I don't even know how you can do it."

I smoothed the cream-colored tablecloth, and thought of how my grandmother had crocheted it for me with such loving care. The two on the adjacent tables were ivory. "Her mother asked us to go. She may be upset with me for what I said to Amanda the other day, but I have to make an appearance. It wouldn't be right if I stayed away. Besides, I think it will help me make my peace with everything and move on."

Gianna shook her head in disbelief. "You're a better person than I am."

"I don't know about that. You're pretty okay in my book."

"Dad keeps insisting we all go, so I guess I don't have much choice either. If he sees anything he likes, he wants me to take notes." Gianna rolled her eyes at the ceiling.

"Okay, he's really starting to carry this funeral obsession a bit too far." Josie limped over to the table and sat in the seat Gianna had vacated.

Gianna's brow wrinkled. "Are you okay?"

I held back a smile. "Josie just had a massage by Lizzie Borden. She whacked with her hands, not an ax, though."

"Ha, ha." Josie narrowed her eyes.

"Uh, yeah, that sounds like the kind of spa treatment I'd want. Did you find out anything useful?" Gianna asked.

I adjusted the slightly crooked venetian blind on the window. "We found out all of Amanda's employees hated her. Of course, we'd already guessed that part."

"Well, duh. Remember who we're talking about." Gianna put her books down to give me a hug. "Are you coming by the house tonight?'

I shook my head. "I have an errand to run. Then I'm going upstairs for a nice, long, hot bubble bath." The television and a quart of double fudge ice cream were on my agenda as well, but they didn't need to know that. I was looking forward to a night of relaxation, topped off by the fact tomorrow was Sunday, and I could sleep in.

"Oh, I almost forgot." Gianna tossed her hair back. "Mom and Dad want you to come by the house tomorrow so that we can all go to the wake together."

I was about to agree, then remembered Vido. "Why don't you guys meet us here? Josie and I have something to do right before we leave."

Josie turned to Gianna. "Yeah, that's a good idea. Rob's going to stay with the kids, so I'll keep your sister company on the ride over."

"Okay. See you guys tomorrow then." She grabbed her books and pushed the front door open.

I sat across from Josie. "Do you want me to drive you home?"

She shifted uncomfortably in her seat. "No, I think I'll be all right. I might need you to push me into the car and tie my hands to the steering wheel, but then I should be fine. Are you sure you don't want me to stay? We've got almost another two hours to go."

"No worries, I can handle it."

"We should close at five every night. Why only on Saturdays?"

I shrugged. "We still don't know when our busiest time is, especially given the last few days. Once we do, maybe we can adjust the hours some."

"Since Amanda's death, we're busy all the time. We're not making enough sales though. Does that count?"

"Smart aleck. I think I'll hit the ATM when I leave here, and then if Mike's agreeable, I'm going to stop by and see him."

"Don't forget your lingerie." Josie grinned.

I pursed my lips together. "Okay, that was so uncalled for."

"Sorry, I can't help myself. Seriously, do you really want to go to his house alone? It's going to spark a lot of old memories for you guys. It might not be a smart move on your part."

"We're both adults. Besides, our relationship has been over with for years."

Josie looked skeptical. "I don't think it's ever been completely over for you two."

I changed the subject. "You should go home to your babies. They need you."

"All right, but I want details."

"I doubt there will be any. Oh." I hesitated for a moment.

"Do you happen to know his phone number?"

Josie eased her aching body off the chair. "Afraid not. He had an apartment on Green Street before. After his mom died, he moved back into her house. Well, it's his house now, I mean."

I sighed. "I don't remember her number. Who knows if it's even the same one? I really hate to stop without calling first." *What if he's entertaining a lady friend?*

"Your grandmother might have it. She knows everyone's number in town."

I rolled my eyes. "I'd rather they didn't know about this. I guess I'll have to take a chance and surprise him."

"I doubt Mike will mind being surprised by you," Josie quipped.

"You never stop. Meet me here tomorrow by 11:30. Vido's due at noon."

"I wouldn't miss it, believe me. With his help, maybe we can start putting the pieces together in this puzzle." Josie waved and made her way gingerly out the back door and into the alley where her vehicle was parked next to mine.

"I hope so." A niggle at the back of my mind made me wonder if I was throwing away money where Vido was concerned. Hopefully I was wrong. I glanced at my phone on the counter, thinking about the new information we'd learned. I should share my findings with Brian. Plus, it would be nice to hear his voice. My face grew warm at the thought.

Oh, what the heck. I prayed he wouldn't be mad at me. I picked up the phone, searched the contacts section, and dialed his number. I waited, heart thumping.

"Officer Jenkins." His voice sounded brisk, and I could detect laughter in the background.

Shoot. I'd forgotten all about his parents' anniversary. "Hi, Brian, it's Sally. Sally Muccio. I'm sorry to bother you."

"You're never bothering me, Sally." His voice filled the phone with warmth and sex appeal.

A tingle ran through me.

"How are you? Is everything okay?"

"Yes. I feel bad about interrupting your day off though."

"Don't worry about it. We're all sitting around having a

cookout in my parents' backyard. I get to chaperone my nieces in the pool." He chuckled. "They keep trying to dunk me."

Somehow I could picture this and laughed out loud. The image of him in a pair of swim trunks was enough to send my brain into overload as well. "I wanted to let you know about something I found out earlier today."

There was a long silence at the other end. "Have you been snooping again?"

"A little." The words started to tumble out before I could stop them. "See, Josie really wanted a massage, so I decided to go along with her to get a facial. We—"

"You were at Amanda's spa?" Brian interrupted.

I exhaled sharply. "Yes. We found out that Amanda offered a bee venom facial to her clients. The technicians mixed the ingredients for it themselves."

There was silence again. "Really. I was there yesterday and didn't know about this."

"Do any of her employees know how she died?"

"Not unless you mentioned it."

I shut my eyes and winced. He was angry. "I didn't say a word, I swear. Please don't be mad."

Brian sighed. "I'm not mad. I appreciate you letting me know and will definitely check into this further when I get back. Now, will you do something for me?"

"Of course." I waited in anticipation.

"Please don't get involved. I don't want to have to worry about someone coming after you too." He paused. "I've got to get going. Can I call you tomorrow?"

"Sure." Dejected, I didn't know what else to say.

"Okay." His voice became sensual again. "Have a good night. I'm looking forward to our dinner later this week." He clicked off.

Relief washed over me as I put the phone back in my purse. Now that the conversation was over, I was glad to have shared my information with him. I thought of our upcoming dinner date. Was I ready for this? At least I had a few days to decide. I removed some cookies from the case that had been baked the day before yesterday and were too old to sell now. I placed them in a box to drop off at the homeless shelter on my way to Mike's.

The bells over the door announced I had a customer. "Be with you in a sec."

"No hurry, honey."

The hairs on the back of my neck stood at attention. I'd recognize the voice of Jeannie Peterson anywhere.

It was silly to fear the woman since I'd known her for years. Even while bending over the case I knew her dark, brooding eyes were fixated on me. I righted myself slowly.

"Hi, Mrs. Peterson, what can I do for you?"

She pointed a finger the size of a sausage at my display case. "One chocolate chip. And Josie forgot my fortune cookie yesterday."

I reached for a bag. "Sorry about that. I'll make sure you get an extra one." I also gave her the cookie with the most chips since I figured she'd probably count them. "That'll be one dollar and twenty-five cents."

Jeannie reached inside her wallet. "Do yourself a favor, sweetie. Get yourself a new partner. Someone's going to take Josie out one of these days. That girl has no personality whatsoever. Never did. I know the things she's said about me."

Yikes. My forehead started to perspire, but I forced myself to smile. "I'll, uh, try to remember that." I reached my palm out to accept a handful of change.

"You're a nice girl. I have a great-nephew about your age. He's drop dead gorgeous. I'll have him call you."

Oh, good grief. "Thanks, Mrs. Peterson, but I'm not ready to date yet."

She reached inside the bag for a fortune cookie and cracked it open, never taking her eyes off me. "I'll have him call you," she repeated firmly.

"Um, okay." I winced.

She glanced down at the slip of paper in her hands, smiled, and met my eyes again. Hers were cold and calculating. "Want to know what it says?"

I didn't dare refuse. I watched her face, remembering the time Josie had gone to her front door unannounced on a dare from me. We'd been about nine or ten. Jeannie had been stirring a huge, black pot on the stove and talking to it. She'd invited

Josie to join her for dinner. Josie, in turn, had shrieked and taken off down the road, where I waited in fear. Afterward, at my house, she swore Jeannie had asked her to *be* dinner, but my grandmother had said Josie heard wrong. Grandma Rosa explained that Jeannie was a lonely woman who missed her dead husband and not the witch from "Hansel and Gretel" we kept insisting she was.

Jeannie cackled out loud. "Get this. 'Things are not always as they appear.' Don't you find that interesting, Sally?"

It was as if she'd read my mind. "Yes, ma'am. Very interesting."

"Don't worry, honey. I know you didn't kill Amanda. I just hope everyone else knows it too. For your sake."

Her eyes searched my frozen face. All I could do was stare back.

She turned her back on me and headed for the door. "Have a good night, sweetie."

I opened my mouth to say "You, too," but only air came out. I watched her push the door open, bells jingling merrily as she departed.

I wiped my sweaty forehead with the back of my hand and glanced at the clock. Five minutes to five. Oh, how I needed to get out of here. What had Jeannie meant? Was she referring to Amanda or to herself? Did she know something about the murder?

I hurried over to lock the front door as my cell phone started ringing. I ran back over to answer it, not bothering to look at the screen first. Maybe Brian had forgotten to tell me something. I smiled. Talking to him would push the visit from Jeannie right out of my mind.

"Hello?"

"How's freedom treating you?"

I sucked in a sharp breath as I recognized the bitter, male voice on the other end of the line. "Colin, why are you calling me?"

"Perhaps you can tell me why I received a call from a cop named Brian Jenkins asking about Amanda Gregorio's death?" Colin snapped in my ear. "Did you kill her?"

"How can you even ask me such a thing?"

"Sal, get real. You were always jealous of Amanda."

My voice started to shake with rage. "Don't you dare make me out to be the bad guy here. *You* were sleeping with her. That's why Brian called, because of your relationship, which might still have been going on until her death, for all I know." *Or even cared anymore.*

"Oh, so you do know this clown?" Colin asked. "Then that's the reason he called me. You told him Amanda and I were fooling around. Anything to try to get more money out of me."

"What money? I never asked you for anything. And I caught you in the act. In our own home to boot, so don't try to deny it."

Colin snorted into the phone. "I'm so glad I divorced you. You really are nuts."

"Excuse me." Anger rose from the pit of my stomach. "I divorced *you.* Our marriage was never sacred. God knows, you proved that through your adultery."

He ignored my comment. "That idiot pig said Florida police might want to question me about my whereabouts that night. So I'm guessing they think I flew up to New York to commit the deed."

"Were you here? In town?" I held my breath.

"I haven't been anywhere near Colwestern. This is all some kind of setup to extract money from me, isn't it? Is this Brian guy your new boyfriend?" His tone was full of venom.

I was so furious I didn't trust myself to speak for a minute. I remembered how I'd once loved this man—or thought I had. Sadly, I didn't even know him anymore. My voice trembled as I spoke methodically into the phone. "The only thing I want from you is to be left alone. Forever."

I clicked off and took several deep gulps of air in an effort to calm myself. For a minute I stood there numb, unable to move. I wiped away a tear that trickled down my cheek and blinked several times. *No. He can't hurt me anymore.* Still, I couldn't help wondering how I had wasted ten years of my life on a man who never really loved me.

CHAPTER THIRTEEN

———

Mike's home was about ten minutes from my shop. The small cottage was located in one of the older neighborhoods of Colwestern. Houses were neat, small, and equally unimpressive. I had driven past his home a few years ago, when I'd come home for a visit, and been shocked to see its run-down condition. The lawn had been overrun with piles of leaves and dandelions knee-high. Paint was peeling off the sides of the house, and the roof was dilapidated. Now it appeared to have done a total turn around.

Fresh paint shone in the bright sunlight, a cheerful shade of yellow beneath a brand new asphalt roof. There was a screened front door I didn't recall, along with a modern porch and wooden steps that gleamed in the sunshine. The old ones used to creak when Mike would reach over to kiss me as we sat on the porch with our arms around each other on lazy summer evenings.

Mental head slap. *Ugh, I'm doing it again.* I checked my face in the rearview mirror. No visible signs of distress from Colin's nasty phone call. After I had calmed down, I'd stopped at the shelter to drop off cookies and gone to the ATM to withdraw half of Vido's requested bribe.

When Colin and I first started dating he'd been charming, but now I realized there were warning signs I'd chosen to ignore. My grandmother had begged me to reconsider marrying him, but I refused to listen. As much as I hated to admit it, I had been on the rebound and anxious to forget about Mike with someone else.

Little things Mike did for me that I took for granted, never happened with Colin. He didn't hold the door, kiss my hand, bring me flowers, or call me beautiful like Mike had. I'd been blind to his true feelings, especially when it came to children, the one thing I wanted most from life. Mike and I had discussed the subject only once, both agreeing we wanted a houseful of kids. True, we'd been young, but Mike had confided that he hoped to be the kind of father he never had—dependable, caring, and always there for his children.

My throat tightened. Ten years later and here I was, sitting in his driveway. Life could be a repetitive chain of events at times.

I eased myself out of the front seat. A Harley and a Camaro I didn't recognize were both parked in the gravel-coated driveway. I hoped he didn't have a lady friend visiting. Josie mentioned he'd dated several girls in the past few years.

I remembered the bike, or at least I thought it was the same one. Mike had only taken me out on it a couple of times. He claimed they were dangerous, and he'd never forgive himself if something were to happen to me.

The front door was ajar, and through the screened door I could see the tiny living room with a beige couch and matching armchair. The walls were freshly painted white with wainscoting on the lower half. Heavy metal music blared from another room, and the sound of feet running on a treadmill was keeping time to it. I knocked loudly on the screen door, hoping he'd eventually hear me.

A black-and-white Shih Tzu appeared from out of nowhere, leaping at the screen and barking. I laughed and stooped down on the other side of the door until I was level with him.

"Hi, Spike. How's the boy?" He wagged his tail and tried to lick my fingers through the vinyl mesh. As I chuckled at his antics, I noticed the sound of the treadmill had stopped.

"He remembers you."

Mike stood behind Spike with a hand towel wrapped around his neck. His gray T-shirt was drenched in sweat. He shooed the dog away and opened the door for me. "Come on in."

Spike raced back over to me, rolling around on the floor while I rubbed his belly.

"I remember when we picked him out at the shelter. He's

got to be near eleven, right? He still acts like a puppy."

"Yep, he's a big baby." Mike turned away from me to remove his shirt.

I tried to keep my eyes on the dog, but it was difficult as I caught a glimpse of his broad, sculpted chest. I struggled to look away. More memories came flooding back—quite pleasant ones. Heat flooded my face. Out of the corner of my eye, I spotted him watching me.

"I'll be right back." Mike left the room, and the screaming of Metallica stopped suddenly. After a few minutes he returned wearing another T-shirt, this one light blue. I watched the muscles bulge through his shirt as he reached in the fridge for a Gatorade. "Want one?"

I swallowed hard. "No, thanks."

"I have soda, or some beer, if you prefer."

My nose wrinkled. "Definitely not."

"Right. Alcohol and you don't mix very well." Mike grinned and gestured toward the couch. "Sit down."

I sank into the comfortable seat, and Spike immediately leaped into my lap. He nudged my hand with his nose for me to pet him. "I'm sorry about your shoes. I'll pay for them."

"I'm not worried about it." He took a sip from the plastic bottle and stood in the archway of the kitchen, still staring at me.

Well, this was awkward. "You've done a nice job with the house. It looks great."

"Thanks. I guess you could say I have my stepfather to thank for that."

I remembered his stepdad well. He'd been horrible to Mike. "What do you have to thank him for?"

"He taught me two things. The construction business and how to take a beating. Well, three things, actually. What kind of father I never want to be to my kids." He sipped at his drink again and continued to watch me. His next question hurt. "How come you and Colin didn't have kids?"

"That's kind of a personal question, you know."

"This is me, remember? I know how much you always wanted children. You used to have a great time babysitting the kids down the road." His tone softened. "I loved watching you with them."

My heart stuttered inside my chest. I didn't want to tell him about Colin's true feelings because I suspected it would open a whole new can of worms. "The timing wasn't right. Besides, it's better we didn't have any because of the divorce. How's the business going?"

"It's steady. I've got work lined up through the end of the year."

"Even in the snow?"

Mike grinned. "I'll be doing indoor jobs then."

"Oh, right." I glanced around, surprised at how neat the place was. Whenever I'd come to see Mike before, it had always been in shambles.

Mike guessed my thoughts. "Yeah, it doesn't seem the same without all of Mom's empty liquor bottles around here, huh?"

I caught a reflection of pain in his baby blues. He'd known more hurt in his twenty-eight years than some people endured during their entire existence on earth. Life wasn't fair sometimes.

"I was sorry to hear about your mother and wish I could have come to the funeral. Bad timing." My marriage had just started to unravel before the death of Mike's mom. When I told Colin I wanted to fly up to visit my parents for a few days, he'd insisted money was too tight, even though we always found a way when he wanted something.

Colin had been too busy with his new bartending career to care about my needs. If I had realized back then how much he enjoyed the attention women lavished on him while he mixed their martinis, I could have gotten out of our sham of a marriage much sooner.

Mike raised his Gatorade. "I got your flowers. It was nice of you to think of me."

Of course I'd thought of him. How could I not? He'd been my first serious boyfriend, lover, and best friend. Years ago, I had had no doubt in my mind that he was the one I wanted to spend the rest of my life with. How things had changed in a hurry.

His eyes never left my face. "You still look exactly the same as you did ten years ago."

I laughed. "Thanks, but I think you need glasses."

"I've got perfect vision. I know beauty when I see it." His voice grew husky.

Butterflies danced in my stomach as Mike came over and sat down next to me on the couch. If I'd been an ice cube, I would have melted on the spot. I cleared my throat, desperately trying to think of a diversion. "I need to ask you something. It's personal."

His mouth twitched. "I like the sound of this already."

It didn't take much thought to guess where his mind was headed. "Actually, it's about Amanda."

Mike's smile disappeared, and the lines around his mouth hardened. "What about her?"

"I was over at her spa today. The technician was talking about her death and happened to mention—" Crap. What was I going to say? *Excuse me, Mike, were you involved with her?*

Mike leaned back against a pillow and reached over to pet Spike, nestled on my lap. "Let me guess. You want to know why I was at her spa, and you didn't think it was for a manicure."

"Something like that."

He pushed a strand of damp hair back from his forehead, revealing a small, deep scar over his left eye where his stepfather had once thrown a beer bottle at him. "Why do you care, Sal? Did you think I was having a fling with her?"

"No, of course not."

"If you must know, she asked me to install a Jacuzzi for her. Of course, with her, she always had to have an angle. 'Sure, Mike. I'll pay what you're asking, but you have to take me out to dinner first.' Or, 'I think I need you to come over to my apartment, so we can discuss the details for the hundredth time. Excuse me while I slip into something more comfortable.'"

My mouth went dry as I focused my attention on stroking Spike's soft fur.

"I never would've taken the job if I'd known she was going to drag it out so long. I'm sorry she's dead, but Amanda wasn't exactly on my favorites list, if you recall. She used to refer to my family as poor white trash." A muscle ticked along his jaw.

"Yes, I remember."

He took another sip of his drink. "And contrary to public belief, I don't date every girl in town."

"That's not what *I* heard." *Ugh, me and my big mouth.* I wanted to pinch myself. Hard.

His lips turned upward into a quirky smile. "Oh, really?"

I shrugged. "Just a rumor I heard. Um, in the bakery one day."

Mike reached over to place his hand on mine. The sudden contact sent a spark through my body. "I may have been out with some other girls, but I wouldn't exactly call it dating." He lowered his voice. "There's only been one woman for me. And I was stupid enough to let her go years ago without a fight."

I sucked in a sharp breath while my cheeks grew hot. "I didn't think you were dating Amanda."

Mike released my hand. "Well, perhaps you feel I'm responsible for her death."

"No." I stared at him in shock. "I know you'd never do something like that."

"Then what *are* you doing here?"

What am I doing here? Spike leaped off my lap and tottered into the kitchen, oblivious to the situation he was leaving behind. I stood, unsure what to say next. Josie was right. It hadn't been a good idea to come. Mike and I had way too much history together.

"Okay." I decided to come clean. "I was curious why you were at her apartment."

Mike eased himself off the couch. "Too bad. I was hoping you came to see me because of what transpired between us the other night."

I didn't answer. The words stuck in my throat.

"Sal, you need to hear me out, once and for all."

"That part of our life is over, Mike. We need to let it go." I turned in the direction of the door.

Mike grabbed my arm. "Would you please listen for once? I think you owe me at least that much."

He was right. The night I found him in Brenda's arms, I ran instead of staying to confront the situation. I could be headstrong and impatient, refusing to listen. When my stubborn streak was paired with his jealous fits, we'd had some epic battles. We never managed to stay mad at each other for very long, though, and the making up that followed had always been wonderful.

I turned back to face him and crossed my arms at my waist. "Okay. I'm listening."

Mike gestured toward the couch. The instant I sat down, Spike reappeared and leaped into my lap again. I stroked him behind the ears while he wagged his tail in acute happiness.

Mike sat at the other end of the couch, careful not to touch me this time. "I was really pissed off when I came back with your drink and found you dancing with Neil Wescott."

I couldn't believe my ears. "He saw me standing there alone and asked me to dance. It wasn't a big deal."

"It *was* the prom."

"Good grief, I didn't want to be mean. He came by himself, the poor guy. Why did you have to make a scene? Were you that insecure about us?"

Mike's jaw tightened. "When I went outside to cool off, Brenda was sitting in her car and called to me. She had a bottle and offered to share."

"I knew you'd been drinking. I smelled it on your breath when I—I found you."

"I swear. Nothing happened."

"So you're telling me you didn't sleep with Brenda?"

Mike's face reddened. "I never said that. But no, not that night."

"You were all over her in the back seat of her car."

"I was drunk. We were only talking at first. She seemed sincere and willing to listen—something you had a problem with at times."

It was amazing that after ten years his words could still hurt me so much. I chewed my lower lip to temper my response. "Go on."

"She'd had a fight with her date too. Said he didn't understand her or some crap like that. She kept talking, blah, blah, and I kept drinking."

"And then you kissed her." I held my breath, waiting for his response.

Mike shook his head vehemently. "No. She kissed *me*. In

fact, I couldn't get her off me." He looked embarrassed by the memory and lowered his eyes to the floor.

Yeah, right. Brenda had been about a hundred pounds soaking wet. I snorted. "From the look of things, you weren't trying very hard."

His eyes sought mine again. "I wasn't thinking straight. When I saw you with Neil, I guess I kind of went crazy. I was always afraid—"

"Afraid of what?"

"Of losing you."

There was silence in the room, with the exception of Spike's heavy panting.

Mike went on. "I spent hours walking past your house when you wouldn't take my calls. I even came to the door, but your father wouldn't let me in."

The memory of my father brandishing a baseball bat brought a pained smile to my lips. "I know. My parents were trying to protect me."

"Finally I thought, well, I'll talk to her Monday at school. But, no. You ran every time I came near you. And then to have Josie do your dirty work for you—what the hell was that about? You didn't even have the decency to tell me yourself we were over? You made her do it?"

I hung my head, not quite sure how to respond. He had a valid point. "I didn't even want to look at you. I was grateful school was ending, so I'd never have to see you again."

"Did you really hate me that much?" Mike's eyes widened in surprise, and his voice grew ragged.

I swallowed, but the lump in my throat didn't dissolve. "No, Mike. It was just the opposite. Why didn't you ever try to tell me later on? Write me a letter, an email? Anything?"

"After Brenda and I broke up, you'd already started dating Colin. I figured one day when you left him, I'd tell you. I didn't think it would last so long. He was always such a player."

I nudged Spike off my lap and stood, fists clenched at my sides. "Gee, well, thanks for sharing that with me. You could have saved me a few years of heartbreak."

"Like you would have listened to me?" Mike's eyes flashed with anger as he rose to his feet. "Give me a break. I always figured one day you and I would get back together. The next thing I knew, you'd married the guy." His tone grew quiet. "I almost lost it when I heard."

My pulse quickened, and I knew I should leave before the situation escalated further. I lifted my purse off the coffee table and turned around to face him. "I'm sorry I never gave you a chance to explain. We both made mistakes we can't undo now. Look, maybe we could try to be friends, okay?" The words sounded peculiar to my ears as I stared at his incredulous expression.

Mike held back a laugh. "After everything we've been through? I don't think I could be your friend, Sal."

My mouth went dry. "I'd be willing to try."

"It would never work. Not for me." He took a step closer.

I watched him, filled with sudden apprehension. "Uh, I'd better be going. Maybe I'll see you at the wake tomorrow."

Nervous, I moved my feet in reverse, colliding with the forgotten coffee table. As I started to fall backward, I shrieked and reached out to grab Mike by the front of his shirt. We both crashed over the table together and onto the floor, him on top of me. Spike yelped and barely managed to escape our tangled bodies. I lay there, trying to catch my breath as Mike stared down into my face, grinning.

"Are you okay?" *Wait, shouldn't he be asking* me *that?*

His eyes blazed with passion, and alarm bells went off in my head.

"Still such a klutz," he whispered as his lips covered mine. I forgot everything as I threw my arms around his neck and lost myself in the kiss. Sensing my urgency, his mouth probed mine, fast and furious. I couldn't think straight. I no longer wanted to think. If only we could move the clock back ten years and do things differently.

Musical notes from my cell startled us both and brought me back to reality. I managed to wriggle out from beneath him and succeeded in smacking my head on one of the legs of the upside down coffee table. "Ouch." My version of *Life's Most Embarrassing Moments,* right here in Mike Donovan's living room.

Mike suppressed a chuckle as he extended a hand to help me up.

Face burning, I reached for my phone that had fallen out of my purse during our acrobatic session. "Hello?"

"Hi, sweetheart." My mother suppressed a giggle.

Oh, Mom, you'd be so upset to know what you just interrupted.

"I was wondering if I could borrow that little black-and-gold striped skirt of yours for the wake," my mother asked.

I paused, trying to collect my thoughts. "Mom, that skirt is a little inappropriate for a wake, don't you think? It barely covers a person's rear, which is why I never wear it." I glanced sideways at Mike who was taking another sip of his drink, grinning.

"Oh, pooh," my mother said, like a five-year-old. "Everyone wears them nowadays."

Teenage girls wear them, Mom. Not middle-aged women. "Can I call you later? I have another skirt that would look spectacular on you with your great legs. I'll have it ready tomorrow when you come to the shop."

"Of course, darling. Love you." She made kissing noises on the other end of the phone and disconnected.

Mike looked amused. "Is Maria still going through her teenage phase?"

"It gets worse every year." I gazed into his eyes, the color reminding me of the ocean on a summer evening. We'd gone to the beach once for a long weekend. To this day, it was still the most romantic trip I'd ever taken. Far better than my honeymoon. *Okay, stop it, Sal. This has already gone way too far.* "I need to get going."

He moved forward and stroked my shoulders. "I don't want you to leave. Stay with me." There was an undeniable hunger in his voice.

I didn't trust myself enough to stay. "I'll see you tomorrow."

Mike glanced at his watch. "What's the rush? Do you have another date with the new cop on the beat?"

Oh, brother. Here we go again. I shook my head in irritation. "You never change. Do you know that?"

"Exactly what is going on with you and Jenkins, Sal?"

My mouth dropped open in astonishment. "There's nothing going on with me and Brian, and even if—"

"So it's Brian now, is it?"

"Even if there was something going on, it's none of your business."

Mike's jaw hardened, and he put his hands on his hips. "Oh. I see how it is. Has he got you wearing a wire? Are they getting this all on tape?"

"What are you talking about?" I asked.

"Tell me the truth! Did your new boyfriend send you here to question me?"

Startled, I opened the screen door a crack and whirled to face him. "I'd never do anything like that. I can't believe you'd even suggest such a thing. And for the record, no, he isn't my boyfriend."

Mike had the decency to look embarrassed. "I'm sorry. I just can't stand the thought of you with anyone else."

I watched him in silence, unsure what to think anymore. There was no doubt in my mind I had strong feelings for him. They'd never gone away. Had he changed in ten years? I wasn't so sure. The insecurities and jealous moods were definitely alive and well.

"I still love you, Sally. I always will." His voice was low and charged with emotion as his gaze held mine.

Panicked, I held my hand up in a protective gesture. "Please don't say any more." This was all too much to absorb right now, so I did what had always come so easily for me.

I flew out the door.

CHAPTER FOURTEEN

"Where the heck is he?" Josie paced back and forth on the vinyl floor.

The wall clock read 12:20 and there was still no sign of Vido on this bright Sunday afternoon. "Maybe we should try calling him again."

Josie sat next to me. "Do you think he's planning to meet us at the wake?"

"Oh, wouldn't that be great—exchanging money with him for all eyes in town to see. Jeepers, he's never been this late before." If Vido didn't arrive soon, he'd run into my parents, and that was one encounter I hoped to avoid.

"Maybe he got drunk last night and doesn't know where the hell he is. It wouldn't be the first time."

I wrapped my hands around my coffee cup for warmth. "How's your back today?"

Josie put her hands behind her head and stretched. "You know, I hate to admit it, but after the initial agony yesterday, I woke up feeling pretty good this morning. Then again, that could be from the fabulous back rub Rob gave me." Her eyes were full of mischief.

I winked in return. "That must be it then."

Josie leaned forward on the table. "You never called me last night. Did you go over to Mike's?"

"Yeah, I saw him." I gazed out the window.

"And?" She propped herself up on her elbows. "Did you spend the night?"

Incredulous, I shook my head. "Where do you get these ideas from?"

Josie made a face. "I wish you'd both admit your

breakup was a mistake and get back together."

"It's too late for that." I took a sip of coffee, thinking about last night, my hasty departure, and what might have happened if I'd stayed. *Oh, Sal, you know what would have happened.* Heat crept into my neck, but Josie didn't seem to notice.

"Well, then, Officer Hottie should be back in town today, right?"

I put down my cup. "I don't want to rush things. My marriage just fell apart, for cripes sake. I can't jump right back into another relationship. Remember what happened the last time I did that."

"Yeah, you did make a major screw up there."

"Thanks for the vote of confidence." I smiled wryly. "You're pretty lucky, you know. You have a husband who adores you and four beautiful kids to boot."

"Hey, you're going to have all those things too. I know how hard this has been for you. I'm so glad you're finally free of Col—" She clapped her hand over her mouth. "I promised myself I wouldn't say his name again. Anyhow, I'm glad you're finally free of jerk face, and I only wish I could have been there to help."

I grinned. "You did help, more than you know. I'm okay now, really, and so relieved it's over with." I didn't mention Colin's phone call from yesterday. I knew Josie would have been sympathetic to my plight, but I needed to put my ex-husband behind me. Forever. "It took me a long while to realize this, but the marriage was what failed. Not me personally."

Josie's eyes gleamed. "You're one tough cookie, Sal."

"No pun intended, right?" I couldn't help myself. "Shoot. Everyone will be here soon. I wish Vido would arrive before they do."

"Who are we kidding? I don't think he's coming. Maybe he had second thoughts. Wait till I get him alone at the wake. He'll be sorry he messed with us." She walked behind the display case and started up the stairs. "I'm going to freshen up. What time are your folks meeting us?"

"They should be here any minute. Dad likes to arrive early." That was an understatement. The last time my father went to a wake, he arrived even before the deceased's family.

Josie rolled her eyes. "I hope he doesn't make a scene."

"Oh, you can pretty much count on that."

She disappeared out of sight. A moment later the bells on the door rang, and in walked my mother, father, Gianna, and Grandma Rosa.

My mother wore a low-cut, black silk blouse with a leopard print skirt that ended halfway down her thighs. She held a compact in front of her face and fussed with her hair.

Gianna looked pretty in a sleeveless, black dress with matching pumps. She stared at our mother and shook her head in disgust, whispering in my ear. "I tried, so help me, I did."

"Tried what, darling?" my mother asked.

Grandma Rosa, dressed in black slacks and a bulky, gray sweater, understood the unspoken message between us. "You look like a tramp," she told her daughter.

"Ma!" my mother gasped. "What a thing to say."

"Hey, Mom," I began. "I'm sure I have a skirt upstairs that would look great on you. Why don't I run on up and—"

My father growled. He was dressed in his one and only black suit, which he'd been keeping the cleaners busy with as of late. In the past few months he'd taken up the habit of attending wakes two or three times a week, even if he didn't know the people. He liked to chat with various undertakers about their services. Phibbins Mortuary, the funeral home where Amanda was being laid out, had an excellent payment plan, but my father had assured them there wouldn't be time for a long-term setup.

"Leave your mother alone. She looks sensational." He kissed her on the cheek. "Get a load of those legs."

My mother grinned at me and Gianna as if to say, *I told you so.*

"My God! Everyone in town will be talking about us." Gianna slumped into one of the chairs, a mortified expression on her face.

"Everyone is already talking about us." Grandma Rosa stared at me in concern. "Well, at least about Sally and Amanda. It is not a smart idea for you to go today."

"I *have* to go, Grandma."

"Why?" Grandma Rosa frowned. "Do you want

everyone pointing their fingers at you and saying, 'There she is—the girl who might have killed Amanda?'"

My face warmed. "I *have* to go." I didn't want to tell them Josie and I were searching for the killer. All I needed was my family causing more problems at the wake. And they were already bound to cause problems.

My father was standing in front of the display case. "Sal, get your papa one of those fortune cookies. I'm feeling lucky today."

Gianna was mystified. "You're going to a wake, and you feel lucky?"

"Sure." Dad nodded. "It's like a dress rehearsal for when my time comes."

"Good Lord." My grandmother made the sign of the cross on her chest. "The man is going bonkers."

I handed the fortune cookie to my father, and he snapped it in two. "Aha!" He waved the paper around triumphantly. "I was right."

"What's it say?" Gianna asked. "Death comes to those who wait?"

"Hey, I like that one, honey. You're so good with words." A broad grin spread across his face as he read from the strip of paper. "*Practice makes perfect.* So fitting for me. *Bellissimo.*" Dad gathered his fingers to his lips, kissed them, and opened them into the air. Then he popped the cookie into his mouth whole. "Needs more vanilla, Sal."

I opened my mouth to say something then checked myself in time. My father was a tough one to please when it came to food. Josie didn't take criticism well, and I was thankful she hadn't overheard.

At that moment, her high heels clicked on the stairs. "Hi, everyone."

My mother went to work on her lipstick. "Hello, dear. How's the baby? Is he over that nasty cold yet?"

"He's fine." Josie smiled. "Thanks for the sleepers you sent over with Sal. They look adorable on him."

"Our pleasure." Mom smacked her lips together.

"Rob's not coming?" My father glanced out the window. Josie shook her head. "He couldn't. We don't have anyone to stay with the boys."

"What a shame." Mom's tone was sympathetic as she added another layer of mascara to her long lashes.

I held back a smile. I knew Josie could have found a sitter. She didn't want her husband to come so that she could be free to focus on the people. If Rob learned she was playing amateur detective, he wouldn't be pleased.

"Well, what are we waiting for?" My father reached for my mother's elbow and started toward the door. "There's going to be a huge crowd, and I don't want to be standing in line for over an hour." Grandma Rosa followed at their heels.

Gianna hung back. "I'm going to ride over with you two, if you don't mind. I need a break from them."

"Fine with me," I said.

Gianna studied both of us. "You guys are up to something. You're thick as thieves. Looking for the murderer, perhaps?"

"Maybe." Josie hesitated as she looked at me.

"Why else would you subject yourself to this mess?" Gianna asked. "I'm sure Mrs. Gregorio won't be thrilled to see you, especially after the other night."

At the mention of Kate's name, my stomach experienced a serious case of the jitters. I blew out a breath. "You're right. This is going to be a mess."

"No turning back now." Josie grabbed her purse from the counter. "We need to do this."

A car horn honked from outside. My father's patience was quickly receding, along with his hairline.

"Okay, let's get this fiasco over with." Gianna ran over to the case and grabbed a fudge cookie. "This will help get me through."

We arrived at Phibbins Mortuary at one o'clock sharp. The small parking lot was already full, so Josie parked her minivan on the street. My father pulled up behind her.

Josie checked her reflection in the rearview mirror. "I'm wearing way too much blush. That's tasteless at a wake." She rubbed some off with a tissue.

"With everything else our family has going on, do you really think anyone will even notice?" Gianna asked.

Josie opened the door. "True enough. Your family always steals the limelight."

I stood on the grass and smoothed the black skirt I had decided to wear with a pair of black, open-toe sandals and a white, linen blouse. My parents had already made their way to the front door, and Grandma Rosa was right behind them. Before they could reach it, the door was opened from the opposite side by an older gentleman in a dark gray suit and black dress shoes, polished until they shone like glass. He nodded toward them and waited patiently for us to arrive.

I blew out a long breath. "Here goes nothing."

We signed the registry for guests and then stood in the line, which had already started to form. My father turned around, his face giddy with excitement. "You see what they did? They have so many people that they opened the expandable wall between Restful Room A and B. That's what I want for mine."

Gianna gritted her teeth, and I patted her on the shoulder.

"You." Someone called out behind me.

I turned to see Mrs. Gavelli approaching. *Oh, no.* I had forgotten about my number one fan.

Mrs. Gavelli stabbed her finger into my chest. "What you think you do? No murderers allowed."

I closed my eyes and wished I could disappear.

"Look, old lady." Josie snapped, her face as red as her hair. "We're here to pay our respects. That's all. Now get off her back."

"Respect?" Mrs. Gavelli spat out the word. "What you know about respect? And who you call old lady?"

"Nicoletta!" My grandmother grabbed Mrs. Gavelli by the arm and led her toward the door. Both of them garbled at each other in Italian while mourners watched in amazement.

The employee shook his head as he quickly shut the door behind them then glared at Josie and me.

I cringed. "This is turning into a freaking disaster."

"Told you so," Gianna said.

Inside the doorway to the double room, I had a clear view of several rows of chairs, some already occupied. My father shrugged off his suit coat and draped it across the back of a comfortable-looking armchair in the rear corner of the room.

My jaw dropped as I watched him. "Dad, you can't save yourself a seat."

"But I just did." He grinned.

Baskets and vases of flowers were everywhere I turned, the air heavy with their perfumed scent. Next to every floral arrangement, various pictures of Amanda were displayed from different stages of her life. There were photos of her as a little girl in a ballerina outfit, her as a teenager with her parents, cheerleading at football games, her first day of school, and her high school graduation.

I spotted a picture of Amanda and Colin and sucked in a sharp breath. They were sitting at a bar together, and Colin had his arm around her. From the backdrop, I could tell it was the part-time gig he had briefly held here in town, before we moved to Florida. A cold chill enveloped my body. How long had the two of them actually been carrying on before I found out?

Gianna whispered in my ear, "I can't believe they'd have the nerve to put that here."

I shrugged. "Not a big deal. Her mother probably didn't even think about it." Still, my face stung as if someone had slapped it.

"Yeah, right." Gianna gave me a doubtful look.

As we neared the front of the room, to the left of the casket I spotted Kate, with Charlotte by her side. They were talking to an older couple and didn't see us.

Charlotte seemed absorbed in their conversation, then happened to turn her head in our direction. She frowned, and her eyes narrowed when they came to rest on me.

"Wow." Josie's mouth dropped open. "If looks could kill. I never knew timid, little Charlotte could be so brazen."

My mother and father had somehow skipped over a few people in front of us and were now talking to Kate and Charlotte. My mother held both of Kate's hands in her own and seemed to be speaking in earnest. Next to her, my father pulled a tape measure from his trouser pocket and showed Charlotte.

"Oh no." My sister covered her eyes. "I don't believe this."

While Gianna and I watched in embarrassment, not quite sure what to do next, my grandmother appeared from out of nowhere. She excused herself to Charlotte and dragged my father away.

"I have someone in the office who needs to speak with you right now, Domenic."

"The undertaker?" His face brightened.

"*Si*." Grandma Rosa nodded. "He has a better tape measure than yours."

My father left Charlotte standing by herself while my mother continued talking to Kate.

Gianna rested her head on my shoulder. "Why can't they ever act normal?"

As I watched my father and Grandma Rosa leave the room, I caught sight of Mike toward the back of the line. His eyes held mine for a long moment, and he smiled. He wore a dark blue suit the same color as his eyes.

Josie noticed him, too. "Dang. He should never be allowed to wear that color. The man is lethal."

Gianna nodded. "Totally fine. Josie said you went to see him last night. Details, please."

I thought again of the kiss we had shared, my heart drumming wildly against the inside of my chest as we continued to stare at each other. I nodded to him, then turned back to Gianna. "Nothing happened. Come on. Let's go."

The people ahead in line had moved from the kneeler in front of the coffin to speak with Kate. The three of us walked toward the casket together, Gianna clutching my arm. We both made the sign of the cross and knelt while Josie stood beside us. Josie didn't care much for religious beliefs. She said she believed in God, and that was enough for her.

The casket was made of ivory and lined with pink satin. Amanda looked as if she were sleeping. Her white, silk dress was similar to what a bride might wear. Golden hair spilled over her shoulders, and a diamond tiara was perched on top of her head.

"I know this sounds disrespectful," Gianna whispered as she bowed her head to pray. "But white on her? Like that isn't a joke."

I couldn't tear my eyes from Amanda's face. Who could have done this? The motive had to be more than plain hatred.

Who stood to gain anything from her death?

A few feet away, Kate glared at us, an icy expression on her face. Charlotte had disappeared. "Come on. People are waiting behind us to pay their respects."

Josie grabbed my hand and walked with me.

Gianna reached Kate first. "I'm so sorry for your loss."

Kate nodded stiffly at her. "Thank you for coming." She glanced at me and Josie.

Beads of perspiration collected on my forehead. "Kate, I wanted to say—"

"Save your phony sympathy." Her eyes flashed with anger. "Charlotte told me what you really thought about my daughter and the things you did to her. What a fool I was to be taken in by the likes of you."

I took a step back, too stunned to say anything.

Josie's mouth compressed into a thin, hard line. "Hold on a minute, Kate. Your daughter slept with my best friend's husband. And Sally never laid a finger on her. You're the one making something out of nothing here."

"Josie, not now. This isn't the time or place," I said quietly.

"We'll see about that, won't we?" Kate's tone was menacing. "Somehow I'll prove that you were involved. At the very least, I'm going to ruin your pathetic little shop, and you won't have a leg left to stand on in this town." She turned her attention to the people waiting uncomfortably behind us. "Jack, Sarah, how good of you to come."

This appeared to be our invitation to leave. My legs were blocks of cement, and I couldn't get them to budge. Gianna gave me a slight push forward, and I lost my balance. I stumbled and fell head first into an elderly man's lap in the front row. Everyone in the room gasped.

Gianna and Josie were quick to help me up. Gianna's face was scarlet, and mine, no doubt, mirrored hers.

"I'm so sorry. Please excuse me," I stammered to the surprised man.

"Drop in any time, honey." He gave me a huge grin. The stern-faced woman sitting beside him frowned. From the dirty look she gave me, I guessed she must be his wife. She muttered something to him under her breath, which I couldn't quite make out.

Kate's eyes were hostile as they met mine.

"Let's get the hell out of here," Josie whispered.

As we walked toward the front door with everyone staring, I caught sight of Mike again, his face focused on the floor. A smile twitched at the corners of his mouth. Well, at least someone found it amusing.

The doorman nodded politely and opened the door for us. As soon as we stepped out onto the large wraparound porch, Gianna exhaled a long breath. "Sweet Lord. Could things have gone any worse?"

"Probably not." Josie wiped at her damp forehead with a tissue.

Gianna reached inside her purse and pulled out her cell phone, which was vibrating away. "Excuse me, guys. Frank's calling. I'll be back in a sec." She sauntered off in the direction of the parking lot.

Josie turned to me. "What do we do now? Because there's no way in hell I'm going back inside. We're not going to learn anything from the outside looking in, either."

"I've no idea." I longed to leave, but was disappointed we hadn't found out anything useful, other than the fact that Charlotte was telling Kate lies about me. I caught sight of my mother, leaning against the rail of the porch, smoking a cigarette. "Mom, I thought you gave those up."

"I'm going to call Rob. Be right back." Josie walked toward her van at a fast clip.

My mother smiled as she exhaled a perfect circle of smoke. "Old habits die hard, honey. Which reminds me, I spotted one of yours back inside."

"Oh, Mom. Not you, too."

"I've always liked Mike. You know that. He's such a sweet guy, and I think you were unfair to him."

I winced. My mother's job wouldn't be complete until I was married again and had bore her a couple of perfect grandchildren. After Mike's heartfelt speech to me yesterday, it appeared she might be correct in her opinion. I sighed but said nothing.

"It's amazing he grew up normal in that family of his."
My mother inhaled a deep drag.

I'd always thought my family was normal when
compared to Mike's. Now I wasn't so sure if we still made the
cut.

I changed the subject. "Where's Dad?"

My mother closed her eyes, lost in her smoke-filled
haze. "Talking to the undertaker, of course."

Probably picking out his coffin. "Is Grandma with him?"

"No, she's around here somewhere with Nicoletta. God
knows what they're doing." She dropped the cigarette butt on the
wooden floor and stubbed it out with her heel, then frowned and
stooped to pick something up.

"What is it?" I asked.

"I bummed a match from Charlotte. She was out here
smoking with me, and I think she dropped these. Make sure you
give them back to her." She handed me a packet of matches. "I'm
going back in to find Daddy. Are you coming?"

I shook my head. "Uh, no, I think I'll stay out here. We'll
probably be leaving soon."

"All right, sweetie." She kissed me on the cheek. "Why
don't you and Josie come by for dinner tonight? Grandma's
making manicotti."

"Okay, I'll call you."

Mom gave a giggle and pranced back over to the door
where the doorman was already three paces ahead of her. She
passed through the entrance while he stared after her, obviously
checking out her legs. I had to give her credit. Most women half
her age didn't look as good in a short, tight skirt. I loved my
mother and could understand her fear of aging, but it drove
Gianna crazy when she didn't behave like a typical mom.

Leaning over the rail, I tried to think of who stood to
gain anything from Amanda's death. Charlotte? Vido? Liza or
Zoe? Jeannie Peterson? True, a lot of people hated her, but there
had to be more of a motivation to kill. Didn't there?

I glanced at the packet of matches in my hand. The cover
was purple with two white dice in the middle and the words
"Snake Eyes Casino" imprinted underneath. Give these back to
Charlotte? I don't think so. *Excuse me, Charlotte, I know you*

hate my guts, but I needed another reason to talk to you. I threw the packet in my purse.

Footsteps tapped the porch behind me, and I turned to see Brian dressed in his dark blue uniform, arms crossed over his broad chest. His eyes bored directly into mine.

My heart skipped a beat at the sight of him. "Nice to see a friendly face."

"I'll bet. Something tells me you're not too popular around here today."

"How was your trip?"

"It was great, but a long drive back." He seemed annoyed about something. "I heard you've been playing detective again. Kate Gregorio called me this morning. She said you and Josie threatened Amanda. She demanded I arrest you. Didn't I tell you to stay out of this mess?"

"Are you going to?" I held my breath.

Brian stared—then a grin broke out over his face. "Arrest you? No. I'd need a little more proof to do that, and I don't believe you did anything. But my opinion's not important here. Amanda wasn't very well liked in town. Anyone who knew about her allergy could have done this."

I thought about Mike and the Jacuzzi situation. Brian needed to know he was innocent. "There's something I have to tell you."

Brian's eyes searched mine. "Well, I have something to tell you, and it's not going to make you very happy."

Fear gripped me. "What is it?"

He placed his hands on my shoulders and gently sat me down on the iron bench. "Vido Falzo was found dead last night in his apartment."

"Oh my God," Josie cried out in alarm. She and Gianna were standing behind Brian.

My mouth fell open, and I stared at Brian in silence, unable to get any words out.

"There's more." He sat down next to me, hat in hand.

Josie's eyes were wild. "For goodness sake, tell us everything."

Brian hesitated for a second. "We're not positive how he died yet, but we have a good idea."

I grabbed his arm. "Do you think his death is connected to Amanda's?"

"Possibly. We're not sure yet." He seemed to be grasping for words. "We found a box of cookies from your bakery in his kitchen. There were five left in the box. Do you remember how many he bought?"

Josie clamped her lips together in a stubborn manner. "He didn't buy them. They were a gift of sorts."

"A dozen." I gave my friend a warning stare. "He also took a dozen of the fortune cookies."

Brian's expression was grim. "It's going to take quite a while for toxicology reports to come back on Vido."

"Amanda's autopsy didn't take that long," Josie said.

He shook his head. "This is a possible drug-related homicide. The tests take a lot longer to complete. They'll have to take samples of his liver and other organs."

My stomach grew queasy at the thought of Vido's internal organs. "You think he died of a drug overdose?"

"The cookies were taken as evidence and tested. They were laced with morphine. Like I said, we don't have proof yet that's how Vido died, but it's a pretty good assumption." Brian's gaze met mine. "We're going to have to treat you as a suspect now."

CHAPTER FIFTEEN

———

"That's ridiculous!" Josie stomped her foot like a child.

My mouth was like sawdust as I struggled to speak. "B-But you said you didn't know for sure he was poisoned, right?"

"We're not positive, no." Brian rubbed the bridge of his nose between his thumb and forefinger. "The evidence does look pretty damning though."

"But the cookies. No. There's no way."

Josie sat down on the other side of me. "He knew something. That's why he was killed. So he couldn't come today."

Brian's face was puzzled. "Do you mean to the wake?"

I didn't want to tell him about our snooping, but it was too late now. "Vido and Amanda spent some time together. They were…" I couldn't bring myself to say the word. The very idea made me nauseous.

His mouth twitched slightly. "Intimate?"

"Yes." My face grew warm.

"Ew." Gianna twitched her nose. "You've got to be kidding."

Brian suppressed a grin. "We knew about that. Several of Amanda's neighbors reported seeing him at her place. We'd already questioned him."

"Did he happen to tell you Amanda thought her life was in jeopardy?" I asked.

He frowned, his voice stern. "What exactly did he tell you?"

I was taken aback by his tone. "He told us that Amanda was afraid someone was trying to kill her. We asked him for further information and—"

"And?" Brian searched my face.

He was going to be furious. "We—"

"I told him I'd give him money if he gave us information," Josie blurted out. "Sal had nothing to do with it."

I shifted in my seat uncomfortably and focused my attention on the wooden floor.

Brian was silent for a few seconds as he processed this information. "I see."

There was no way I'd let Josie take the rap for this. "No, it was my idea. I asked him to tell us what was going on. Vido wanted five hundred dollars and personalized baking lessons from Josie."

For a brief second, Brian looked as though he might explode into laughter. "Personalized baking lessons?"

"I'm sorry. I wasn't trying to interfere with the investigation, honest. I need to get my sales back up." I stared at him in earnest. "If we have many more days like the last few, I won't have a business for very long."

He hesitated. "I need to talk to you about that as well. I recommend you shut the place down for a while."

"What do you mean?" Panic set in.

Brian clamped his lips together. "As soon as word gets out about this, especially if the toxicology reports come back saying Vido was poisoned, the Health Department is going to descend upon you and force you to close."

Josie had tears in her eyes. "I don't believe this is happening."

"Would you two ladies let me talk to Sally alone for a minute?" Brian asked.

"Of course. We'll meet you at the van, Sal." Gianna put her arm around Josie, who started to sob as they walked toward the road.

A lump formed in my throat. "Everything started off so great. We had a nice write-up in the paper, orders for parties were pouring in, and now this."

Brian sighed. "Please don't be upset."

"How long will I have to stay closed?"

He shrugged. "Two weeks at the most. Hopefully."

"Two weeks," I gasped.

"I'll try to put a rush on the report. No guarantees though."

"What am I going to do? I can't close for two weeks. I have bills to pay, and Josie has four kids to feed. I need to find out who did this."

"There are more important things to worry about besides your business right now. It may sound insensitive of me, but I'm concerned about you. This is serious. I don't want you to get hurt. I couldn't stand that." Brian stroked my palm in a circular motion with his thumb while I struggled to stay focused on what he was saying. "Promise me you'll stay out of this. Leave it to the police. That's what we're trained for."

I didn't answer.

"Well?"

I exhaled deeply. "I'll try."

"You're not a very good liar." Brian gave me a long searching look, then released my hand and strode toward his squad car.

My stomach convulsed with dread as I watched him leave. I turned my head to see Mike standing in the parking lot next to his Camaro, arms folded across his chest. As soon as our eyes met, he climbed into his car and drove away. *Great. I just can't do anything right today.*

I got to my feet and walked over to where the minivan was parked. Gianna and Josie were leaning against the vehicle. "Let's get out of here."

Grandma Rosa approached us from the parking lot.

"Where were you?" I asked.

"I brought Nicoletta home. I borrowed the car keys from your papa. Instead of fitting your father for a casket, they should measure him for a straitjacket." My grandmother made the sign of the cross on her chest.

Josie grimaced. "Rosa, what's her problem? Why does she hate Sally so much?"

"It's all right." My voice faltered. "I don't need to know." The truth was I didn't want to know. I wasn't sure how much more bad news I could handle today.

My grandmother cradled my face between her hands. "She does not hate you, *cara mia*. She really cares for you a great deal."

I drew my eyebrows together. "I don't understand."

"Do you remember Johnny's mother? Nicoletta's daughter, Sophia?"

"A little." I waggled my hand back and forth.

"She died when you were a little girl." Grandma Rosa patted my cheek. "You look a lot like her."

"So what?" Gianna asked.

My grandmother went on. "Sophia was a crackhead. Young and stubborn. A little like you in that manner. But she ran with the wrong crowd and died of an overdose. I think in some ways, Nicoletta associates you with her daughter, and she is trying to protect you. She has never been the same since Sophia died."

I bit my bottom lip hard. "All the times she harassed me when I was a kid, and you never told me?"

Her large brown eyes were solemn. "I thought she would stop when you came back home. She simply cannot help herself, sweetheart. Nicoletta and me—well, we are old ladies. We have nothing left but our children and memories."

I flinched as I remembered unkind thoughts I'd aimed at the old woman whenever she'd yelled at me. "Well, this day keeps getting better and better."

Grandma Rosa shook her finger. "None of you are to ever breathe a word about this. It is our little secret." She gave all three of us a kiss on the cheek. "Okay, you girls go. I will take the crazies home." Without another word, she turned and walked toward the front door of the funeral home.

Josie watched her leave. "You guys are so lucky to have her. She's like an encyclopedia of wisdom and knowledge all rolled into one."

"I guess I should go join the crazies." Gianna leaned over to hug me.

"Don't you want to ride back to the shop with us?" I asked. "Have a coffee?"

"I think I'll go home and take a nap. See you for dinner." Gianna smiled at Josie. "Mom wants you to come too."

She shook her head. "I need to get home to the little monsters. Some other time, thanks."

As we drove back to the shop, I couldn't help thinking about how my life had become total chaos since Amanda's murder. My business was teetering on the edge, and our deliveryman was dead. Mike had admitted he still loved me while I, in turn, was confused about my feelings for him. Brian, whom I had grown fond of quickly, just informed me I was under suspicion for murder. No wonder my head ached. I reached into my purse for some Tylenol.

Josie interrupted my thoughts. "What did Brian say after we left?"

I swallowed the pills dry. "He wants us to stay out of the investigation. He said it's dangerous."

"Well, he has a point. If Vido was murdered, it's because he knew something. The killer might think you know it too."

"How can I back out of this? Now Brian says we have to close for about two weeks."

Josie's mouth fell open. "That long?"

"Don't worry, I'll figure out something for you."

She frowned. "I'm not taking charity from you. You'd keep paying my salary while living back home with your wacky parents. I know you."

I didn't want to scare Josie, but what would happen if they never found the person responsible for Amanda's death? My stomach revolted at the thought. There was no way I could back off the killer's trail now.

Josie pulled the van into the alley behind the shop.

"Do you have to rush off? We really need to come up with some kind of game plan." I glanced toward the back door, and a chill ran down my spine. "Did I forget to lock the door?"

Her face paled. "I saw you lock it."

We both jumped out of the vehicle and rushed toward the building. A huge chunk of the wooden door was missing, and it stood wide open, daring us to enter. We glanced around inside with trepidation, fearful someone might be lying in wait for us. My jaw dropped to the floor when I saw the prep area. In the two hours since we'd been gone, the place had been completely trashed. Ingredients had been dumped from shelves and spilled onto the floor. Glass storage jars lay shattered.

We trudged through the mess and made our way through

the storefront, uttering no words due to shock. I was totally unprepared for the sight before my eyes, and a strangled cry escaped from my throat.

Our intruder had taken the strawberry frosting from inside the fridge and smeared it all over the walls. One side of the display case had been shattered, perhaps by a hammer or someone's foot. Most of the cookies had been emptied from the case, and the floor was littered with a mass of crumbs and glass shards. Several of the crumbled pastries were ground fine, and I found myself wondering if the thug had been brushing up on his tap-dancing skills.

Josie grabbed my arm and pointed at the back wall above the cash register. In pink strawberry frosting, someone had crudely written, "Back off or die, bitches."

"Oh my God." Her voice trembled. "Call Brian."

I covered my face with my hands, not wanting to look anymore.

Josie shook me by the shoulders. "Call him!"

Trembling, I reached for my purse, knocking it onto the floor and into a pile of chocolate chip cookie pieces. I fumbled inside the bag until I located my cell. My hands shook as I searched for his number, pressed the button, and waited, breathing hard.

He answered on the second ring and must have recognized my number. "Sally, this isn't a good time right now."

"Brian." It was a faint whimper—all I could manage.

"What is it?" Brian's tone was alarmed. "What's wrong?"

I picked up the broken stand Rob had made for our wall. Tears fell from my eyes as I spotted one of the little porcelain figures with his head ripped off. Ignoring the mess, I sank onto the floor. "Please come to—to the shop. Some-somebody's trashed it."

"Are you all right?"

I nodded mutely.

"Sally, answer me!" Brian yelled into the phone.

"I'm okay," I sobbed.

"Try not to touch anything. I'll be right there." He clicked off.

Josie sank down onto the floor and wrapped her arms

around me. We said nothing as we rocked back and forth, holding each other as if we were drowning.

CHAPTER SIXTEEN

Josie and I sat in silence at my kitchen table. I ran my fingers over the smooth surface of the drop leaf, flinching as thoughts of the break-in entered my mind. Instead, I tried to focus on how I'd purchased the table and its four matching chairs at a nearby yard sale, talking the owner down to a mere twenty dollars. I'd been very proud of my bargaining skills that day.

It was past six o'clock, and we were waiting for Brian and another policeman to finish their investigation downstairs. Pictures had been taken and my insurance company notified. I was thankful for the policy because even though I didn't own the building, my business needed the protection. The insurance representative informed me that the amount for a new display case would be covered, which was a huge relief. I didn't know about the ingredients or my Cuisinart mixer, which had also been destroyed. That was sure to cost a pretty penny to replace. No money would be coming in for a few weeks, and now I had repairs to make, on top of a major cleanup.

I exhaled sharply and stared at my green speckled Formica countertop. An unopened bottle of Merlot sat there, just waiting for me to open it. Gianna had given me the wine as a housewarming gift. It would be easy to indulge and forget my troubles, but with my low tolerance for alcohol, not the smartest idea.

Josie sighed and reached for her coffee cup. "What are we going to do, Sal?"

I rested my weary head on my arms. "Someone's trying to warn us to mind our own business. They think we know something."

"I hate to admit it, but I'm getting scared." Josie's eyes

glistened with fear.

My stomach was tied in knots. "I know. Me too."

There was a tap on my door, and Brian walked in. He gave us both a sympathetic smile. "We're all set. We've gone through the shop, made note of damages, and taken some pictures. You guys can start cleaning up, if you want. You said nothing was taken, right?"

I shook my head. "I didn't see anything missing. Definitely no money. The shop's closed on Sundays, so the drawer was emptied last night."

He made a note on his pad. "Well, at least you don't have to rush to clean anything up. You have more than a few days."

Josie snorted. "Gee, that's comforting to know."

"Jos." I shot her a warning glance. "It's not his fault."

Her face reddened, and she eased herself out of the chair. "I'm sorry, Brian. I know you're only trying to help. I'll go see if there's anything I can salvage from the ruins."

"I'll start on the walls." I got to my feet and started to walk past Brian.

"Hey." He touched my arm. "Are you angry with me?"

I shook my head, refusing to meet his gaze.

"No, I'll go tackle the walls." Josie glanced from me to Brian. "You come down whenever you're ready." Her high heels clicked on the wooden staircase.

Brian lifted my chin in his large hand. "You're upset I asked you to close the shop."

My eyes were moist as I stared back at him. "It's not you. Honest. I feel so violated right now. Not to mention angry."

Brian put his arms around me, and my heart thumped faster. "Do you know why I didn't want you snooping around? Because I was afraid something like this could happen. I mean, what if you guys had come back early from the wake and found the intruder? He could have—hurt you." His expression darkened.

I understood what he meant, but couldn't bring himself to say. Josie and I both might have been killed.

"I don't know what the insurance company will cover. My policy will probably skyrocket since I didn't have an alarm system installed." I was determined not to cry again and gulped back a sob. "This might be the end of my shop."

Brian tightened his grip around me. "Everything is going to be okay. I promise you I'm going to do whatever I can to find this creep."

He stroked my cheek gently, and from the look in his eyes, I thought he was going to kiss me. I waited, but nothing happened. Something seemed to be holding him back. He released his hold and then walked me toward the stairs, closing the apartment door behind us.

I clenched my fists while surveying the damage, furious at the monster who'd done this. I'd lived with loneliness and betrayal the last couple of years. There was no way I would add fear into the mix. The killer was determined to ruin my life as well as Josie's, and I wanted him stopped.

Josie had donned some plastic gloves and filled a bucket with baking soda and water. She was cleaning the frosting mess off the walls. She gave me an encouraging nod, and I thanked my lucky stars for her. I didn't think I could have handled this by myself.

I managed a smile for Brian. "Thanks for coming. You were a lifesaver."

"Hey, anytime your life needs saving, I'm happy to oblige. Or if you need anything else." He dropped his tone a notch. "Would you like me to stay and help clean up?"

I shook my head. "No, you're on duty. Thanks for the offer, though."

Brian reached for my hand and glanced over at Josie, absorbed in her work. "Let's have that dinner date. How about Tuesday night? I'd *really* like to get to know you better."

Although sorely tempted, I worried about starting something so soon. My track record with men wasn't very good. "I-I don't know, Brian. I think it's kind of soon for me after the divorce and everything."

"I understand. But you do have to eat, right?" His warm eyes teased me, and I melted under his gaze.

Maybe I was being silly. Plus, I *really* liked him. "Yes."

"We'll only talk. And eat, of course." He held up his right hand. "Scout's honor."

I laughed. He made it tough for me to say no, and there

was something about him and his boyish charm that I found so appealing. Sweet, kind, uncomplicated, and easy on the eyes. The complete package. *What can one dinner hurt?* I gave in. "Okay."

Brian's face lit up. "Great. Now behave yourself, and another thing, lay off the gas pedal."

"What do you mean?" I asked, confused.

"Last week, I spotted you going fifty in a thirty-mile-an-hour zone." He shook his finger at me then reached over to take my hand again, massaging it between both of his. My breath caught in my throat. "I should have pulled you over and given you a ticket."

"Why didn't you?"

"I figured you'd start crying and didn't want to see those big, beautiful, brown eyes get all watered down." He hesitated for a second. "I've been watching you for a while."

"Oh, really?" I teased him. "Are you some kind of a stalker?"

His eyes locked on mine. "Only when I see something I like."

Oh, my. "I bet you let everyone off the hook."

He roared with laughter. "I issued over one hundred tickets last month. You're the *only* one I let off the hook. Like I said, I had my reasons." His tone grew serious. "I've got to get going. Please be careful. I don't want anything to happen to you. Call me if you need me. Anytime, day or night."

"Okay." *My knight in shining armor.*

Brian released my hand. "I'll talk to you tomorrow, beautiful." He strode to the door, turned around, and smiled, giving me one last appraising look before he exited the shop. I waved my hand in front of my face. *Dang, it was warm in here.*

Josie faced me, hands on her hips. "Well, at least something good came out of this mess. You and Officer Hottie have a date."

"You were listening." I tried to conceal my grin but failed miserably.

"Hey, I never like to miss out on the good stuff. And he *is* hot. Maybe not as hot as Mike, but pretty damn close."

"Would you quit? We're only having dinner." I went into

the back room for another bucket and dumped in some baking soda. "How's it coming off?"

"Slowly, but it doesn't seem to be hurting the paint. By the way, Gianna's on her way over. She said she'd be here within an hour to help."

"Did you tell her what happened?"

"Your father heard the alert over his scanner. They called my phone when you didn't answer. Must have been while you and Brian were upstairs making out." Josie flicked a drop of water at me as I walked by.

I wiped my cheek. "We weren't doing anything. He was here on business, remember?"

"Oh, yeah. He's strictly all business around you."

I grabbed a sponge and set to work on removing our personalized message. I didn't want to look at it anymore. "So if the murderer did this, they weren't at the wake after all."

"They could have been." Josie wrung out her sponge. "The viewing was until five o'clock. They might have come here, trashed the place, and gone over afterward."

"Did you see Zoe and Liza at the funeral home?" The *B* in bitches vanished before my eyes.

She shook her head. "Maybe they showed up after we left."

My sponge was quickly turning the same shade as Pepto-Bismol. "What do you think about Charlotte?"

Josie stopped to consider. "I guess anything's possible. She seemed to be fond of Amanda, though. Why else would she put up with her crap for years? You're forgetting she was at the wake too. The entire time."

"I know. That's what's so frustrating about all this."

"Okay, let's break this all down. I mean, who do we have as suspects? Liza, the crazy massage therapist. Maybe Zoe. There are other technicians at the shop we haven't met yet. They could be suspects as well. We know they all hated Amanda. Maybe Charlotte was involved. We even thought it might have been Vido, remember."

"What about Jeannie Peterson?" I asked.

Josie narrowed her eyes at me. "The Wicked Witch of the West? Why would you suspect her?"

"When Jeannie was in here the other day, she mentioned that Amanda got her just desserts. And she came back last night, after you'd gone home. She..." I stopped. There was no way I was going to tell my friend what Jeannie had said about her. "Um, she said she knew you didn't like her."

Josie snorted. "Gee, she sure knows how to hurt my feelings. The woman is a nutcase, but there's no way she did it. How could she have even gotten close enough to slip something into her smoothie? Amanda wouldn't let Jeannie anywhere near her. She hated her cackling guts."

She had a point. "I'm trying to consider all options here."

"Then you have to consider Mike, too."

"Why? Because he comes from an abusive family? The idea is ridiculous."

Josie smiled. "My, aren't you quick to defend him."

I ignored her teasing. "Look. Mike had no reason to kill her. He was installing a Jacuzzi at the spa. That's all."

"By the way." Josie scrubbed the wall around the front door. "Mikey was watching you and Officer Hottie talking at the wake. He didn't look too happy."

"What else is new? He seems to be everywhere these days." I found it amazing that I hadn't seen Mike during the first few weeks I was back in town. Then again, I'd barely stepped foot out of the shop. Now there was no escaping him.

She waved her sponge in the air. "Getting back to Charlotte. She'd have easy access to the money and bee venom they kept at the spa. Maybe she even had a key to Amanda's apartment. She fits the profile spot on."

I laughed. "The profile? What, are you Sherlock Holmes now?"

"Oh, you know what I mean. She's the perfect suspect." Josie picked up the bucket and carried it into the back room for another refill.

"Yeah, except for one thing. She was at the wake today and couldn't have done this. I think we already covered the fact that she can't be in two places at once."

Josie reappeared with a fresh pail of water. "You had to ruin it for me, didn't you? Still, what does she do all day?"

"What are you talking about?" I walked past her to

empty my bucket.

"Well, Liza said Charlotte was hardly ever at the spa, and Zoe hadn't seen her since Tuesday, the day before Amanda was murdered. What does she do with her time? Maybe she has a boyfriend." Josie chuckled. "I'd love to see what kind of guy would date her."

"I don't remember her ever dating anyone in high school. And for someone we always considered so meek, she sure didn't waste any time filling Kate's head with evil ideas about me." I recalled what Kate had said about ruining my business and shuddered. She definitely had the power to do it. "Do you think Kate could have had something to do with the murder? No, wait, forget I said that. The idea's just crazy."

Josie reached for a broom and began sweeping the floor. "I can't picture Kate plotting her own daughter's death. I could see Charlotte involved, though."

"Wait a second..." I remembered the talk I'd had with my mother earlier at the funeral home and headed upstairs for my purse. I pawed through it until I found the matchbook she'd given me and ran back downstairs to show Josie.

"*Snake Eyes Casino,*" Josie read aloud. "What does this have to do with anything?"

"Charlotte had this. My mother bummed a light from her. Do you think she goes there? Maybe she's got a gambling problem?"

"I guess anything's possible, but it may not mean anything. I think I have an idea where this place is, right before the border to Niagara Falls. About an hour's drive to get there."

My mind raced. "I think we should go. We might learn something that would help. Seriously, what do we have to lose?"

"Not tonight," Josie pleaded. "I'm too exhausted to even think about it right now."

"Yeah. Me too. How about a road trip tomorrow?"

"Why not?" The bitterness in her voice was apparent. "It's not like we have a business to run or anything."

I glanced around at the mess. "If the killer hasn't been found by the time the toxicology reports come back on Vido, we're done for. We know he died from eating the cookies."

"Sal, Brian's right. This was a warning. We could be

next."

"As long as we stick together, we'll be fine."

"But why waste our time on Charlotte?" Josie asked.

"If she has a gambling problem, maybe the spa was having problems too. Money problems."

"So you think she might have been embezzling from the spa to pay for her habit?"

I paused, my sponge in mid-air. "I think we have to at least consider it."

Josie emptied cookie crumbs into the garbage can. "It's not much to go on but all we have right now." She yawned. "Let's stop. Call Gianna, and tell her not to bother coming down tonight. We've got most of the frosting off and can deal with the rest tomorrow. What else do we have to do?"

I dropped my sponge back in the water and glanced around. At least the place was starting to look a little more presentable. "Yeah, there's no need to rush, that's for sure. What time do you want to leave tomorrow?"

"How about 1:00?" Josie placed the broom and dustpan in the corner. "I'll spend a little time with Rob and the kids first, and then we can put in a couple of hours cleaning this place up."

"Fine. Hey, do you have any pictures of Charlotte?"

Josie wrinkled her brow. "Only from our high school yearbook, when you and I were juniors, and she was a senior. Had I known it was necessary, I'd have arranged to take a selfie with her at the wake today."

"Stop being a smart aleck. Bring her picture from the book then. She hasn't changed at all, and we can ask people at the casino if they've seen her."

"Your sexy cop is going to need to move a little faster. With something besides you, that is." She tossed me a dishtowel so I could wipe my hands. "I'll look for the yearbook tonight. What about your copy, if I can't find mine? Have you been taking a trip down memory lane lately?"

She knew me too well. "I think it's still packed away from the move." That was a lie, for I knew exactly where the book was. Last night, when I'd returned home from Mike's, I'd spent a good portion of the evening rummaging through both my junior and senior yearbooks. There were pictures of Mike and me all over both books. We'd been named best couple, in addition to princess and prince at the junior prom. The senior prom, of course, I longed to forget.

My grandmother's words about making a choice flashed through my mind. Now I knew what and whom she was referring to.

CHAPTER SEVENTEEN

————

The bells tinkled over the door behind me as I stood on top of a ladder, reaching for a glob of frosting near the ceiling. "Sorry, we're closed."

The ladder tilted slightly, and I shrieked. A pair of solid arms grabbed me around the waist and lifted me down. I whirled around to see Mike.

"Thanks," I said in surprise.

"Anything for a damsel in distress." Mike slowly removed his hands while his eyes surveyed the condition of my shop. "What the hell happened?"

"Someone broke in and vandalized the store."

"Are you all right?" His jaw hardened, and he stole a peek in the back room. "Is Josie okay?"

I nodded. "We're both fine. Josie's at the post office, but she'll be right back. We have to run an errand in a few minutes. The shop will be closed for a while."

"Didn't you have an alarm system or a surveillance camera?"

I hesitated. Mike had always been a big advocate of security systems. I'd noticed the impressive alarm hookup by his front door the other day. "I was getting around to it, but—"

Mike drew his eyebrows together. "But what?"

I twisted a sponge between my hands. "I was waiting until my finances got a little better."

"I see. Did the vandals take a lot of cash?"

I forced a laugh. "They didn't take any money. That was the only good thing to come out of this."

Mike leaned against the counter, watching me. He was wearing his work uniform of jeans, steel-toe boots, and a sleeveless, black T-shirt that showed off his hardened biceps to perfection. His tanned face made his eyes appear even bluer, and he smelled of spicy aftershave.

I wiped my sweaty palms on a dishtowel. "Outdoor work today?"

Mike nodded. "I'm putting a new roof on Julie Fitzpatrick's house. I took a quick lunch break and decided to stop by and see you. I was going to say everything looks great, but that would probably be a lie, huh?"

"Fair enough." I smiled. "Would you like something to eat? Most of our stock has been destroyed, but I'm sure I could find you something."

"Thanks, but I'm not hungry. Well, not for food, anyway." His mouth tightened as his eyes lingered over me.

I swallowed hard and concentrated on scrubbing away at an imaginary spot on the wall.

"I'll pick up a system for you and install it."

"No, thanks. I'll take care of it myself."

"Don't be so damn stubborn, Sal. Please let me do this. It would make me feel a lot better, knowing you're safe."

"When I can afford to buy one, I'll let you know and pay you accordingly."

Mike pursed his lips. "I don't think you'll have much of a choice. The insurance company might insist you put one in, unless they go ahead and cancel your policy."

A tremor of unease ran through me. I hadn't thought about that possibility. "Shoot. Maybe you're right."

"It doesn't have to be anything elaborate like the one over at Amanda's place. Something simple, and my fee will be practically free." His lips turned upward in a quirky smile.

My body temperature skyrocketed. "Did you install hers?"

"That was the initial plan. I had another job going on at the time, and she didn't want to wait. Big surprise there. She chose Arthur's Alarm Company, which was fine with me. I wasn't looking for an excuse to spend time with her." His eyes searched mine for assurance I believed him.

"How well do you know Charlotte?"

He shrugged. "Not very well. I mean, I remember her

from high school, but that's about it. She's always been afraid to open her damned mouth. Especially where Amanda was concerned. Now that you brought her up, I remember hearing them argue last week. I thought it was kind of strange, with Charlotte being so timid and all. She was crying her eyes out. I guess Amanda really gave it to her."

I dropped my sponge back into the water. "You don't know why, do you?"

Mike's face was full of suspicion. "What's this all about? Are you a detective now? Betsy Drew in the making?"

"Nancy Drew." I grinned.

"Whatever. You know I was never much of a reader."

I stripped my plastic gloves off and threw them in the garbage. "I don't know. It's a theory I'm working on."

"I actually got a call from her this morning."

"Betsy Drew?"

Mike laughed. "Aren't we sarcastic? No, I mean Charlotte."

My ears pricked up. "What did she want?"

"She said business had slowed quite a bit since Amanda's death, and they were going to hold off on the Jacuzzi for a while. No big deal. It would have been an easy payday for me, but I'm fine without it."

"The spa seemed to be doing well enough the other day when I was there. The technicians said they don't see much of Charlotte. That's interesting, especially since she's in charge now." I grabbed a broom from the corner and started sweeping, mulling this over in my mind.

"Amanda did make a snide comment to me after their argument. Something about Charlotte was never there when she needed her. Said she should pay me to put a tracking system on Charlotte's car, so she'd know where she was at all times and with whom. I'm pretty sure Charlotte overheard. Amanda talked to her in a condescending tone all the time. I don't know why Charlotte didn't haul off and smack her."

I sighed. "From the sound of things, she would've had to get in line."

That got a smile out of him. "Do you think she's responsible for Amanda's death?"

"I don't know. I mean, anyone could have slipped the bee venom in her drink."

Mike's eyes widened in surprise. "Is that how it happened? So it was deliberate, with her allergy and all?"

Oops. Me and my big mouth. "That's what Brian seems to think." *Uh-oh.* I was really on a roll now.

The lines around Mike's mouth hardened. "Of course. I'd forgotten Officer Jenkins knows everything. He's not your type, Sal. I don't trust him."

"He's a cop investigating a murder."

"It doesn't matter. There's something sneaky about him."

I put my hands on my hips. "I seem to remember you saying the same thing about Joe Thurston in high school. Right after you punched him, that is."

Joe had been sitting next to me one day at lunch while I waited for Mike. Quiet and somewhat reserved, he'd accidentally spilled a drink on my lap. The poor guy had been beside himself and tried to help me clean it up until my jealous boyfriend came over and punched him in the face, no questions asked.

Color rose in Mike's cheeks at the memory. "I was a little headstrong in those days."

I cocked one eyebrow at him. "A little?"

"Don't change the subject. Someone's telling you to back off. Let Jenkins and his friends handle this whole mess, and please stay out of it." He extended his arms out wide as he glanced around my shop, his expression darkening. "I'm worried about you."

I moved across the room to dump a dustpan full of cookie crumbs into the garbage. "My entire business is at stake here. Josie's livelihood and mine, too. No, I'm not going to stay out of it."

"You're still as stubborn as ever." He cursed under his breath. "I think we should talk. Would you please turn around, and look at me when I'm speaking to you?"

I whirled around to face him. "We talked the other night."

A devilish grin spread across his face. "If memory serves, we didn't talk that much."

My body tingled, and I blew out a breath. "I don't think

it's a good idea."

"I promise. We'll only talk. I'll keep my hands under control the entire time." I watched while he stuffed them into the pockets of his jeans to demonstrate. His eyes twinkled at me. Damn him. He knew I could never resist those baby blues.

"What did you have in mind?"

"If I told you what I really had in mind, you'd never agree."

He really was impossible. "Please be serious."

Mike reached for my hand. "Can we have dinner together tomorrow night? I'd like to cook for you."

"We're not a couple anymore, Mike." There was a lump in my throat. "I'm not going to your house for dinner."

He gazed at me, a haunted expression in his eyes. "If it wasn't for a stupid misunderstanding, we'd still be a couple. Married. With a bunch of kids."

I bit my lower lip hard while trying to decide what to do. "If I agree to come, will you leave me alone after that?"

He looked at me, thunderstruck. "What does that mean? You need time to date other people? Like your new friend, the cop?"

The green-eyed monster was back. In truth, I wasn't sure he'd ever left.

"No. I just got divorced, remember? The biggest mistake of my life was marrying Colin. Lord knows I've made others too." I stared at him pointedly. "I can't be seriously involved with anyone right now. I need time to sort things out first."

Mike was silent for a minute. "Okay. We'll have dinner. That's all. Afterward, if you don't want me bothering you again, fine. I'll give you your space. Seven o'clock okay?"

"Sure."

Mike started toward the door, then turned back to look at me one last time. "I've made a lot of mistakes too, Sal. But my biggest one was letting you go."

* * *

"Do you have the yearbook?" I winced when my car hit a pothole the size of the Niagara River as I steered onto the thruway. All I needed now was to add vehicle repairs to my growing list of debts.

Josie patted her purse. "All set. I tore the page out with Charlotte's picture on it. So I noticed Mike leaving. What was that all about?'

At the mention of his name, my face heated. "He wants me to have dinner with him tomorrow night so that we can talk."

"Busy girl. What about Brian? Didn't he ask you as well?"

I switched lanes and checked my speed, alarmed to find myself going seventy-five. Brian was right. I did have a lead foot. "Shoot. I forgot. What am I going to do? This is becoming a mess."

"How can two guys fighting over you be a mess?" Josie asked.

"I'll deal with them later. By the way, Charlotte called Mike this morning to halt the installation of the Jacuzzi at the spa."

Josie didn't seem surprised. "If they're hurting for money, well then, yeah, that would be a smart thing to do."

"Doesn't Charlotte's family have money? Her dad and Amanda's father were brothers, right?"

"Yes, but Amanda's father had all the dough. I remember my mother telling me he kept the rest of the family well provided for, though. He paid for Charlotte's college tuition, car, and so on."

"Interesting how she and Amanda never went to private school." I switched lanes again to pass a Subaru that dared go the speed limit.

"Don't you remember Amanda's excuse for that? 'My parents want me to be like everyone else. A regular person.'" Josie rolled her eyes. "It was more like, I really don't want to be here with you commoners, but I have no choice."

The sign for Exit 49 was approaching. Josie glanced at her watch. "We're here already? Gee, that was under an hour."

"Forty minutes." I spoke with pride.

"Better watch out, or you'll get a ticket. Oh, wait, I guess you've got that covered now." She chuckled.

The GPS told me to take a right and proceed straight for

another five miles. The houses quickly changed from middle-class range to apartment buildings sprayed with graffiti. A crowd of teenage kids was gathered on one corner, smoking and jeering at one another. The girls wore skintight jeans and tube tops, while the boys sported undershirts and jeans that hung halfway down their legs to reveal plaid boxer shorts. I wondered why they weren't in school. Then again, I probably didn't want to know the reason.

"Pull your pants up," Josie shouted out the window. She was rewarded with the middle finger and loud catcalls.

I stopped for a light and glanced over my shoulder. "Please don't get them started. What if they decided to run after us?"

Josie snorted. "Bunch of homies. How can you run with your pants on the ground?"

The GPS told me to take a left then announced, "You have reached your destination."

We pulled into a small parking lot with cracked blacktop and a large, green Dumpster that occupied most of the space. A dilapidated, two-story building with peeling, brown paint stood before us. On top of the asphalt roof, where several shingles were missing, a sign flashed *Snake Eyes Casino*. Like Charlotte's matchbook, a pair of dice was displayed on the sign. Almost all of the bulbs on the letters were blown out. I wrinkled my nose as we got out of the car. A sewage problem was evident.

Josie looked around in disgust. "What a dump. Why the hell would she come here?"

"I've no idea." Mystified, I watched the Dumpster with caution, half expecting someone to jump out and attack us. "Let's see what we can find out."

A sign directed us to use the side door, which we did. We carefully climbed the three cement steps, which were starting to crumble in various spots.

Josie gritted her teeth and opened the steel door.

The room was dimly lit, and the smell of smoke and stale beer hung heavily in the air. A small bar was set up in the left corner, an overweight barkeep absorbed in reading the classified section of the newspaper. A television was propped up next to him on a card table. To our right were several slot machines making assorted beeping noises and flashing bright colors across their screens. A security guard stood next to a cashier's window, chatting with the man on the other side. We walked past them into another room where one lone couple sat in front of a machine, making out and groping each other. Everywhere. We averted our gaze, turned around, and hurried back into the main room.

"Well, I guess now we know what purpose the dim lighting serves." Josie scratched at her arm. "My skin feels like it's crawling with something. I'll bet there are fleas in this place."

"Probably worse." The stench of the room was already starting to make my head ache as we advanced toward the shady-looking security guard. He was heavyset, his shoulder-length, brown hair matted, and he sported a full beard in desperate need of a trim. He laughed with the male cashier while taking puffs from a foul-smelling cigar that made me nauseous. They stopped talking as Josie and I approached with trepidation.

"Hello, beautiful ladies." The guard looked us both up and down several times. "What can I do for you? Or better yet, what can you do for me?"

His foul breath was adding to my growing discomfort. "We're wondering if you could answer a few questions for us." I tried to resist the sudden urge to flee.

He grinned, revealing broken, stained teeth. "Listen, honey, I don't know what you two got planned for here, but don't worry. Ain't nobody gonna watch. Except me, maybe."

Ew. My stomach rumbled and not from hunger.

Horror was written all over Josie's face. "Um, that's not why we're here."

The guard surveyed Josie with a sadistic smirk, then turned and rested his gaze on my chest. The man behind the cage waggled his tongue at me. Suddenly I longed for a hot, cleansing shower.

"Well, it happens that we both break for lunch soon. We'd be glad to assist you lovely ladies." The guard winked at me.

"Ah, no. We're hoping you can help us find someone." I motioned to Josie, who removed the yearbook page from her purse. I folded it in half and pointed at Charlotte's picture. "Do you remember ever seeing this woman in here? The picture is over ten years old, but she still looks the same."

He glanced from the picture to my face. "What's in it for me?"

I shook my head in disbelief. Everyone had a price tag these days. "What do you want, Mister…er…"

"The name's Hank." He reached for my hand, but I backed away. "Not very friendly, are you?"

"Look, Hank." Josie sneered. "Are you going to help us or not?"

He took a puff of his cigar. "Fifty bucks."

I opened my mouth in astonishment. "Do you actually have anything to tell us if we give you the money?"

"Sassy little thing, ain't ya?" Hank chewed a piece of his cigar while keeping his eyes fixated on me. He turned and spat in the direction of a nearby wastebasket. He missed his aim, and the remnants hit the floor instead. "Yeah, I got something to tell. I seen her."

"You *saw* her." Josie stared at him in irritation.

"What are you, an English teacher?" Hank glared, then turned to me and held out his hand. "Fifty smackeroos, baby doll."

I blew out a sigh and reached into my purse for the money I'd taken from the ATM for Vido. I handed Hank a fifty-dollar bill. "Okay, now talk."

"She's in here all the time," he said. "Two or three times a week. I never got her name. She don't talk much to nobody."

I chewed my bottom lip. "Does she come in alone? What does she do?"

Hank stared at me like I was some type of moron. "She ain't ever alone. Got it? Hangs with some other broad. They always go in the back room." He pointed in the direction of the couple, still slobbering all over each other.

My mouth fell open as Josie and I stared at each other in shock. "What did the other woman look like?" I asked.

Hank shrugged. "I can't describe her. Think her hair's blonde. She ain't got one of those faces that sticks in my memory. You know what I mean?"

I sincerely doubted there was much that stuck in Hank's

memory. "Are you sure it was the same woman each time?"

He scoffed. "Of course I'm sure. They're regulars. The dark-haired broad—she plays the machines while she waits for the other one to arrive. And she likes the Off Track Betting. Don't think she wins much. Told me she and the other broad were going away soon."

Josie put her hands on her hips. "Is that a fact?"

"You can put that in your cigar and smoke it, honey." Hank licked his lips. "You two little gals wanna go grab a beer with some real men?"

I glanced around, waiting for some real men to materialize. "Uh, thanks for the offer, but we have to run." I fished in my purse for one of my business cards and handed it to Hank. "If you see her again, would you please let me know? And maybe you could try to get a better look at her friend next time, too?"

"That ain't just her friend, honey." He chuckled.

My face grew warm. "Well, maybe you could try to describe her?"

Hank glanced at the card and read aloud, "*Sally's Samples, made fresh daily.* What you got for me to sample, honey?" He blew a kiss at me, and slipped the yearbook page and my card into his pocket.

"Oh my God." Josie yanked my arm and pulled me toward the door. "We need to get out of this sleaze-filled abyss now."

Hank yelled after us. "Hey, come back tomorrow. There's live music at night, and I got the moves, baby."

"Whatever you do, don't look back," Josie hissed in my ear. "We might get turned into stone."

CHAPTER EIGHTEEN

———

Back in the car, Josie grabbed a hand wipe and rubbed it violently all over her arms. "I feel like I've been digging ditches all day."

I shuddered. "That place was so disgusting, but at least we know why she goes there now."

"So she's gay." Josie shrugged. "What's the big deal?"

"It's not a big deal to us, but it might be to someone else."

Josie was silent for a moment. "Do you suppose Amanda knew and threatened to tell? Maybe Charlotte was afraid of someone finding out. Or…her partner was."

I took my eyes off the road for a brief second to stare at my friend. "I hadn't thought of that. Gosh, I wish we knew who she was."

Josie stretched back in the seat. "So timid little Charlotte's gay, and she may have a gambling problem. What if she stole money from the spa, and Amanda found out? You should call Brian and tell him."

"Tell him what, exactly? We don't have any proof this even connects back to Amanda's murder. And I'm sure he'd be thrilled to learn I've been doing more snooping."

"Uh-oh." Josie studied my face. "I know that look. You've got something else in mind." She watched me drive past our exit. "Where are we going now?"

"I think we need to have another chat with Liza and Zoe."

Josie sat upright. "Are you nuts? The only way that ogre touches me again is over my dead body."

"Relax. We'll see if they're willing to answer a few

questions. Outside of the massage room."

She snorted. "I hope you have more cash, because that seems to be the only thing getting people to talk these days."

As I pulled into the parking lot of Amanda's Retreat, I realized there might be a problem with my plan. "What'll we do if Charlotte's there?"

"Guess we'll have to wing it. Come on. Let's get this over with."

A different receptionist was seated at the front counter today. The young girl appeared to be fresh out of high school, or perhaps even still in it. Her long, dark hair was pulled back in a ponytail, which revealed a face with alabaster skin and crystal-clear blue eyes.

She smiled warmly at us. "Hi, I'm Connie. Do you have an appointment?"

I returned her pleasantries. "Actually, Connie, we'd prefer to speak with Liza or Zoe for a minute. It concerns a product they used on our skin Saturday."

Connie frowned. "Oh no. Which one of you had a reaction?"

"She did," Josie and I said in unison. We stared at each other in muddled confusion.

"Well, I mean Josie had the reaction. Of course, I'm concerned for her well-being." I started to babble, unable to stop myself.

Josie gave me a look I interpreted as *shut up, you're blowing this.*

Connie stared at me with regret. "I'm sorry, there are no refunds given."

"We don't want a refund."

Josie mumbled under her breath. "I sure as hell do."

Connie checked the computer screen in front of her. "Let's see. Zoe started a facial a few minutes ago, but Liza should be free shortly if you want to talk to her."

"Oh, great." Josie groaned. "I should have known."

I gave her a nudge with my arm. "That will be fine. Thank you."

"Would you like to take a seat in the waiting room?" Connie asked.

I was about to agree then shook my head. "We'll keep you company here, if that's okay."

Connie smiled. "Oh, of course."

Josie leaned over the marble counter. "So have you worked here long, Connie?"

"About six months." As Connie took a sip of her smoothie, I couldn't help but flinch. "I go to the local community college, so I split my hours with another girl."

"Terrible shame what happened to the owner." I watched her face closely.

"Did you know Amanda?"

I hesitated. "I wasn't friendly with her." God knows I spoke the truth.

Connie glanced into the waiting room where one young woman sat absorbed in a magazine. "No one was. She was a real witch. Everyone here hated her."

I raised one eyebrow. "What was so bad about her?"

"She treated us all like slaves." The bitterness in Connie's voice was apparent. "All she ever did was complain that the place wasn't making enough money. I mean, give me a break. I get minimum wage here. Amanda should have been making a fortune, yet she claimed she was losing money. That's not why I hated her though."

"Well?" Josie propped herself up on her elbows.

Connie's delicate complexion turned a bright red. "She accused me of stealing. Can you believe it? I've never stolen anything in my entire life."

"Did the register come up short?" I asked.

"She claimed the books were off. I mean, it's not like she ever even looked at them much, not until last week when she wanted to buy a Jacuzzi. Some hot-looking guy was going to install it for her." Connie stopped to fan herself with a napkin. "I think I drooled on myself, he was so fine."

I was getting tired of hearing this. "Is that so?"

"Oh, yeah. She told him to come by her house, and she'd give him his deposit." Connie's smile was wry. "He seemed pretty annoyed, too."

Josie gave me a look as if to say, *I told you so.*

"Yeah, I don't think he was interested in her. Who could

blame him, right? I'll bet that part about giving him his deposit was code for—"

I leaned over the counter to interrupt. "What happened when she looked at the books?"

She hesitated. "Amanda started yelling at her cousin. I think she accused her of taking some money too, because Charlotte was crying."

I remembered Mike's comments from earlier. Something for us to go on at last.

Josie drummed her fingers on the counter. "We know Charlotte. Um, have you ever seen her in here with a—friend?"

Connie wrinkled her forehead. "I don't think Charlotte has any friends."

This was a touchy situation. "Does anyone ever call on the phone for her?"

Connie's smile faded as she glanced from me to Josie in sudden alarm. "Are you guys, like, detectives or something?"

I shook my head. "We only want to know what happened to Amanda."

Connie's face turned the color of sugar. "Well, um, no one here killed her. I mean, we all liked her. Honest."

"Gee, that was a quick turn around," Josie whispered.

I tried to reassure the young girl. "We're not accusing anyone. We—"

"What the hell are you two doing in here?"

I froze and counted to five before I spun around. Charlotte stood behind me wearing a black sweatshirt, the hood pulled up over her head. She clutched two brass candlesticks, which she thumped on the counter in front of Connie. "A guy named Earl Schmidt bought these from me. He's already paid and will be coming by tomorrow to pick them up. "

"Aren't these from the waiting room?" Connie fingered the heavy objects. "Why are you selling them?"

Charlotte glared at the young girl. "You're not here to ask questions. Just do your job, okay?" She stood tall and glanced from me to Josie. "I asked why you were here."

I fought to remain calm. "I-uh, was here for a facial on Saturday and wanted to ask Zoe about the products she used."

"I don't believe you. You were snooping, and I'm going

to tell Kate. She already hates you both." Charlotte's eyes glittered as she peered over her glasses at us.

"Go ahead and call her. There are a few things we'd like to tell her too." Josie put her hands on her hips and glared back.

Charlotte's jaw dropped. "What are you talking about?"

I wished Josie hadn't said anything. I didn't want to make Charlotte aware of the fact that we were on to her. I decided to play dumb. "What did you say to Kate? You know neither one of us would do anything to hurt Amanda."

She tapped her foot and gave me an impatient stare. "I don't know anything of the sort. You hated Amanda because she slept with your husband and was so popular with men. Guess you just don't know how to keep a guy."

"And obviously you don't want to." Josie narrowed her eyes.

Charlotte froze while I cursed my best friend in silence.

"What did you say?" She spat the words out.

"I said obviously you have no problem with guys." Josie glanced at her watch. "Oh my, look at the time. We should be going."

"Are you sure you don't want to wait for Liza?" Connie asked. "She should be done with her client any minute."

"No, Connie, we really need to leave." My heart drummed inside my chest. "We already know what products to ask for next time."

Josie and I both waved to Connie and started for the door.

"Are you sure you don't want to make another appointment?" Charlotte sneered at us. Her voice sent an icy chill through my body. "Don't come back here again or the next treatment you get will be very bad for your skin."

CHAPTER NINETEEN

———

When the light at the intersection turned green, I plowed ahead. "We still have no proof she's involved."

Josie's mouth dropped open as she gawked at me. "Are you kidding? She threatened us."

"I know, but we need something more concrete."

"I think you should call Brian and fill him in."

"Oh, yeah, that's sure to go over well." I could already hear his voice in my mind. *Didn't I tell you to let the police handle this?*

Josie blew out a breath. "Okay, so we don't have proof Charlotte killed Amanda. She did have a motive though. Amanda might have known about her little friend and threatened to tell the world. Plus, there's the fact she may have been taking money from the business, and now she's selling off the antiques?"

"If we knew who the other woman was, maybe it would all come together." I pulled up in front of the shop. "Might as well park here. They'll be coming to fix the back door tomorrow."

"Why not ask Mike to do it?" Josie teased. "I bet you'd get a premium discount."

I stuck my tongue out at her in a childish manner, then glanced across the street and froze. A black Cadillac was parked next to the curb. The driver's door opened, and Kate Gregorio emerged.

"Oh, great," Josie groaned. "What's she going to do now? Set the place on fire?"

"Great." I rubbed my temples in agitation. "Maybe she's got Brian on his way to arrest me as well."

We both got out of the car and waited for Kate to cross the street. She was dressed in an expensive, black Valentino suit. With a pang, I remembered Amanda's funeral had been held earlier this morning.

Kate's cheeks turned scarlet when she forced her red-rimmed eyes to meet mine. She glanced up and down the street nervously. "I was hoping I could have a word with you, Sally."

I wondered if she was going to lecture me again, but I didn't have the heart to refuse her request when I looked into those despondent eyes. "Of course." I unlocked the front door, then held it open for Kate to enter first.

She stepped inside and gasped aloud as she observed the condition of my shop. Although the frosting had been cleaned up, garbage was still strewn all over the floor, and the shattered case was clearly visible. "My goodness, did you have a break-in?"

I nodded. "Someone's been threatening us."

Her worn face turned a sickly gray. "Do you mind if I sit down?"

I held out a chair for Kate and seated myself across from her. Josie remained standing at my side.

Kate traced a pattern along the tablecloth with her slim fingers. "I wanted to apologize for my actions yesterday. I allowed myself to be swayed by other people's thoughts and don't usually act like that."

"It's okay. You're going through a horrible ordeal right now."

She blinked back a tear. "I lashed out at you because you threatened Amanda. I don't believe you harmed her, but it was so easy to place the blame on you."

That's what the killer wants, too. I gave Kate a wan smile. "I understand. Let's forget it, all right?"

She reached out to grab my hand in hers. It was like grasping a glacier. "I haven't been truthful about the entire situation."

Josie sat down and leaned forward. "What does that mean?"

Kate blew out a sharp breath. "Instead of blaming you, I should have been paying more attention to the activities at

Amanda's Retreat. The president of Colwestern Bank called me this morning. It seems…" Her voice shook. "Charlotte has been making some very hefty withdrawals out of the spa's account."

Josie gave me her *I told you so* expression.

"Well, she is authorized to make withdrawals, right?' I asked.

"She's the accountant of record." Kate nodded. "But the bank president is a friend of mine, and he became concerned. In the last few weeks, Charlotte has withdrawn over one hundred thousand dollars."

"Holy cow." Josie's blue eyes were wide with astonishment.

Kate shifted in her seat. "Charlotte said you threatened Amanda at your shop. What you don't know is she later informed me you mixed up a special batch of cookies for Amanda with bee venom when you heard she was stopping by."

I was horrified by the lie. "That's not true. We think the bee venom came from the spa. Were you aware they used it there?"

Kate's eyes filled with tears as she nodded. "Amanda was so proud of her idea to feature the anti-aging facial. She wanted to be just like the big-city spas. But it's ludicrous to believe her employees would have anything to do with her death. She handpicked every one of those girls. I don't know what to think anymore. The final straw came when the bank called me. Charlotte withdrew twenty thousand dollars this morning. The account is nearly out of money. How does she expect the employees to get paid?"

"Obviously she doesn't care." Josie frowned.

"You're right about that." Kate wiped at her eyes. "I've given her a home, pay all her expenses, and this is how she treats me?"

I knew Charlotte's parents had relocated shortly after Amanda's father died, but Charlotte chose to remain in the area. It sounded like Kate had been pretty good to her niece, but she still desired more. Josie told me she'd heard Charlotte's father had had a huge falling out with his brother shortly before he died. Rumors were that it was money related.

Kate went on. "She's probably waiting around for me to

die now. Then she'd inherit everything."

I flinched at the words. *Could this be Charlotte's next plan?* "I need to ask you something personal about Charlotte. Does she—um, have friends over to the house?"

Kate was thoughtful for a moment. "Now that you mention it, I don't remember her ever inviting anyone. She's really not the outgoing type."

"No one at all? Boyfriend? Girlfriend?" Josie glanced sideways at me.

"No one I can think of," Kate said. "Of course, I'm away from home a great deal during the day because of my charity work, so anything's possible."

I decided to get it over with. "We think Charlotte might be gay."

Kate's eyes grew large and round, then she nodded slowly. "Yes, I thought of that, too. I wasn't positive, but there were a few signs. If it's true, I'm hurt she never confided in me. I mean, she knows I would have supported her lifestyle choice. I love her like my own daughter."

If Charlotte isn't worried about Kate knowing, then who? "You said Charlotte has withdrawn all of the money from the business account?"

"There's about ten thousand dollars left. How generous of her to leave that much." Her voice dripped with sarcasm. "I've frozen the account. I'll pay the employees out of my personal funds until I figure out what to do with the spa."

I had a stab of sympathy for Zoe, Connie, and even Liza. "So you have no idea who Charlotte's partner might be?"

"The day Amanda died she said she wanted to talk about Charlotte. I pressed for details, but Amanda said she'd come back, and we'd chat later in the evening. Of course, we never got a chance." The lines around Kate's mouth tightened. "I know what you're thinking, and you're mistaken. There's no way Charlotte killed Amanda."

I gave her hand a slight squeeze. "I know you don't want to even consider she'd do such a thing, but the fact remains—"

She interrupted my speech. "You don't understand. She couldn't have done it. Charlotte wasn't even in town that day. Amanda had her attending some seminar about facials over in

Buffalo. She didn't return home until eight o'clock that evening."

Josie and I looked at each other in confusion.

"Are you sure she was there?" I asked.

Kate nodded. "Positive. The police checked the records. She signed in at the seminar about nine o'clock that morning and left at seven in the evening. Several people reported seeing her there as well."

"Another one of our theories bites the dust." Josie folded her arms and rested them on the table.

"Whoever did this must have been with Amanda when she went back to her apartment." Kate glanced at me in sympathy. "I spoke to her on the phone that afternoon, and she told me she was coming here. If someone was there, they would have heard the same thing. They wanted you to take the blame."

A light bulb went on in my head. "Wait a minute. So maybe Charlotte wasn't at Amanda's apartment, but what if her partner was?"

Kate placed her trembling hands in her lap. "I know the money laundering is horrible, but I refuse to believe Charlotte would orchestrate the killing of her own cousin." She searched my face. "And I never really thought it was you. To tell you the truth, I thought it might have been that Vido character she hung out with."

"You heard about his death?" I asked.

"Yes. The police think that he knew who the killer was, which, of course, put his life in jeopardy. I'm sorry he's dead, but I'll never understand why Amanda associated with him." The color rose high in her cheeks. "I never told anyone this, but my daughter was some kind of a sex addict."

I struggled to erase from my mind the mental image of Amanda and Vido together while Josie kicked me under the table.

Exhausted, I rubbed my eyes. The last few days of stress and sleeplessness were taking their toll. "Have you thought about having Charlotte followed? Even if she didn't kill Amanda, it's possible she may know who did."

"I suppose I could." Kate twisted a handkerchief between her hands. "I think the police may be planning on it as well."

As if on cue, the bells over the door chimed, and Brian walked in. He glanced from me to Kate in surprise. "Ladies. What's going on?"

I stood, ready to defend myself. "Kate came to tell me about Charlotte and the problems with the spa."

Brian's expression was grim. "I see. Well, I need to talk to you. In private."

What now? I gritted my teeth and turned to Kate. "Please excuse me for a moment." I led the way into the back room, with Brian at my heels. I wasn't positive we were completely out of earshot and no longer cared. I had nothing to hide.

I whirled around and placed my hands on my hips. "Okay. What did I do now?" My patience was wearing thin.

"For once, *you* didn't do anything. Your ex-husband was arrested last night in Florida."

My breath caught in my throat. "Colin? No. He couldn't have. I mean—"

Brian held up a hand. "Let me finish. A police officer came to his place of work last night to ask him some questions about Amanda. Colin started a fistfight and was arrested for assaulting an officer."

Josie appeared in the doorway, a sheepish look on her face. "Sorry, I was listening." She came over and draped an arm around my shoulders. "Thank God you're not with that loser anymore."

"My sentiments exactly." Brian studied me. "Are you okay?"

I put my face in my hands for a second and sighed heavily. "Yeah, I'm not surprised. He was furious when he called the other day."

Josie's mouth fell open. "He called? You didn't mention that. What'd he want?"

"Only to harass me." My voice trembled. "He accused me of trying to make trouble for him. He was angry the police were questioning him and tried to blame everything on me. Big surprise there."

Brian folded his arms. "He doesn't have an alibi for that night. He could have flown up here from Florida in about two hours. We're checking plane records, but haven't found anything so far."

I remembered Kate in the shop. "We'd better get back out front. I don't like leaving her alone."

"I'll bet she was listening too." Josie kept her arm around my shoulders as we walked back into the storefront.

Kate was still sitting at the table, handkerchief pressed to her mouth as if it were bleeding. She stood as we approached.

"I think I'd better go." Her voice shook, and she took a step forward, then staggered. Brian jumped forward and caught her in his arms. He gently placed her back in the chair.

"I'll get some water." Josie raced into the back room.

I pulled another chair up and lifted Kate's feet onto it, despite her feeble protests. Josie returned with a paper cup and held it to her blue-tinted lips.

"I'm sorry to be such a bother." Kate's voice was faint.

I rubbed her shoulders gently. "You're not a bother at all."

"Is that your car across the street?" Brian asked, and Kate gave a slight nod. Brian put his hand out for her keys. "I'll drive you home. I'll have another officer meet us at your house and bring me back here for my cruiser."

"Oh, no." Kate looked appalled at the suggestion. "I can't let you go to all that trouble."

Brian helped her to her feet and guided her toward the door. "I insist. You're in no condition to drive."

Kate sighed and handed him the keys. As they walked by me, she grabbed my hand in a fragile grip. "Thank you for being so understanding."

"Take care of yourself." My heart ached for her.

Brian turned around to give me a stern look. "Don't go anywhere. I'm not finished talking to you."

CHAPTER TWENTY

———

It was past six, and my stomach growled from hunger. I hadn't eaten anything since that morning, when I had grabbed bagels for Josie and me from the little bistro down the street. I had a sudden, overwhelming urge for Grandma Rosa's comforting Italian cuisine.

I sat down at a table to call my parents' house. Grandma answered on the second ring.

"What's for dinner?" I asked.

"Eggplant parmesan and a nice green salad," my grandmother said. "We eat in half an hour. You are coming?"

Brian was due back any minute, and I didn't dare leave before his return. "Yes, but I might be a little late."

"Whenever you get here is fine." Grandma Rosa started talking to someone in the background. I heard my mother giggling, and my grandma sighed loudly into the phone.

"Tell Mom I'm not bringing a date."

Grandma Rosa snorted. "No, that is not what she wants. Your father would like you to bring him some fortune cookies. He is wondering if he should play the lottery tonight. If he wins, he said he is going to buy a gold casket and put it in the living room."

Good grief. This morbid fascination of my father's had to stop. "Okay, there's a few left in the back room. I'll bring him whatever we have."

"I am glad you are coming, *cara mia*. I need to talk to you." With that, my grandmother clicked off.

All of a sudden, everyone needed to talk to me. Perhaps my grandmother wanted to advise me about the opposite sex again. One never knew what she had in mind.

Josie appeared in the doorway of the back room, purse slung over her shoulder. She watched me inquisitively as I strode past her and grabbed the remaining fortune cookies out of a plastic container on the shelf, stuffing them into a paper bag. We'd only been able to salvage a handful of the treats after the break-in. There was no sense in making any more until we were ready to reopen.

"Has dear old dad got a hankering for a fortune? Oh, wait a second." Josie leaned over and grabbed a cookie from the bag. She waved it in front of my face while covering her eyes and chanted in a sinister voice. "Do not wear your best suit today because you may need to be buried in it tomorrow."

"Not bad. Maybe you should work for Hallmark or something. Start writing these sayings, and we won't have to buy them anymore."

"Yeah, like I'd have the time." She squeezed the cookie a little too hard, and it cracked in her hands.

"Nice going."

"Oops. Pops will have to make do with one less." Josie reached down to retrieve the slip of paper from inside. As she read it, she gave a loud bark of laughter.

"What now?"

She read aloud in a dramatic voice. "It says, 'Do not throw caution to the wind tonight.'" She chuckled and threw the strip and cookie into the garbage. "This cookie is nine years too late. I don't have to worry since Rob got his vasectomy."

I shook my head at her and grinned. "You're hopeless."

Josie observed me carefully. "I can stay for a little while if you need me to."

I stuffed the bag of fortune cookies into my purse and made my way back to the table. "No, thanks. I'll be fine."

"I don't know about that. He looked kind of ticked off at you."

"Believe me, I'm getting used to it. Listen, I think we need to go back to Snake Eyes tomorrow."

Josie wrinkled her nose. "Ew. But that place is so vile."

"Maybe we don't have to go inside. Just case the joint, so to speak. We've got to find out who Charlotte's partner is, and this is the only way I can think of."

"It might be days before they show up," Josie protested.

I stared at her pointedly. "Can you think of anything better?"

"Well, Kate's going to have her followed, right?"

I shrugged. "Who knows? Kate's dealing with quite a bit right now. We can't count on that."

Josie mulled this over for a second. "Fine. It's not like we have anything else to do around here anyway."

"Good. Let's plan to leave here about eleven in the morning. The new case should be installed by then, and we'll be free to go."

She knit her eyebrows together. "How are you going to pay for that? I mean, sorry, it's none of my business, but—"

I hated to alarm her, but with things getting dire after the break-in, she needed to be fully aware of the situation. "It's going to take the last of the money my aunt left me. I hope the insurance check comes through soon."

Josie clutched my hand in a death grip. "Sal, if something happens and we still can't open the shop by next week, what—" She stopped in the middle of the sentence, but I knew what she was trying to say.

"I don't know if I'll be able to make my rent next month. I'm good for September, but if we can't reopen for a while and the Health Department gets involved, we might be done for." I blinked hard, trying to prevent tears.

Josie squeezed my hand. "We'll get through. You'll see."

The front door opened and Brian walked in. He tossed his hat onto a chair and sat down next to me. "Kate should be fine. She called her doctor to come over, but my guess is she's suffering from stress and exhaustion."

"I'm glad she's all right." I got to my feet. "Would you like a cup of coffee? I've got a great dark roast—"

Brian caught me by the arm. "Sit down, please. I want to talk to you."

"Should I leave?" Josie asked.

Brian shook his head. "I'm going to read her the riot act, and you might as well stay and hear it too. It would save me from tracking you down later."

"Wonderful." Josie leaned against the wall.

My stomach twisted into a giant knot. "Okay, I know what you're going to say."

The lines around Brian's mouth hardened. "I came to tell you about Colin, and what do I find? You hitting Kate Gregorio up for information. Again, I'm asking you to stay out of this investigation."

I clapped one hand over my eyes. "Brian, please try to understand. She came here. We didn't go to her."

"That is true," Josie said.

Brian cleared his throat. "It doesn't matter. I told you to please let me do my job. Don't you think the police department is capable of finding the killer?"

I removed my hand and met his gaze. "Of course I do, but my entire business is at stake here. I have to *do* something."

"Has the autopsy been completed on Vido yet?" Josie asked.

Brian's smile appeared pained. "I told you ladies it's going to take several days for the toxicology reports to come back. Maybe longer."

I tapped my fingers on the table. "But you did say the cookies were laced with morphine?"

"Yes, the drip kind." Brian watched me curiously.

"Where would a person get that?" Josie wanted to know.

He shrugged. "It could be prescribed for someone. My mother used some last year when she broke her wrist. I imagine it might be difficult to figure out how much to give someone to kill them."

I was deep in thought. "But a doctor would know, right?"

Brian nodded. "I'm sure he would. Stop speculating though."

I clutched his hand. "Brian, I think Charlotte is involved. Maybe she didn't kill Amanda, but she could have killed Vido. She might have had a friend helping her."

"Don't you think we've thought of her? I know about the finances at the spa. It still doesn't make Charlotte a killer. A person of interest, yes, but not a murderer. She had an alibi."

"There's more. She's gay. Kate didn't know for sure, but she suspected. I think Charlotte's partner could have killed

Amanda. Maybe they were acting as a team."

Brian was thunderstruck. "How did you find all this out?"

"Um, we—" I couldn't meet his eyes and glanced toward Josie for help.

Josie picked up her purse. "Well, I've got to get home to the kids. See you tomorrow morning. Night, Brian." With that, she rushed out the door.

Some best friend, deserting me in my hour of need.

Brian watched her depart then looked at me, arms crossed over his broad chest, his Greek god-like face stern. "I'm waiting for an answer."

My insides filled with dread. "Josie and I did a little snooping yesterday. We found a place Charlotte likes to frequent. It's called Snake Eyes Casino."

Brian's jaw tightened, and his eyes blazed into mine. Nervous, I glanced down and busied myself with fingering the tablecloth. He said nothing for a full minute. I wondered if he was counting to ten, or perhaps ten million, before he was going to start yelling at me.

When he finally spoke, however, his voice was cautionary. "I know that place. It's a hellhole. A woman was raped there last week. Promise me you won't go there again."

I didn't answer.

"Sally, I'm not kidding around."

"I can't just sit here and wait." I grabbed a handful of my hair and twisted it in exasperation. "If this keeps up, I won't be able to pay my rent next month. This is my livelihood we're talking about."

Brian placed his hands on my shoulders. "I told you. Let us handle it. Don't you trust me?"

"You know I do, but—"

He pushed the hair back from my face. "No buts. I have enough to worry about without having to think about you, too." He ran a finger over my lips, and my heart stuttered inside my chest. "Okay, maybe that came out wrong. I like thinking about you when I'm stuck in my squad car during the middle of the night."

He placed his hand behind my neck, pulling me toward

him. I closed my eyes and let his mouth devour me. His lips were moist, warm, and delicious. The kiss seared through every part of my body. When we finally broke apart, I longed for more.

Brian stroked my cheek. "Very nice. So, dinner tomorrow night?" He whispered as he kissed me again.

"Yes." My brain had zoned out.

"Good." Brian eyes sparkled. "I get off duty at six. I'll pick you up here at seven." He hesitated. "We'll eat at my place, if that's okay with you."

Heat crept into my face. "That sounds nice." *And hot.*

Brian got to his feet and put his hat on. "Until tomorrow, beautiful." He opened the door and quickly disappeared into the night. Josie had the right name for him. He was Officer Hottie.

* * *

"Dang." Gianna watched me in amazement from across our parents' dinner table. "I've never seen you eat so much."

I looked up from my second helping of eggplant parmesan to glare. "Pass the garlic bread, will you?"

"It is good." Grandma Rosa nodded in approval as she walked into the kitchen. "You need the food. You are all skin and hair."

I raised one eyebrow at her. "Do you mean bones?"

"That is good, too."

I had arrived at my parent's house at seven o'clock. They had already eaten and disappeared upstairs to watch television, or so they said. My mother's giggling, which resembled that of a schoolgirl's, found its way back down to the dining room table. We knew exactly what they were doing.

"They're just like rabbits." Disgust was written all over Gianna's face.

My grandmother reappeared with coffee for me and gestured toward the plates. "Gianna, you start stacking the dishes. I need to talk with Sally."

Gianna groaned. "Come on Grandma, can't I stay?"

Grandma Rosa yelled at her in Italian.

"Okay, okay," Gianna grumbled as she took the plates into the kitchen.

My grandmother reached into her housecoat pocket and placed a check in front of me. "A little something to help you out with expenses."

"What's this?" A check for five thousand dollars. My jaw dropped. "Grandma, I can't accept this."

"You will take it," my grandmother ordered. "Use it for the new case in the shop and to help pay your rent, if needed."

My eyes filled with unshed tears. "I need to do this on my own."

"Baloney. What good is it to have grandchildren if you cannot help them once in a while?" Grandma patted my arm. "Thanks to your great-aunt Luisa, my sister, I am able to give you this. God rest her soul." She made the sign of the cross. "Gianna will use her money toward student loans, and you have used yours for the business. Me, what do I need the money for? My whole world is right here. You take this, and pay your bills, and if you have enough left over, give Josie some. The poor girl has never had anyone looking out for her, and she and Robbie need the money."

I sobbed as I threw my arms around her neck. "You're so good to me."

My phone started ringing as Grandma hugged me back. She retreated into the kitchen while I stared down at a number I didn't recognize. Not a Florida area code, but I wasn't taking any chances. I prayed it wasn't Colin asking for bail money and pressed ignore on my phone.

Grandma Rosa reappeared with a dish of spumoni for me. As I savored the mixture of pistachio, cherry, and chocolate ice cream, I marveled at how lucky I was to have this wonderful woman in my life. Family was everything. True, my parents were a bit crazy at times, but I had never doubted their love for me or Gianna. And Grandma Rosa was in a class by herself. Too bad someone like Mike had never been able to experience this special bond of family.

Mike. "Oh no."

Grandma Rosa frowned. "What is wrong?"

"Mike asked me to dinner tomorrow night."

Her mouth turned upward in a slight smile. "Did he? This is very good news."

"You don't understand." Frustrated, I put my head in my hands. "Brian asked me, too. For the same night."

She appeared even more pleased as she cleared the rest of the dishes in silence. I glanced at her in accusation. "You knew this was going to happen. That's what you meant when you said I would have to make a choice."

My grandmother tapped her forefinger against her white hair. "See? I always know." With that, she disappeared into the kitchen again.

My phone pinged to tell me I had a new voice mail. I was about to play it back when a text from Josie arrived. *Ellen and I meeting for drinks. Her Dad back in hospital. Not looking good. Wanna come?*

I sighed. The only thing I wanted right now was my soft bed. I texted back. *I'm beat. Will send prayers. Going to bed. See you in a.m.*

She shot back a quick, *Okay.*

Grandma Rosa came into the dining room as I got to my feet. "You are leaving already?"

I kissed her on the cheek. "I'm sorry, Grandma, but I've got to get some sleep." I threw my arms around her neck. "Thank you so much. I love you."

She patted my back. "I love you, too, *cara mia.* You go home and dream about your two Prince Charmings. You deserve much happiness. It is time for you to shine."

Gianna reappeared, dish towel in hand. "You're going?"

I leaned over to hug her. "I need sleep. Bad. Maybe I'll see you tomorrow."

As I opened the front door, I came face to face with Mrs. Gavelli. She wrinkled her nose at me. "Why they let you out of jail?"

"Nicoletta." My grandmother frowned. "Knock it off."

I remembered what my grandmother had told me and leaned down to give the old lady a quick buss on the cheek. When I straightened up, her eyes clouded over. "Good night, Mrs. Gavelli."

As I drove off into the night, I reflected on my entire situation. The check from Grandma Rosa was a huge relief, even though I didn't like taking her money. A short-term solution to my problems, but it would have been useless to argue with her. We were both stubborn in that respect.

Tomorrow night still seemed far away, but it had become apparent I would have to turn someone down for dinner. If I refused Mike, he'd be furious. Brian might be more understanding, but he'd probably be hurt as well. *How did I get myself into these messes?*

Maybe I should refuse them both. My first priority now was finding Amanda's killer. If I kept searching for the person against Brian's wishes, there was a good chance he wouldn't want to date me anyway. My brain was starting to hurt, and I was too exhausted to make sense of anything right now. Things would look better in the morning.

As I unlocked the front door, I remembered the voice mail. Throwing my keys on to one of the tables, I reached for my phone. If it was Colin, I'd press delete.

"Hey, sweet thing." A hoarse, low-pitched male voice breathed into the phone. "It's Hank from Snake Eyes."

Ick. My skin started to crawl at the very mention of his name.

"Since you were so nice about throwing the fifty my way, I thought I'd give you a freebie."

The eggplant wasn't helping my stomach, and I had a sudden urge to retch.

Hank droned on. "I seen your little friend leaving with her buddy a couple of hours ago. Figured you'd want to know."

My ears perked up with excitement. Charlotte must have gone to the casino right after I'd seen her at the salon. Too bad she'd already left. How long would we have to wait for her to make another appearance?

His voice turned breathless as he chuckled. I winced and prayed the message would be over soon. "Got a good look at her friend's face this time. Like I told ya, she's blonde, kind of plain. I knew I seen that face before."

I waited with bated breath.

"She went to high school with your pal. Pretty much been under your nose the whole time, huh." The message ended with his maniacal laugh, and a chill went through my body. I stared at the phone in confusion. Went to school with her? How would he know?

Then it dawned on me. The page Josie cut out from her yearbook.

I flew up the stairs. In my haste, I stumbled and tripped on one of the steps, banging my knee in the process. I groaned in pain and hobbled into my bedroom, grabbing the yearbook out from under my bed, where I'd been studying it the other night. I laid it on my comforter, remembering how seniors were each designated a fourth of the page.

The blood pounded in my ears. I already knew whose picture I'd find. The same person I'd had drinks with last week, who also happened to be a nurse and could easily lay her hands on a supply of morphine.

The same person that my dearest friend, Josie, happened to be with right now.

I flipped through the pages in a crazed frenzy until Charlotte Gregorio's mousy face stared back at me. Right above her picture, smiling and laughing, was the one I feared.

Ellen George.

CHAPTER TWENTY-ONE

———

Don't panic. Josie's okay. She has to be.

Bruised knee forgotten, I ran back down the stairs for my cell and dialed Josie's phone. It rang three times before her voice mail kicked in. "This is Josie. You know what to do." A beep sounded.

"Damn it," I whispered into the phone. "Josie, call me as soon as possible. It's urgent."

I scrolled my contacts section and pressed the number for her home phone. Rob answered on the third ring. The kids were screaming like they were on the warpath, and I tried to keep my voice from trembling. "Hi, Rob, it's Sally."

"Hey, Sal. What's going on?"

"Um, Josie texted me a while back and said she and Ellen were headed out for a quick drink. Did she happen to mention where they were going?"

He chuckled. "No. She never gives me details like that. I'm only her husband, you know."

I tried to laugh, but it stuck in my throat. "So you have no idea where she is?"

"Can't help you there. Something wrong? Is the shop okay?"

The baby started crying in the background, and I longed to join in. My teeth were clenched together in an effort to keep them from chattering. Above all, I needed to maintain a calm head in hopes of finding Josie. *Why didn't I ask where she was going?*

I didn't want to worry Rob yet, especially with four kids left in his charge. "The shop's fine. I wanted to talk with her—about something else. Do you remember what time she left?"

"Let's see." Rob paused for a moment. "It had to be about seven thirty. I'm guessing she'll be home around nine since I need to work at ten. I'll have her call you." He hung up without another word.

"Thanks," I whispered to the air. My hands were shaking. What could I do? Was she with Ellen and Charlotte somewhere? Would they harm her, or had they already? *No. Don't think like that.* I dialed Brian's number and got his voice mail. *Great.*

"Brian, it's Sally. Please call me right away. I'm worried about Josie." I clicked off and grabbed my purse and keys while making a beeline for the front door, careful to lock it on my way out. I hurried to my car and sped off into the darkness.

They might be anywhere. *Think, think.* My head started to spin as I considered the options. I shot into the parking lot of nearby Giuseppe's Grill. I slammed on the brakes, jumped out of the vehicle, and raced inside.

The layout was similar to Ralph's, but larger with a separate dining area. Since it was a Monday evening, the place was quiet. Three men sat at the bar drinking, and two couples were having dinner in the next room. I ran in to check the ladies room, but it was empty. No Josie, no Ellen, nothing. The bartender stared at me with a question in his eyes, but I didn't have time for him. I ran back to my car, tires squealing as I zoomed out of the parking lot.

Ralph's was next on my list. I raced over to the pool table in the back room. A couple of bikers were involved in a game and glanced up at me curiously. Ralph himself was stationed behind the bar. His big belly rose and fell as he laughed at some private joke with a lone customer seated on one of the bar stools. My heart lurched when I realized who it was.

Mike turned around and gazed at me with affection. He started to smile, but when his eyes met mine, his expression changed to one of concern.

"Ralph." I tried to keep my voice steady. "Have you seen Josie tonight? Or Ellen?"

Ralph scratched his silver head. "No, honey. I don't think I've seen either one since you guys were here last week."

"Okay, thanks." I whirled around.

"Sal." Mike caught my arm. "What's wrong?"

A sob escaped from my throat. "Mike—" My eyes grew moist, and I knew I was going to lose it soon.

He put his arm around me and led me toward the front door. "Come on, we'll go talk outside."

We stood on the front porch, a warm wind shaking the large oak trees nearby. Less than a week ago, I'd kissed him and made a fool of myself in the exact same spot. Nearly half a lifetime ago, we'd shared our first kiss as a couple here. Fate seemed to keep pushing us back together. Agitated, I forced the romantic thoughts out of my mind. I had to concentrate on Josie now.

Mike held my hands. "Out with it. What happened?"

I stared at the worry in his beautiful eyes and trembled. "Josie's in trouble. She went out with Ellen tonight for a drink."

"So? Josie's a big girl, remember?"

"I'm pretty sure Ellen had something to do with Amanda's murder, and I'm so scared. She might h-hurt her." Tears ran down my face.

"Hey." Mike brushed at my cheek with his thumb. "It's okay. We'll find her. I'll take you."

"Are you in any condition to drive?" I asked, doubtful.

Mike's eyes widened in surprise. "I only had one beer. I'm not like my mother, Sal."

"Sorry, that's not what I meant. But I can't wait—I've got to get going."

He clutched my shoulders. "Did you call your friend at the police department?"

I caught a hint of jealousy in his words but chose to ignore it. "I left Brian a message, but he hasn't called me back yet."

"I heard on my scanner that there was an armed robbery outside of Colwestern." Mike drew his eyebrows together. "He might have been called there."

Fear gripped me. "What if Ellen hurts her?"

He glanced toward the parking area. "Don't talk like that. She's going to be fine. Is your car in the lot?"

I nodded mutely.

"Okay, we'll take yours. Mine's back at the house. I'll run

in, pay for my beer, and be right back." He stared at me with a stern expression. "Stay here. I don't want you going alone."

"Please hurry." I clutched his arm.

Mike cradled my face in his hands and gazed into my eyes with a longing that made my entire body ache for him. "Wait for me, baby. I promise I'll take care of everything." He pushed the door open and disappeared inside.

The musical notes of my phone startled me. I reached into my purse and breathed a huge sigh of relief when I recognized the number. "Josie!"

"Hey." Her voice was quiet. "Where are you?"

"I'm at Ralph's, looking for you. Where's Ellen?"

"She went home." Josie's tone sounded strange.

"Are you all right?" The panic rose inside me again.

"I'm fine, but—I have a flat tire. Um, Rob can't leave because there's no one to watch the kids. Can you pick me up?"

"Of course I'll pick you up. Where are you?" No response. "Josie, where are you?"

"Calm down." Her voice became a soft whisper. "I'm at Amanda's spa."

Puzzled, I stared at the phone. "Why are you there?"

"Ellen wanted me to meet her. She went to have her nails done before they closed. Poor thing is so upset about her Dad. She needed a little relaxation."

"Josie, don't see her again. She's Charlotte's partner, and I think she's dangerous."

"No, that's not true." She sighed into the phone. "Impossible."

"You sound really weird." I had a sudden, impulsive thought. "Have you been smoking weed?" She hadn't done any in years, but who knew?

There was silence for a few seconds before she spoke again. "A little. Please get here soon. I don't want to be alone."

"Okay, sit tight. I'm on my way." I rushed to my car and started the engine.

As I was pulling out of the lot, Mike ran toward me. "Hey! What the hell do you think you're doing?"

"Josie's okay," I called out my open window. "She got a flat tire over at Amanda's spa. I'm going to pick her up."

"Let me go with you." Mike gripped the door. "I'll fix it for her."

I shook my head. "We'll leave it there tonight. I want to get her home safe and sound."

Mike glared at me and tried to open my door. "Stop being so stubborn."

"I'll call you later." I peeled out of the lot and glimpsed him in the rearview mirror. He'd lost his balance as I sped off and fallen into the road. He stared at my retreating car in exasperation.

"Damn it, Sal!" He screamed after me.

Just like old times. I knew Mike meant well, but it was better to go without him. I'd apologize for my hasty departure later. Josie wouldn't want anyone to see her in a drug-induced state. After I picked her up, I would phone Brian again and have him locate Charlotte and Ellen.

I raced into the parking lot of Amanda's spa. Josie's minivan was sitting there, and a BMW was parked a few spots away from her. Light shone from one of the upstairs windows, and I breathed a huge sigh of relief. Maybe she was inside talking to the technician. I recalled her doing some strange things in the past when she was high.

Thank God for the flat tire. I bristled at the thought of her even considering driving after smoking marijuana. How could Josie be so selfish? She had children to think about. We were going to have a long talk, whether she wanted to or not.

The van was empty. I trotted toward the front door, somewhat more relaxed now. Maybe I'd take Josie back to my parents' house for a while. I didn't want Rob to see her like this. He'd be furious if he knew. I'd call him after I got her settled and thought of something to say.

I knocked on the door, but there was no response. Light still blazed from the upstairs window, but the bottom floor and receptionist counter were silhouetted in darkness. I rapped again.

"Josie?" I called out. There was no answer.

What the heck is she doing? The doorknob turned easily in my hands. A flicker of light beckoned me from the stairway to the right. "Josie?"

A muffled sound came from behind me, and I whirled

around.

A heavy object crashed onto my head from out of nowhere. There was no time for me to react as it made contact with my skull. Stars danced before my eyes, and an intense wave of pain spread throughout my body. My hand reached out to grab the counter and keep from falling as I trembled violently.

Someone roared with laughter from behind me and pried my fingers loose from the counter.

I sank into the darkness.

CHAPTER TWENTY-TWO

———

Slowly I opened my eyes, squinting at the bright light. My vision was blurred as I glanced around in confusion and realized I was lying on the cedar floor of Amanda's sauna.

Josie knelt next to me on the floor, peering at me in concern. "Are you okay?"

I tried to sit up but groaned and fell backward. "Ugh. What happened?"

"That bitch Charlotte knocked you over the head with one of those brass candlesticks." Josie's face was streaked with dirt, and she had tears in her eyes. "I'm so sorry. They made me call and give you that pretend story about getting a flat tire."

My head throbbed unmercifully. I closed my eyes then reopened them, trying to adjust to the light. I ran a hand over my right eye and winced. It was swollen and painful to the touch. "Did they hit me in the eye, too?"

"Charlotte and my so-called friend Ellen threw us in here. When Ellen dragged you across the floor, she hit your face with the door." She clenched her jaw. "Accident? I don't think so. They were laughing at you."

"Nice." I blinked several times, and thankfully, the blurriness started to diminish. "Where are they now?"

Josie had her right arm wrapped around her left one as if shielding it. "I don't know. They're planning some type of getaway."

I surveyed the small, paneled room. It was warm, but not unbearably hot. Yet. "Do you think they'll come back?"

"Oh, I'm betting on it. They want to know whom we've told. Then they'll take care of us." Josie cringed as she continued to protect her left arm. "I think it's broken."

I struggled to sit up again. Gently, I touched her arm, and she whimpered in pain. I tried to control the rage in my voice. "Who did that to you?"

"Ellen. It hurts like hell." Tears ran down her face. "They're going to kill us, Sal. I'll never see Rob or my babies again."

I clutched her right hand. "Yes, you will. We're going to be fine." I prayed my voice sounded confident because my body was consumed with terror.

"It's all my fault. I never should have gone with Ellen, but she sounded so depressed on the phone." She bowed her head in her lap. "I should have known she'd never come visit the spa. Some nurses can't even wear nail polish, did you know that? Plus she hated Amanda, so why would she come here? God, how stupid I am."

"Stop talking like that. How'd they get you inside?" I asked.

Josie lifted her head and blushed as her eyes met mine. "I didn't know the spa closed at seven until I checked the sign on the door. Ellen told me to come on in when I got here because one of the technicians was staying late for her. I thought it was kind of weird when I didn't see any other cars." She sighed. "And now I've dragged you into this too."

"It's not your fault." I put an arm around Josie's shoulders, careful not to hurt her again. "Did they hit you over the head?"

Josie shivered, despite the heat. "No. When I rounded the receptionist counter, I spotted Charlotte coming toward me. That's when I knew it was a setup. I headed for the door, but Ellen pulled me back by my hair." Her enormous, blue eyes were wild with fear. "They've got a gun."

The realization of what was going to happen to us slowly began to dawn on me. Blood pounded in my ears. I didn't want to die this way.

Josie wiped her eyes. "So they forced me down the hall, and I got pissed. This was before I knew they had the gun. I lunged at Charlotte, but Ellen yanked my arm behind my back. I'm pretty sure it's broken."

Anger rose from the pit of my stomach. "They're not

going to get away with this."

"Does anyone know you're here?" Josie's voice was thick with hope.

I prayed Mike had followed me, but why should he? I'd almost run him over during my hasty getaway. "I think we're on our own."

"At least I won't die by myself," Josie sobbed into my shoulder.

I clung to her, tears forming in my eyes until a noise caught our attention. The door opened, and our assailants walked in. We both sat upright.

Charlotte walked over to me, pistol in hand. "Did you have a nice nap?"

"Great, thanks for asking." I gritted my teeth.

"Talk." Ellen's hostile eyes focused on mine. "Did Vido tell you about us?"

I shook my head.

"Don't lie to me." Ellen shook her finger in my face. "Who else knows?"

"So you're gay." Josie glared at her. "No offense, but why would anyone care?"

Ellen's eyes filled with surprise. "You don't get it. If my father knew, I'd be history. He'd change his will, and I'd be disinherited."

Charlotte nodded. "I was disinherited because my father had a stupid fight with his brother. It wasn't even my fault."

"Ellen killed Amanda because she knew you two were lovers, didn't she?" It was all clear to me now. "And you, in turn, killed Vido."

Charlotte sneered at me. "You're smarter than you look. I mean, two guys did cheat on you, after all." She and Ellen went off into peals of laughter.

I clenched my fists but said nothing.

Josie's nostrils flared. "Loser. At least she can *get* a guy."

In a flash, Ellen reached over and punched Josie in the face. She fell backward on the floor.

"Leave her alone!" I screamed.

Josie muttered something inaudible as blood seeped from her nose. I reached in my jeans pocket for a tissue.

The hammer clicked on Charlotte's gun. "What's in your hand?"

"It's only a tissue." I glowered at her. "Can I please help my friend?"

Charlotte waved the gun and shrugged.

"Are you okay?" I tried my best to stop the bleeding and managed to at least stem the flow. My hands shook, and the bile continued to rise in my throat.

"Ugh," Josie groaned. Her nose was already starting to swell.

Furious, I turned on Charlotte and Ellen. "Let her go. She's got four kids who need her. You can do whatever you want with me, just let her go."

"Aww." Charlotte pretended to wipe fake tears away while Ellen laughed. "How touching. Such a good friend. Well, that's impossible. She knows too much." She pointed the gun at me again. "Speaking of which, who else knows?"

Mike. "No one."

"You're lying." Charlotte took a step closer.

My brain went into overload. "I swear. No one. Kate came to my shop this afternoon. She thought you might be gay but said that didn't matter to her. She wouldn't have treated you any differently. She loves you. She didn't know about Ellen and neither did I, not until tonight."

Charlotte tipped her head back and roared with laughter. "That bitch. Did she ever care anything about me? No. It was Amanda this and Amanda that. 'Charlotte, can you pick Amanda up after school? Can you stop and get her dry cleaning?' That's all I was ever good enough for, to be Amanda's maid. And she was adopted, for crying out loud. She wasn't even a real Gregorio."

"Is that why you had Ellen kill her?" I tried to stall for more time. *Please, Mike, please have followed me here.*

Charlotte stared at me, astonished. "You really are stupid, you know that? I put up with years of Amanda's crap. And for what? To be treated like a charity case by her and rich, old auntie. When Amanda found out about Ellen and threatened to tell, we had no choice but to kill her. If Ellen's father knew the truth, she would lose everything."

Ellen nodded. "That old man is so close-minded that I'd have been left out in the cold, just like Charlotte."

"How did Amanda find out?" Josie held the blood-stained tissue to her nose.

Ellen pursed her lips. "That scumbag Vido spotted us together at a casino and told her. When I saw him in your shop the other day, I knew he'd blab. That slimeball would have sold his own mother out for five bucks."

She had a point there.

"It was all so easy." Ellen snapped her fingers. "I waited until Charlotte was out of town and had a tight alibi. Then I went over to pay Amanda a visit. She was in the kitchen making her smoothie, on her way out the door. I begged her not to say anything. Let me tell you, I should have been an actress, that's how damned convincing I was. Amanda got a phone call and left the room for privacy. I overheard her telling someone she hadn't eaten and was going to stop by your cookie shop. Charlotte had given me the bee venom earlier. I stirred some into her smoothie, lifted the EpiPen out of her purse, and *voila*. Instant death, and the world is rid of that slut."

I sucked in a sharp breath. "So you guys planned this after Amanda and I had the argument at my bakery. You wanted to pin it all on me."

"Very perceptive of you, Jessica Fletcher." Charlotte winked at Ellen. "We are pretty proud of our ingenuity."

"It all worked like a charm." Ellen's eyes flashed with anger. "That is, until you two had to butt in. I liked you, Josie. If only you had minded your own business. I did try to warn you both."

I drew my eyebrows together in amazement. "Trashing my shop was your way of warning us?"

"You should have backed off." Ellen's eyes glittered. Then she laughed. "I did have fun with that frosting though. Kind of like being a little kid again." Her expression immediately soured. "My parents never even let me make mud pies in the backyard. No friends over, no dates, nothing. They let me go to the prom, but by then I knew I didn't even want to be with a guy. That's why Charlotte and I get along so well. We both know what it's like to be virtual prisoners in our homes."

I was silent for a few seconds as I mulled this over. They'd given me my answers, but it was imperative to keep stalling for time. "So Ellen killed Amanda, and you took care of Vido?"

"Of course. Easy peasy, as you Italians would say." Charlotte giggled.

I made a face. "No one uses that expression in my family."

"Oh, whatever. So how'd you find out about us?" Charlotte pointed the gun at Josie. "If I think you're lying, I'll kill Josie right now. In front of you."

I swallowed hard. "A guard at Snake Eyes Casino."

"Did you tell your little cop friend about it?"

I prayed she'd believe me. "No. I wish I had though."

Relief filled Charlotte's voice. "Good. This is better than I thought. No one suspects anything?"

"I don't know." My tone was doubtful. "I mean, Kate knows about the withdrawals from the spa's account."

"Too bad, so sad. I deserve that money. My father was cheated by his greedy brother." Charlotte glanced at her watch. "Now I'm afraid we must bid you two good-bye, or I'll miss my plane."

"Where are you going?" Josie asked.

Charlotte and Ellen smiled at each other.

"I guess it doesn't do any harm to tell you. I'm leaving for South America." Charlotte withdrew a ticket from the pocket of her long, flowery skirt and waved it at us. "One way, of course. That's why I needed the money this morning. With all the cash I've taken, there's enough to tide me over for a few weeks."

I turned to Ellen. "Aren't you going too?"

She shrugged. "I can't leave until my father dies and I get my inheritance. Lucky for me, he's in a coma. The doctors don't expect him to last the night."

"That's a shame," I mumbled, not knowing what else to say.

Ellen sneered and folded her arms in triumph. "It really isn't. This worked out perfect for us. No one even knows I'm involved, with the exception of that perverted security guard at the casino, and I can take care of him if I need to. Everyone will think Charlotte's guilty, especially because of the withdrawals. Once Kate discovers she's gone, there'll be even more reason to suspect her. No one can pin anything on me. Well, except for you two, that is." Her icy tone sent shivers through my body. "And we know for a fact that you won't be around to tell anyone."

Charlotte laughed. "Maybe we didn't even have to kill Amanda—if we'd known your father was going to kick the bucket so soon. Oh, well. She so deserved it."

Ellen grinned. "No worries, hon. I enjoyed killing your cousin. After the hell she put you through, it was my pleasure."

My stomach did flip-flops, and the urge to retch was overwhelming. These two were definitely twisted. How would we ever get out of here alive and away from these lunatics? We could try to charge Charlotte and the gun, but with Josie injured that wasn't a smart move. At least one of us would wind up dead. Would anyone think to look for us here?

I thought of Hank at Snake Eyes. It was a long shot he'd ever come forward with the information, especially if Ellen got to him first. He didn't even know why I'd asked about Charlotte. Mike knew, so perhaps some justice would come out of this after Josie and I were gone. I bit my lip, determined not to let them see me cry. *Why didn't I tell Brian about Ellen on my voice mail?*

"If the old man dies tonight," Ellen said to Charlotte, "I can arrange the funeral and be out there in a week or so. My attorney told me I'd get my money right away. No one else has any claims to the estate, and I'm the executor. I can't wait till he's gone."

I gasped in horror. "How can you say that about your father? He gave you life."

"Life?" Ellen grabbed the gun from Charlotte and pointed it at my head in a rage. I held my breath, afraid to make any sudden sound or movement. "What life? I've never had any life because of that man. He's always been overbearing and a control freak. He molested me and my sister, Emma, when we were children. Did you know that? No, because my mother wanted it hushed up. Thanks to him, my sister killed herself, or don't you remember?"

Josie's eyes filled with terror and she nodded slowly. I

remained perfectly still as I recalled the incident. Emma, three years Ellen's senior, had committed suicide as we were starting junior high. The exact reason she had taken her life had never come to light. Her parents only said at the time that she had issues.

"I'm sorry. You've been through a lot," I whispered, hoping to win her trust and perhaps get her to move the gun away from my head a wee bit.

Charlotte put her arm around Ellen. "It's all right now. You never have to go through that again."

"Yeah, I know." Ellen sighed and smiled at Charlotte. "Come on. Let's get you out of this loser town."

Charlotte walked over to the stove in the corner of the room. We watched while she poured a pitcher of water on the stones. She jumped back in a hurry as the pile hissed and steam erupted.

Ellen moved the gun away from my head, and I was free to breathe again.

"I don't like the idea of shooting anyone. It's not my style. Nurses clean up messes, we don't like to leave them." She giggled. "Poisoning is more my thing. Or—baking people to death." Her eyes glittered like a maniac's.

Charlotte's smile was evil as she glanced at Josie. "I'm sure your hubby will be wondering where you are eventually. It will all be over soon though. You'll both be nice and toasty shortly. Oh, pardon the pun."

My blood ran cold as Josie and I stared at each other in horror. They weren't going to shoot us after all. We would be left in the sauna to roast to death.

"Please don't do this. Come on, Ellen, I thought you were my friend," Josie pleaded with her.

Ellen laughed. "I don't have any friends, except for Charlotte. You can't trust anyone in this world."

Charlotte pursed her lips. "Hmm, so true. By the way, how long have you two been best buds?"

"Since we were eight." I struggled to breathe normally. "When Josie moved here from Maine."

"Right. So you're true friends. It's fitting you should die together then." Charlotte nudged Ellen. "This is so appropriate.

They're both bakers. And that's how they'll die—being baked to death." They both nearly collapsed with mirth.

Josie frowned in disgust. "Wow, way too funny."

"Josie's family needs her. Please let her go, she won't say anything," I implored.

Ellen's irritated eyes found mine. "We've been over this. How stupid do you think I am?" She glanced at Josie with mock sympathy. "Don't worry. Rob's a good-looking guy. I'm sure the kids will have a new mother soon." She gave us a little finger wave. "Bye, ladies. Enjoy your spa night."

The door slammed shut with a finality that echoed in my ears. Through the small window, I saw Charlotte pause for a moment. Then the click of a lock sounded. All was quiet with the exception of hissing noises emanating from the stove.

Josie got to her feet with my assistance and started yelling at the top of her lungs. "Help us, someone!"

"We've got to get out of here." My forehead was already starting to perspire. I scanned the room for something to break the window with. The benches were built into the floor, and there was nothing else in the room, save the stove with its two hundred degree rocks. I glanced at the plastic pitcher on the floor. Holding my breath, I flung it at the small pane of glass over the door. It bounced off the window and fell to the floor. I exhaled sharply. "Plexiglass."

Josie's breathing was labored. "I can't stand the heat. I'd rather freeze to death." There was a flicker of hope in her eyes. "They took my cell phone away after I called you. You don't happen to—"

Crestfallen, I shook my head. "I left it in the car. They'd have taken it anyway when they knocked me out, I'm sure."

The thermometer on the wall read 120 degrees. I beat on the door with my hands until they were bruised, then alternated with kicks, yet it refused to budge an inch. Sweat fell off my face in great droplets. I thought of my parents, grandmother, Gianna. Mike and Brian. What about all the things I dreamed of doing one day? Expanding the shop, entering baking contests, going to Italy, having children. My sweat mixed with my tears. *No.* I wouldn't give up. I was determined to fight till the bitter end.

"Somebody help us, please!" I screamed at the top of my

lungs until my voice was hoarse. I pushed my entire weight against the sauna door.

At that instant, the door was yanked open. A rush of cool air engulfed me, and I fell into a pair of strong, masculine arms. Someone scooped me up and carried me into the waiting room, where I was placed in an armchair. Josie was laid down next to me on the couch.

Brian wiped my face with a handkerchief, his face a mask of worry. His eyes didn't leave mine as he reached down to his belt for his radio and barked into it. "Officer Jenkins here. I need emergency medical service at nine Hollow Road right away. Name of the establishment is Amanda's Retreat. We have two women with injuries here. Hurry."

He clicked off and knelt before me, cradling my face between his hands, eyes full of concern. "Are you all right?" His fingertips gently touched my swollen eye.

I nodded and tried to force back tears.

Brian gathered me in his arms. "It's okay. You're safe now."

A woman's voice blared through his radio. "We've apprehended the two female suspects on Hollow Road."

"Got it." Brian rushed over to the coffee bar and returned with two cups of water. He handed one to his partner and placed the other in front of my lips. "Drink slowly."

I looked over to see if Josie was okay. Brian's partner was holding her head up so that she could drink. She met my gaze and gave me a thumbs-up. "We made it, kid."

The water tasted wonderful on my parched tongue. Brian grabbed the cup from me and then reached for my hand. "I'm so sorry I missed your call. There was an armed robbery outside of town. I didn't even know you'd left me a message until Mike Donovan managed to get hold of me."

I blinked, not sure I'd heard him right. "Mike called you?" That was the last thing I'd expected.

Brian nodded. "He told me you were in a panic looking for Josie and heading over to the spa to pick her up. He was worried you might be in trouble and asked me to check on you."

I was relieved Mike had called him, but why didn't he come himself? The old Mike I remembered would have driven through the spa's front window on his Harley to rescue me. Maybe he didn't care as much as I'd thought.

"He mentioned that he asked you to wait for him, but there was no holding you back. Said you were a raving lunatic." Brian raised his eyebrows at me.

"I wonder why he didn't come himself." I didn't realize I'd spoke the words aloud until I caught Brian's puzzled expression. "I mean, he's always been one to take charge and do things on his own."

Brian's mouth tipped upward in a slight smile. "He couldn't come. He's at the OnCall Clinic."

Panic gripped me. I tried to stand, but my legs were shaky, and I stumbled against Brian.

"You're not going anywhere." His strong arms placed me back down in the chair, and he grinned.

Why does he think this is funny? "Is Mike all right?" *What the heck happened to him?*

"He's going to be fine." Brian held back a laugh. "He said you ran over his foot."

CHAPTER TWENTY-THREE

––––––

"Come on, Jos, can we please get out of here?" I tapped on the bathroom door.

"Out in a minute," she called back.

As I glanced around the hospital room, where Josie and I had spent the last couple of hours, my desire to go home was overwhelming. Everything about hospitals bothered me—the smells, sterility, needles, and of course, blood. I could go on and on. If I ever had children someday, I didn't know what I'd do. Perhaps a home birth would be in order.

Gianna and Rob were in the waiting room, ready to take us home. In addition to my black eye, the doctor said I had a mild concussion and recommended I stay the night, but they weren't going to force me. Since I had no intention of remaining there any longer than necessary, this was a very good thing. For their sake.

Josie's nose was broken and her shoulder dislocated. The doctor urged her to remain, but she had refused as well.

"I need to go home and see my babies." She had explained this to the doctor as she wept on my shoulder.

There was a knock, and Brian peered around the door at me. He grinned as he strode over to where I was standing and put his arms around me. "I wanted to stop by and see how you were doing."

"A little sore. But I'll be fine, thanks to you." *And Mike.*

He caressed my cheek with his fingers, and then his smile faded. "Charlotte and Ellen are in a holding cell for the night. They'll be transported to a prison downstate tomorrow."

"What's going to happen to them?"

Brian sat on the edge of the bed and pulled me down

beside him. "Don't worry. They'll be going away for a long time, maybe even life. Ellen cracked like a walnut and told us everything. It was Charlotte's idea to kill Amanda after she found out about their relationship. Ellen carried out the deed because who would think to suspect her? And of course, Charlotte had an alibi."

"Clever on their part, I guess." I trembled as the image of those two came to mind. One thing was for sure. I was never going to set foot in a sauna again.

"In turn, Charlotte did in Vido. She had Nurse Ellen buy the cookies from you and taint them with enough morphine to kill him. Charlotte delivered them on the pretense she was going to give Vido a little action in return for his silence."

"Gross." I wrinkled my nose.

Brian smiled. "When Vido went to slip into, shall we say, something more comfortable, Charlotte switched the cookies he got from you with the lethal ones."

"And Ellen wrecked the shop while we were at the funeral with Charlotte."

"Yes. They thought they had it all planned out. Well, until they ran into your super sleuthing skills, that is." He turned me to face him and caressed my back with his hands until I all but went limp from his touch. "Maybe we should hire you on the force. At least you'd be more pleasant to look at than my current partner."

"Do you have good benefits?" I teased.

"The best." He brushed the hair back from my face, gazed into my eyes, and kissed me. I put my arms around his neck while his hands splayed down my back and then moved to my waist, pulling me closer. He devoured my mouth, and I was a willing participant. "Mm. Better tasting than a chocolate chip cookie."

Someone cleared their throat behind us. Josie stood there, an embarrassed look on her face. "Um, excuse me. I don't want to interrupt anything, but I'd like to go home."

Brian grinned in embarrassment. "How are you feeling?"

She wiggled her right hand back and forth. The left one was in a sling. "They gave me pain meds. Luckily my arm's not broken, but the shoulder's dislocated. Thank God I'm right-handed." She smiled at me. "With Sal's help, I can start making some more doughs tomorrow."

"Tomorrow?" Brian's voice was shocked.

"We don't let any grass grow under our feet." I slipped my hand into Brian's, and he squeezed it. "Gianna will be at the shop when the new case gets delivered tomorrow morning. Josie and I hope to get down there before noon, and Gianna's promised to help us with some baking. If all goes well after the rest of the cleanup, we can reopen the next day for business."

Brian shook his head. "You ladies should really take it easy for a couple of days. You've been through quite an ordeal." He gave me a quick kiss. "I've got to get back. Call me in the morning after you've gotten some sleep?"

"Okay." I released my hand, reluctant to see him leave.

He started to stand then looked at me. "Don't forget about dinner tomorrow night. Unless you have other plans now."

My stomach lurched. *Does he know about Mike asking me to dinner?* "What are you talking about?"

"I'll be back in a minute." Josie walked out into the hallway.

Brian reached for my hand again and massaged it between his. "Mike called me about a dozen times in the last hour. He's worried sick about you."

"Is he still at OnCall?" I asked.

"No, he's home. He wanted to come, but I told him you were fine."

I winced. I wouldn't blame Mike if he was furious. Who the heck runs over a person's foot—not once, but twice in the same lifetime?

"You still have feelings for him." It was a simple statement.

"I don't know." I lowered my head, refusing to look at Brian.

He lifted my chin until our eyes met. "It's written all over your face, especially when you heard he'd been hurt. Deny it if you want, but I can tell. And it's pretty obvious how he feels about you."

"I didn't mean to lead you or Mike on in any way. Please believe me."

"Sal, it's okay. You're still vulnerable from the divorce."

I blew out a breath. "God, I hate that word. I think this might be too soon for me."

He nodded in understanding. "I know. And if so, I'm willing to wait. I'd still like to take you to dinner tomorrow night. We can take things slow, as slow as you want. But if you aren't over Mike, we shouldn't be starting anything."

"Brian—" I began.

He shook his head. "I won't compete with ghosts, Sal. I'm not going to date a girl who's still in love with someone else. I just don't work that way."

My heart sank at the words, and I didn't know what else to say.

He leaned over and kissed me on the cheek. "I hope you'll give me a chance. I think we could be really good together."

My face grew hot as I stared into his brilliant green eyes, mesmerized. There were so many things I wanted to say to him, but the words refused to come out.

Brian stood and adjusted his hat. "Call me in the morning, and let me know what you've decided. Night, beautiful."

With that, he was gone.

I put my aching head into my hands. *What am I going to do now?* Yes, he was right. I did still have feelings for Mike and probably always would. I was drawn to him like a magnet. Now that I knew the truth about what had happened ten years ago, things had grown more complicated. I was being forced to choose between these two men, whether I wanted to or not. And considering past experience, I was very bad when it came to making decisions about the opposite sex.

Josie opened the door and walked over to me. "Are you going home or planning to camp out here tonight? I know your love of hospitals, so I'm guessing not." She glanced at me with concern. "What's wrong now? Did you and Officer Hottie have a fight? He was kind of short with us out in the waiting room."

I sighed. "What am I going to do? Brian and Mike both asked me to dinner tomorrow night."

"Oh, yeah, I'd almost forgotten." Her face broke out in a

wide grin. "So who are you going with?"

"Help me, Jos. I don't know what to do."

She stared at me for a long moment. "You're still in love with Mike."

I didn't answer.

"It's okay to admit it, Sal."

I clasped my hands together as if in prayer. "I don't know. Maybe I'm being nostalgic, remembering all the old times. He's still as jealous as ever."

"He doesn't want to lose you again." Josie sat down next to me. "Now Brian is an absolute doll. Sweet, calm, and heaven knows, I love a man in uniform." Her eyes twinkled. "No woman would kick him out of bed for eating cookies."

I chuckled. "You mean crackers."

"Not in your case." Josie winked, and we laughed together.

She leaned her head on my shoulder. "Did you ever stop and think why Mike's so jealous?"

"Because he's possessive."

Josie made a face. "No, dummy. I think he was always afraid he'd lose you. Then, bingo, it happened. Try to look at it from his point of view. Who else in this world has he ever been able to love and be loved by, besides you?"

Mike's words from the other day echoed in my head. I blew out a breath. "Gee, thanks for makings things easier for me."

She put her arm around my shoulders. "I can't make these decisions for you. No one can. Hopefully this time you'll do what's right. For you. That's what really matters."

Gianna peered around the door. "Ready to go, love?"

"I'll see you at the shop around noon. And thank you," Josie whispered in my ear.

"For what?" I asked, puzzled.

"I'll never forget what you said to those two whack-a-doodles tonight. Asking them to let me go and keep you instead." Her eyes filled with unshed tears.

As I stared at my best friend, a sob escaped from my throat. "Go on, get out of here. Your family's waiting."

"See you tomorrow. Oops, I mean later today. Night."

She stopped to give Gianna a hug and left the room.

Gianna threw her arms around me. "You're going to take my bed tonight. It's more comfortable than the one in your old room."

I shook my head. "I'm not putting you out of your room. I'm fine."

"No arguments." Gianna put her hands on her hips. "And I'm taking the day off from studying tomorrow. After I help you guys get the shop in order, Frank and I are going to the beach and then dinner. It's all because of you. You showed me tonight that life is too precious to waste."

My heart was full as I stared at my baby sister. "You're what's precious to me. Did Mom and Dad leave?"

"A little while ago. It's way past the loving hour for them." She made a face. "Grandma's waiting up at the house for us. She said she was going to fix you something special."

My mouth watered. "Special means fattening. Gosh, I hope she made cheesecake."

"I think you may be correct."

We walked outside to the parking lot while I checked my phone for messages. There was a lone voice mail from Mike.

"I wanted to make sure you were okay." He paused for several seconds. "Jenkins said you were fine. Call me back. It doesn't matter how late it is, I want to hear your voice."

My heart was in my throat.

Gianna watched me with a worried expression. "How's your head?"

"It's okay." I hesitated. "Would you mind if I made a quick phone call before we go home?"

She glanced around the well-lit parking lot and grinned at me in a teasing manner. "Go ahead. I'll wait in the car. Tell Mike I said hi."

I pressed the callback number on his message. Although it was nearly one o'clock in the morning, he answered on the first ring. "Hi, beautiful."

"I'm so sorry about your foot." I leaned against the building. "Are you okay?"

He laughed. "Just like old times. You and that lead foot of yours. Some things never change. Are *you* okay? Jenkins said you had a concussion and black eye. I've half a mind to go down to the jail and pay those two psychos a visit."

"I'm fine. It's over with now. With any luck, I won't ever have to lay eyes on either one of them again." I paused. "You saved our lives."

"No. Jenkins did that, not me."

"If you hadn't called him—" My voice started to shake, and I steadied it. "Thank you," I whispered hoarsely.

There was silence on the other end. "Are we still on for dinner tomorrow night? I'd love to cook for you."

"How can you manage with a broken foot?" I asked in disbelief.

"My foot's not broken. Only two toes this time. Your aim must be getting better." We laughed together, but then his tone grew serious. "I wouldn't care if I'd broken both arms. I'd still want you here with me."

I shut my eyes tightly, desperately searching my brain for words. "I can't give you an answer right now."

"I know there's something going on between you and Jenkins."

"Mike, can we talk about this later? I'm about to fall over with exhaustion, and Gianna's waiting for me in the car. We're just about to leave the hospital."

"Tell Gianna to bring you here. Come stay the night. Let me take care of you." His voice was sensual and tempting. A rush of heat swept through my body.

"I can't. My parents are expecting me at their house." Silence ensued between us, and I gazed at the bright stars above my head.

"Call me when you get up then?" Mike asked. "Let me know what you've decided."

My knees trembled as I stood by the emergency room entrance, the warm wind rushing by me. "Decided about what?"

Mike sighed. He sounded tired. "Jenkins told me you were having dinner with him tomorrow night. I think it was his attempt to get me to stay away from you."

"I didn't mean for it to turn out like this."

"I know. For the record, I didn't tell him I'd asked you to dinner as well." He paused as raw emotion filled his voice. "If you decide to go with him, there's nothing I can do about it. You know how I feel about you, and that's never going to change. There's still something between us, and you know that too. It doesn't matter how long I have to wait. You're well worth waiting for."

A tear rolled down my cheek before I could stop it. "Mike, I—"

"Call me when you get up." Mike's tone was quiet, but firm. "Good night, Sal. Sleep well."

CHAPTER TWENTY-FOUR

As anticipated, I tossed and turned all night. My head ached, and I spent a good deal of time reliving the conversations I'd had with Mike and Brian, both of which weighed heavily on my mind.

Everyone in the house was worried about my concussion and the possibility of me sleeping too long, which was never really an option. My parents took turns checking in on me. At five o'clock in the morning, Gianna gently shook me awake after I'd finally managed to fall into a dreamless sleep.

My father stopped in around six for a brief chat and to show me a picture of a casket made from gold. He lifted the window shades so that I could view the magazine better, and I squinted as the bright sunlight hit my eyes. "Look at this baby. I bet it's nicer than King Tut's was."

My mother rapped on the door about seven o'clock. She was all gussied up in a red, silk suit that stopped midway down her thighs. "You rest, honey." She smoothed the hair back from my face and kissed my cheek. "Grandma's here if you need anything. I've got inspections today."

My ears pricked up. "You sold a house, Mom?"

She laughed. "Oh, no dear, not yet. I'm only helping another realtor out. I'm getting close, though. You can't rush these things."

Definitely not.

At eight o'clock, I couldn't stand it anymore and rolled myself out of bed to take a shower. I stood under the spray for a long time, letting the hot water soak into my sore limbs and hoping for a miraculous solution to my problems.

While dressing afterward, I stole a glance in the full-length bathroom mirror. My face was pale and my right eye a spectacular shade of purple. I sighed. I didn't exactly look or feel like dating material right now. With my luck, I'd start snoring away at the dinner table. *Whose* dinner table still remained to be seen though.

I descended the stairs, and the pleasant aroma of bacon filled my nostrils. I breathed deeply and also inhaled the rich smell of coffee brewing. *Ah.* Simple things like this made me so grateful for my life today.

My grandmother was bustling around in the kitchen. She looked at me in a disapproving manner when I walked in. "You should be resting."

"I can't sleep."

She kissed the top of my head and opened the oven, where she'd been keeping a plate warm for me. There was an omelet with peppers, onions, and tomatoes, large enough for four people. She placed bacon and a croissant on the side of my dish.

"Grandma," I said, alarmed. "I can't eat all of this."

"You eat. It is good for you."

I was hungrier than I thought. As I plowed through the meal, Grandma Rosa sat down next to me and appeared pleased with herself. She placed her hand gently over the egg on the back of my head. "It still hurts?"

"A little." I hated to worry her.

She clenched her fists in her lap. "When I think of what I would like to do with those two crazies—"

I patted her hand. "It's okay. Josie and I are fine now."

She grunted. "Josie, maybe. You—no, you are not fine. You tossed and turned all night. I watched you like a hawk. I know why you are upset. It is time for you to choose."

"How do you know that?" Her comprehension skills never ceased to amaze me.

She tapped her bony finger against the side of her head. "Old people like me, we have good noggins."

"Dad too?" I asked.

She waggled her hand back and forth. "Him, not so much."

I blew out a long breath. "Grandma, it's not the end of the world, so why am I acting like it? They both want to take me to dinner tonight. That's all. I just have to tell someone no."

"Who did you decide on?"

Before I could respond, someone pounded on the kitchen door. Grandma got up to open it, and in walked Mrs. Gavelli.

"Hello, Mrs. G." I braced myself for an insult.

"You no hello me." She gave me her best irritated look. "Why you here, sittin' like lazy person?"

Grandma Rosa mumbled something under her breath. "Crazy old bat. She got hurt last night. How stupid are you?"

Mrs. Gavelli huffed at me. "You gotta get over to your shop."

"Gianna's there."

"Yah, well, you got people looking in windows. They ask if you open. Gianna, she not know what to tell them. And you got no fortune cookies." She glared at me with impatience. "What I gonna do with you?"

I held up my hand. "Hang on one second." I walked back into the living room and grabbed my purse from the coffee table. With all the excitement last night, I'd forgotten to give my father the fortune cookies he'd requested. I picked up the paper bag, and it slipped out of my hand, cookies spilling onto the table. I hastily shoved them back into the bag and returned to the kitchen.

I gave the bag to my grandmother. "These are for dad. Remember? He asked for them last night."

Grandma Rosa grunted. "Your father needs more than fortune cookies. He needs a swift kick to the seat of his pants."

I handed one cookie to Mrs. Gavelli. "We'll make some fresh this afternoon for you." I prayed she'd take it home to read so that I wouldn't get yelled at again.

"Let me see." *Nope, no such luck.* Mrs. Gavelli snapped the cookie in two while I held my breath. She gasped.

Uh-oh. I flinched as I waited.

My grandmother leaned over her shoulder. "What does it say?"

Mrs. Gavelli stared at both of us, her eyes full of wonder. "It say, *Your love life will soon be happy and harmonious.*"

Darn, maybe I should have kept that one for myself.

She shook the cookie at me. "How you know about Mr. Feathers?"

I held back a smile. Ronald Feathers was almost eighty years old and hard of hearing. Like Mrs. Gavelli's husband, his wife had died many years ago. I didn't realize the two of them were an item.

My grandmother's face confirmed my suspicion. I decided to have a little fun and tapped the side of my head with my index finger. "The spirits must have told me."

Mrs. Gavelli snorted and pointed her finger in my face. "Psychic powers. But you no scare me. I still tell you what you do."

I leaned down to give her a kiss on the forehead.

She looked at me and smiled. Then she pinched my cheek. Hard. "You—you better be good girl. And stay away from my grandson when he home. You no go in the garage with him again."

"Mrs. G, that was over twenty years ago."

She waved her hand dismissively. "That what they all say."

"Go home, *pazza*." My grandmother spoke with affection.

Mrs. Gavelli started out the door then turned around. "You no forget, poker tonight. Eight o'clock."

"I will bring the booze." Grandma Rosa watched her leave then nodded toward me. "She is a flip."

"I think you mean trip," I said.

"Yes, that too." She cleared my plate away from the table and put it in the sink. "So we were talking about Mike and the young officer. Who are you going to say no to?"

I sighed with frustration. "I don't know."

"You still love Mike. Do not lie to your grandmother."

"It's not that simple."

She grunted and opened the dishwasher. "Nothing in this life is simple. You should know that by now. You pushed Mike away many years ago, and you married that clown instead. That is why you are so scared now. You are afraid to make a big mistake again. Remember what happened last time?"

"I thought Mike had cheated on me. I was devastated."

"*Si,* and you spent days crying in your room. Then Colin asked you to go out with him, and you accepted."

I deftly raised one eyebrow. "So?"

"So you are afraid the same thing will happen. And you will make a mistake now like you did before." She reached over and patted my hand.

"Yes." She'd hit the nail right on the head. "You're right. What should I do?"

She shook her head and smiled sadly. "Sally, my love, I cannot tell you what to do. There is only one way to choose, and you did not do it last time with Colin. You need to do it now."

"What way?"

"You have to choose with your heart. Last time, you chose with your gut. Do not make that same mistake again."

I started to mull this over when chimes from the doorbell sounded in the living room. Grandma Rosa made a face. "It is like the Grand Central Station around here."

I placed my hand on her arm. "Don't worry. I'll see who it is."

She pursed her lips and turned away to stack the dishwasher. "No one stays home anymore."

I glanced through the peephole and was shocked to see Kate standing there with a basket of flowers in her hands.

She smiled at me with slight hesitation. "Sally, I wanted to see you. I was down at your shop, and Gianna told me you were here. I'm sorry it's so early. Would you mind if I came in for a minute?"

"Of course not." She swept past me gracefully, sweet lilac perfume pinching my nostrils. Kate was dressed to the nines in a beige, Anne Klein suit with a matching Gucci pocketbook. I might as well have been a homeless person next to her in my worn jeans and T-shirt.

Kate handed me the flowers. "I hope you're doing better. Officer Jenkins called last night and told me what had happened. He also said you suffered a concussion and Josie dislocated her shoulder." She clucked her tongue as she surveyed my face. "Oh, your poor eye. I'm so sorry I involved you in this."

I sat on the couch and beckoned her to sit beside me. "It's not your fault. I wanted to be involved."

She gazed down at the brown shag carpeting, and her lower lip trembled. "It's a very bitter pill to swallow when you find out your own niece is responsible for your daughter's death."

And I thought I had problems. I couldn't imagine what she was going through. "Have you seen Charlotte?"

Kate shook her head. "No, and I don't intend to. She's the one who's dead to me now." She stared at me in earnest. "I wanted to thank you for everything you did to help, and once again, I'm sorry for my accusations. I wasn't thinking straight and was too busy listening to the real murderer. It's so hard when you don't know who to trust."

I leaned back against a throw pillow. "What will you do with the spa?"

"I'm going to keep the place open." Kate dabbed at her eyes with a tissue. "It will be a good investment. Besides, I hate to think of all those people unemployed. Perhaps my new daughter will want to run it someday."

"New daughter?" I was puzzled.

Kate's face lit up. "I've started proceedings to adopt a teenager from China. My attorney doesn't think it will take long to push the paperwork through. I know this seems terribly soon after Amanda, but I need someone to share my life with. I'm not brave enough to be by myself. I'm hoping to fly out next week to meet her."

"I think that's wonderful. She's a very lucky girl."

Kate smiled. "Thank you. I know there's a certain amount of risk involved. I mean, she's not a baby or even a toddler like Amanda was. We all have to take chances in this life sometimes. They're necessary to our well-being."

Interesting how Kate's philosophy applied to me.

She rose. "Well, I wanted to say thank you and bring you a token of my appreciation. I've arranged for flowers to be delivered to Josie's home as well."

"That was very kind, but you didn't have to do anything." I got to my feet as well.

She paused. "I would like to ask you a favor."

"Of course, anything."

"I'm planning a memorial service for Amanda this coming weekend at the house. The affair after the funeral was so dry and formal. I want to honor her memory in a special way, by gathering my relatives and a few close friends. Perhaps have a slideshow dedicated to her. I'd love for you and Josie to be there. Please extend the invitation to your entire family as well."

I touched her hand and smiled. "Of course. We wouldn't miss it."

"I'd also like you to cater the desserts. I'll need about three hundred cookies. All assorted varieties."

My eyes popped. "Are you serious?"

Kate nodded. "Absolutely. Will you have enough time?"

"We'll make the time." I couldn't wait to run down to the shop and get started.

"Wonderful." She reached over to give me a hug then opened the door. "Thank you again. I'll be in touch later this week about the order."

I shut the door quietly behind her. I sank down onto the couch, crossing my legs underneath me and buried my head in my hands. I wanted to call Josie and see what time I should pick her up. She was going to need all of my help this week with the state her arm was in. It looked like my little cookie shop was going to be saved after all. A huge wave of relief washed over me, and I said a silent prayer of thanks. My first worry was over.

My second problem still remained. I decided to wait and call Josie after I'd made the dreaded phone call. Grandma Rosa was right. I was afraid—so afraid to make another mistake. I'd wasted the last ten years of my life in a mistake. Things would be different from now on. Time to live life to its fullest potential.

I finally admitted to myself what everyone else already knew. I still loved Mike and probably always would. He'd put my safety first last night when he'd called Brian to rescue me, not able to be there himself. This spoke volumes about him. He was not the same person who once hit a guy for helping me clean soda out of my lap. Maybe if I'd given him a chance to explain the Brenda situation way back when, we'd still be together. I'd never know the answer now.

However, I wasn't sure love was enough to overcome all of the obstacles still standing in our way. Mike had matured, but there would still be jealousies and insecurities to deal with if we gave it another try. My relationship with Colin had made me gun-shy, and trust no longer came easy. Mike's painful childhood had affected his life in ways I might never fully understand. Could we make it work the second time around? Would love conquer all?

Then there was Brian. Sweet, sensitive, considerate. He was good at his job, and it was hard not to admire him and his profession. I looked forward to getting to know him on a more personal level. His world appeared orderly and uncomplicated. That in itself was something I longed for—and needed—in my life. He was everything a girl dreamed of. Sparks flew when we were together. I wasn't in love with him yet, but I could envision it happening.

When I first dated Colin, I'd been on the rebound and anxious to forget Mike. Years later, when he asked me to marry him, I thought I loved him. I'd invested five years in the relationship by then and didn't want to walk away. Had I been responsible for the divorce since I'd brought baggage into my marriage? No, I knew that was Colin's fault. I hadn't been unfaithful like him, but perhaps he always sensed my heart was somewhere else.

As I leaned over my purse to find my phone, I noticed a single fortune cookie sitting there. It must have rolled over the side of the table when I had spilled the bag earlier. I settled back onto the couch with both the phone and cookie in my lap.

As I rubbed the cookie between my hands, I marveled at how customers always made such a big deal out of the ridiculous fortunes. Some seemed to consider the words a personal horoscope for them. I'd never been a believer in the little strips of paper or any other type of magic, for that matter. Yet something niggled my brain to read the message inside. *Why not? What have I got to lose?*

Holding my breath, I snapped the cookie open. A chill drifted down my spine as I read the words.

The answer you seek is in your question already.

Yes, I had known the answer all along. There would be no mistake this time.

Choose with your heart.

I ran my hand over the face of my iPhone and scrolled through the contact numbers until I located the desired one. I touched the screen and with bated breath, waited to hear his voice come on the line.

He answered on the second ring. "Hey, beautiful."

"Hi. Look, I'm sorry, but I can't make it tonight."

Fortune Cookies

2 large egg whites
½ teaspoon vanilla
⅛ teaspoon cinnamon
½ cup sugar
⅓ cup flour

Typed or handwritten fortunes (Make at least two inches long so that you can see where they are when the cookie is folded)

Approximately 4 ounces chocolate chips for dipping (Toll House, Reese's, or Heath-flavored, whichever you prefer)

Sprinkles (optional)

Preheat oven to 350 degrees Fahrenheit, and grease a metal cookie sheet. In a medium sized bowl, stir together egg whites, vanilla, cinnamon, flour, and sugar. The batter should be very loose. If not, feel free to add a few drops of water.

Scoop about a tablespoon of batter and pour onto the cookie sheet in a circle. Use the back of a spoon to smooth the circle out and make a thin layer to form a medium sized cookie. Only bake a couple of cookies at a time since they harden quickly upon removal from the oven. Bake cookies for about 6-8 minutes, only until the edges begin to brown.

Remove the cookies from the oven. Then use a thin spatula to remove them from the tray. Immediately place the fortunes in the center and fold the cookie in half. Pinch the open edges inward and together to create the fortune cookie shape. Cookies harden instantly after they are formed, so you want to try to get this right the first time.

After all cookies have been baked and shaped, melt the entire amount of chips in the microwave for about 30 seconds on medium heat. Afterward, dunk the rounded edge of the cooled cookies into the chocolate. Immediately roll in sprinkles, and let harden. Place on parchment paper. Makes about one dozen cookies.

Josie's *Genettis*

6 eggs
1 cup vegetable oil
¾ cup sugar
1 teaspoon baking powder
1½ teaspoon anise extract
4 cups flour

Confectioner's sugar and nonpareils

Preheat oven to 325 degrees Fahrenheit. Whisk together eggs, and then add vegetable oil, sugar, baking powder, and anise extract to the mixture. Stir together, then add the flour by small amounts until mixture is no longer sticky.

Roll out into a rope and then break out into six-inch long sections that should be about the thickness of a pinky finger. Wrap in coils upward like a beehive, and place on a parchment lined cookie sheet. Bake for 12 minutes or until the bottom is brown. Cool. Cookies can be frozen in an airtight container to be frosted at a later time or can be dipped in a glaze consisting of ½ cup confectioner's sugar with a few drops of water. Keep adding a few drops at a time until it's at the desired consistency. If the glaze is runny, just add more sugar. After topping, sprinkle with nonpareils before the glaze sets. Makes approximately three-dozen cookies.

Grandma Rosa's Braciole

For the rolled meat:
1 pound flank steak
2 cloves garlic, roughly chopped
½ cup roughly chopped Italian parsley
3 ounces pesto
¼ cup grated Romano cheese
Salt and pepper

Pound meat to desired thinness. Spread pesto on top of meat. Sprinkle salt, pepper, parsley, and grated cheese over pesto. Roll the meat and secure with butcher's twine.

Pan fry the braciole in olive oil until browned on each side. After meat is thoroughly cooked, submerge the braciole in tomato sauce. Serve over pasta.

Grandma Rosa's Ricotta Cheesecake

1 box of yellow cake mix
2 pounds ricotta cheese, drained (the whole milk kind works best)
4 eggs
¾ cup granulated sugar
¼ teaspoon vanilla extract

Preheat oven to 350 degrees Fahrenheit. Prepare the cake mix according to directions on the box, and pour into a 13x9 inch greased pan. Mix together all the other ingredients. Pour ricotta mixture over the cake mix, leaving the outside edge open. Bake at 350 degrees for one hour. Sprinkle with confectioners' sugar and cut into cubes.

ABOUT THE AUTHOR

Catherine lives in Upstate New York with a male dominated household that consists of her very patient husband, three sons, two cats and dogs. She has wanted to be a writer since the age of eight when she wrote her own version of Cinderella (and fortunately Disney never sued). Catherine holds a B.A. and dual major in English and Performing Arts. She has worn several different hats over the years, including that of secretary, press release writer, newspaper reporter, real estate agent, and most recently auditor. In her spare time she enjoys traveling, shopping, and of course, a good book.

To learn more about Catherine, visit her online at
www.catherinebruns.net

Enjoyed this book? Check out these other novels available in print now from Gemma Halliday Publishing:

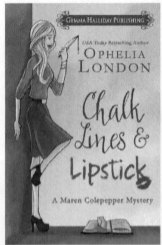

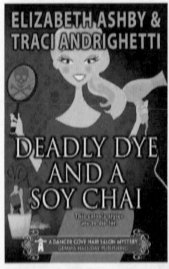

Made in the USA
Las Vegas, NV
26 November 2024